CURSED DRAGON

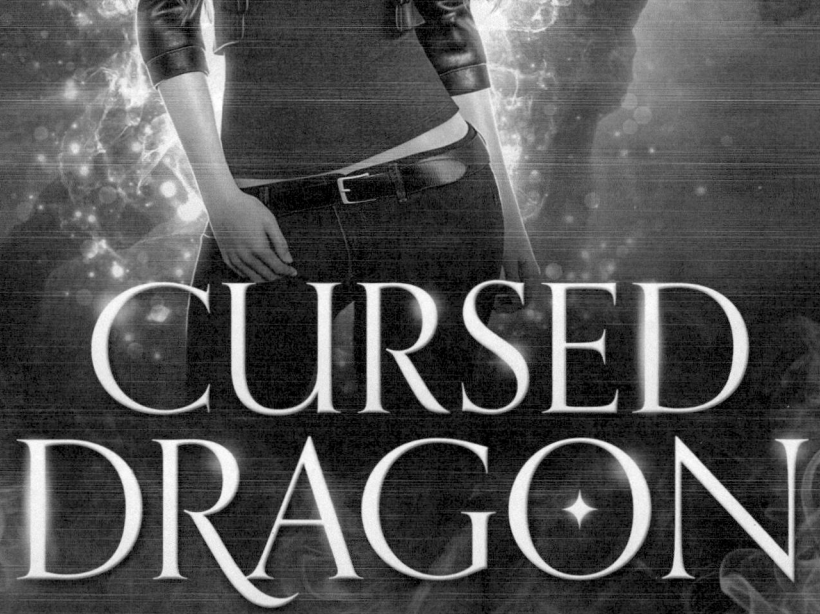

This is a work of fiction. Names, characters, places, and incidents either are the product of the author's imagination or are used fictitiously.

No part of this book may be reproduced or used in any manner without written permission of the copyright owner except for the use of quotations in a book review.

Cursed Dragon - Creatures of the Otherworld
WWW.BROGANTHOMAS.COM

Copyright © 2024 by Brogan Thomas

All rights reserved.

Ebook ASIN: B0CW1H38DS
Paperback ISBN: 978-1-915946-15-7
Hardcover ISBN: 978-1-915946-16-4

Edited by Victory Editing, Tina Reber, and proofread by Sam Everard
Cover design by Melony Paradise of Paradise Cover Design

For my hubby

CHAPTER
ONE

"Good evening." I attempt to smile politely at the next customer without stretching my cheeks or making much of an expression. Enough for my lips to move but not enough that I can't feel my face by the end of the shift.

Retail is lovely.

The job demands you smile as you scan irate customers' frozen Yorkshire puddings, all the while paying you minimum wage.

Also, the name badge is mandatory. They are so stupid. As if customers use them to say how amazing you are. Nah, they only ever want to complain. Not that anyone complains about me, as I'm a nice person and good at my job.

But having your name pinned to your chest isn't the best idea. If I had a tenner for every time some creepy guy points at my left breast and says, "If that one is called Kricket, what's the other one called?" Hardy har har. Hilarious.

No badge, you get a verbal warning, and I can't... I hate getting yelled at, and I can't afford another warning. I'd lose this job, my home, and possibly my life.

It's been a long week.

Today the name on my badge is *close* to Kricket. Karen's badge was lying conveniently on the manager's office desk when I came in, and I might have pilfered it before my shift and changed in the staff room amidst the posted reminders: SMILE, YOU ARE NOW GOING ON STAGE.

Yeah, it's a *stage.*

I had hoped for a choreographed dance—a retail flash mob—to practise performance-worthy smiles. I'd be so lucky. Nope, sorry, it's a bloody supermarket. Now I believe they're lucky we all turn up for our shifts.

If the staff room signs aren't annoying enough, there's a giant yellow smiley face next to the mirror. The flickering overhead tube lights make everybody look washed out and sick. Oh, and if you wear too much makeup, you're written up.

And heaven forbid you colour your hair. Mine is red, and I've lost count of how many times I've been accused of using box dye or an illusion spell. Once, I had to grab my phone to show family and baby pictures. We all have bright red hair, and even Mum is a strawberry blonde.

The customer I smiled at—lip twitched for—doesn't bother to acknowledge me as she unloads a massive pile onto the till's belt. She sticks her hand into a ratty bag, and a hard-boiled sweet disappears in her mouth.

She makes this slurping, spit-filled, wet sucking sound with her tongue.

Ew. I wrinkle my nose and sigh. I can't stand lip and mouth sounds. *Eating. Breathing.* Oh, and annoying phones that bloop and beep also send me into an eye-twitching rage.

There's this one staff member—every keystroke on her mobile sounds like a raindrop. *Bloop. Bloop.* I swear to fate when she texts her husband, I want to grab the handset and stuff it out the nearest window.

I won't. That's rude. But it drives me crazy.

My hands move automatically while scanning, my mind wanders, and... That's when I see the gargoyle.

A peacekeeper.

He moves with dangerous grace, each step deliberate. His eyes, glowing faint green, sweep over the aisles, ever watchful, ever guarding. He doesn't seem to notice the people who scatter out of his way.

The peacekeepers frighten me, and his presence here is unusual. They rarely come inside and have everything they need within their buildings, so he isn't here to buy anything. I've never seen this guy before. I'd remember his face.

Not that I stop to chat with the gargoyles; technically, I'm a rule-breaking criminal and it's best not to stand out for any reason. *Unless you want to get caught.* I should be freaking out—every instinct tells me to be freaking out with him so near, and I am.

But there's something else. Something that makes my heart beat a little faster for reasons that have nothing to do with fear. I can feel myself blushing.

Blushing. Me. I'm sure my face has turned the colour of my hair. I've never considered a gargoyle attractive, but watching him move... It's a weird combination: terror and attraction.

I don't like it. Is this what my friends feel when they swoon over muscles and forearms? The peacekeepers usually scare the crap out of me way too much to find them attractive, but this man—this peacekeeper—is beautiful. *I bet he doesn't chew with his mouth open.*

The gargoyle stops at the end of my queue, his wings folded tightly against his back. My heart pounds and I feel tingles running up and down my arms as his eyes brush over the line of customers. They briefly land on me, and his gaze narrows to a single point of connection.

He's terrifying, yes, but there's a flicker of something else—curiosity maybe? Or is it my imagination?

Sweet Eater impatiently clears her throat, and I snap back to reality. I force myself to focus, scanning the next few items with trembling hands. The peacekeeper resumes his patrol, and I keep my eyes fixed on what I'm doing until he leaves the building.

I should be relieved.

But the absence of his magical signature feels like a loss to me.

To get rid of Sweet Eater, I scan faster, whizzing her items into the bagging area. She keeps sucking, slurping, and unloading her massive trolley, oblivious to my antics. When she notices the enormous pile-up, she glares, tuts, and throws her ratty bags at my face.

I wince as a handle flicks against my nose and I get a whiff of smoke and rotten fruit that clings to the plastic. *Lovely.* Using a cucumber, I push the bags as far away as possible into the bagging area. I'm not touching them.

Fortunately, we're discouraged from helping customers pack—a co-worker squished a loaf of bread once and cracked a dozen eggs, causing store policy to change.

Sweet Eater takes the hint. Leaving a half-full trolley, she stomps past me and sweeps the shopping willy-nilly into her stinky bags with a wave of her arm.

The next customer, a skinny lad in his early twenties with three items in his hands makes a pain-filled noise in the back of his throat.

I do my best customer smile, with a bit of cheek action—"Shouldn't be long now, sir"—and continue to fire the stuff at Sweet Eater until I run out of things to scan. Then I separate items to make her bagging easier.

Still glaring and having a mini temper tantrum, she stomps back to her trolley, shoves the rest of her stuff on the belt, and slams the items down—the till creaks in protest. A two-hundred-gram pack of Traditional Jellied Eels is the first casualty.

The nauseating scent of salt and dead fish permeates the air. Is an eel a fish? I shrug; I think so. Now I'm kind of glad that she's only eating sweets. She could be munching on one of those things.

The strange floating eel in the package looks off. Now that it's leaking, it smells off—disgusting. The thought of eating jellied eels makes me want to hurl. It's a down-South thing, a London delicacy, not here in this glass prison up North.

"I need another one of those." Sweet Eater points with a long pink fingernail.

Yeah, no shit. "Of course, madam." My smile is strained as I press the help button to invoke the flashing light at the top of my till. It turns on with a *bong*. "I'll get a member of staff over to help, and they'll fetch you a replacement."

Sweet Eater narrows her eyes as if it's my fault she beat the eel into submission.

I give her my best *sympathetic* customer service smile—the one I've practised in the mirror. It's a skill. Too much of a smile and I've been told I come across as patronising. Too little of a smile and they think I'm being rude.

The smile stays on my face as I gather half a dozen crappy plastic bags and bunch them together so as not to get any fishy grossness on my hand, then lean across and gingerly encase the stink, leaving the barcode up so I can scan it.

From under the till, the massive blue roll and spray cleaner come out next. Using the cleaning stuff makes my hands go bright red. It's horrendous, so I'm extra careful. I groan when the customer attempts to put more things on top of the eel mess. Does Sweet Eater not see... I sigh and count to ten in my head, then with another five-star polite smile, gingerly push everything away from the liquid ooze with a sweep of my forearm.

"If you would please stand back, I just need to clean this mess up before it gets on your other items." I dramatically wave the bottle of cleaner for emphasis and the shop's camera's sake. If there is a health-and-safety inquiry—for example, I splash her eyes—I have covered myself with a dramatic wave.

Just as I predicted, Sweet Eater doesn't budge an inch. My smile falters, and I raise an eyebrow. *Move, lady.* She narrows her eyes as if I said that out loud and rocks back a teeny-tiny step.

"Please, if you would move back a little more?" I get a scowl for my trouble, but she moves. "Thank you so much."

I love my job. I love my job.

I liberally spray, unroll the blue paper, and using a plastic bag again as a hand protector, mop up the eel juice and put the soggy tissues alongside the damaged packet. Spray and wipe, spray and wipe. I wrinkle my nose. I hope they don't put me on this till tomorrow as I'm sure some fishy liquid has leaked inside, and it will be ripe.

The guy behind watches mournfully at the tills going faster around us and then mumbles he always chooses the wrong lane.

Me too, buddy, me too.

I turn and press the light and bell again. Then go back to scanning.

"What are you doing?" Sweet Eater snarls.

Huh? "I'll scan the damaged eel and complete the transaction while we wait for the replacement."

Mr Three Items Guy perks up.

"You will not." She prods at my face with her finger. "I won't get pulled by security because of your incompetence in not scanning the correct item."

I blink at the finger millimetres off my nose. "But I will be scanning it."

"It won't be the one I'm taking home!" She slams her hand down. "If you scan the damaged one, mine won't show on the system."

I lean back and tuck a strand of hair behind my ear. How do I put this? "Erm, it doesn't work that way. The till system doesn't recognise them as individual products as they all have the same barcode."

She growls at me. The hard sweet in her mouth rattles against her teeth, and a bit of red spit works its way out from between her lips and drips down her chin. Her face goes bright red as she draws in a big breath.

Uh-oh.

"I will wait for my packet of jellied eels!" Now that she has everyone's attention, she sniffs, folds her arms underneath her breasts, taps her foot, and gives me a look of death. "The youth of today—*you*, girl—need better training or perhaps a few nights in a cell."

Nice one. My shoulders hit my ears, and it takes *all* the crappy customer service training I've been inflicted with over the years not to get mad or cry.

The guy behind whines.

I want to whine with him.

The tills time us. If we don't process each customer in a set amount of time, it lowers our average rating. Then we get extra *training*, and management doesn't say it, but for weeks, even after your average time comes up, you get the shitty shifts like this one—Friday night of a full moon when all the weirdos like to shop.

As if on cue, a customer in the produce aisle starts making monkey sounds and throws bananas at other customers. You honestly can't make this stuff up. This place is wild. And not in a good way.

I wonder what that gargoyle is doing.

CHAPTER
TWO

FINALLY, the shift runner stomps towards me, chewing gum. Oh fate, it's one of those days. "What do you want" —*chomp, chomp*—"till six?" She says the words without taking a breath of air or looking at me, and gum almost falls out of her mouth as she grins at the banana thrower.

I show her the eels. "Can we have a replacement please?"

"Sure, I'll be one second." She holds up a single finger.

The runner will not, in fact, be a second. "Could you take—" I attempt to get her to take the damaged, stinking package away, but she's off on a slow slog reminiscent of a snail crossing the store.

My cheeks hurt with smiling at the growing line of

sighing and fidgeting customers, and I continue scanning Sweet Eater's shopping until we are all politely waiting for the replacement grossness to return. This entire interaction is going to ruin my average rate for sure.

Inwardly, I want to cry. I'm nineteen. I should be going out with my friends on a Friday night. It would be so lovely. Instead, I'll be stuck here forever, working.

I drum my fingers on the edge of the built-in aluminium scales. I guess it's my own damn fault. Naturally, I'm not a follower. I'm contrary like that, and I've never mindlessly followed the rules, making me unpopular.

Really unpopular.

I'm not the most pleasant person to be around at the best of times. My mum has told me hundreds of times that I'm too honest for my own good and don't understand which thoughts should be kept to myself and which should be let out. So now I keep my mouth shut. All the questions I have kind of bounce around in my head and come out in other ways.

Magical ways.

When I was a kid, I questioned everything. I asked *a lot* of questions. I wouldn't shut up, and my curiosity and blatant naivety about how the world worked put a black mark on my name.

I got tagged as a problem.

They told everyone at school, including my friends, that I had mental difficulties, and they dragged me through psychological testing, which I failed dismally.

That's why my job allocation is retail.

I can't be trusted to do anything else.

Put the troublemaker on sixteen-hour shifts stacking shelves, let her deal with angry customers six days a week, and see the life sucked out of her. She won't be asking questions anymore, mwahahah.

Well, stacking shelves has made me fit, and there's something kind of relaxing about facing all the labels the same way. It's satisfying to fill an empty shelf, so screw them. I like people.

Most people.

Sweet Eater eyes my name badge. *Karen*, she mouths passive-aggressively as if to motivate me to move faster.

I want to throw my arms in the air and yell, "Look, lady, I can't make the runner move any quicker!" But I don't.

She isn't trying to remember my name 'cause of my sparkling personality. When she gets home, Sweet Eater will fire up her computer and go to the store's review site to moan about my poor customer service.

Meh, she's entitled to her opinion. But more fool her. My official name badge is still attached to yesterday's garish green polo shirt and currently sitting at the bottom of the washing machine, all nice and clean.

I wince. *Sorry, Karen.*

If Sweet Eater does complain, I'll own up and take the hit.

Stupid name badge.

I hate it here. Not just the supermarket but *here. This*

town. This supernatural community of around five thousand living in what I not so affectionately call the glass prison—though it's not made of glass.

No, it's a massive, immovable, powerful wall of a ward that stretches around and over the town's nine-mile circumference.

I once asked my dad why no one thought having a vast warded circle in the middle of England was strange. He shrugged and said, "Kricket, people believe what they're told."

The circulating consensus back then was that a spell had gone wrong and they had to evacuate the town and block it off.

Trapped.

We are all trapped here.

Others say we're protected. Safe. But what is safety when you can't see anything beyond your cage? *Besides. It's not that protected.*

Everyone—or almost everyone—in town has dragon blood.

Cool, huh? *Dragons.*

Some say dragons evolved to be able to turn into human form and not vice versa. Some state these human-shaped dragons are ten feet tall and must have specially made clothing. That they're beautiful. But dragons, real dragons, are rare. I've never seen one, and *I don't want to see one.*

No, thanks. I'm tiny, squishy, and *crunchy*.

This town is full of the lost and the stolen. A mix of

creatures, entire families grabbed in raids to snap up all people with the correct DNA.

Anyone with the blood of dragons.

We came here when I was six and my twin brothers were babies. Mum had a complicated birth, and Aleric, the youngest twin, had a medical issue that resulted in them taking a DNA sample. Within days, our entire family was uprooted and relocated here.

We've been squirrelled away here for the past thirteen years, nice and safe. It's not just English people either. People from all over the world were ripped away from their lives and dumped in this town—to rot.

Oh, I'm sorry. Even in my thoughts, I must get it right. The propaganda script is that we are to be kept safe and *protected*, along with our unique alienesque blood.

Shady as fuck if you ask me.

No one asks me.

I don't enjoy being in a cage, in a town I can't escape. I find it strange that some long-dead relative of mine bonked a dragon and consequently we're stuck here.

I wish I weren't trapped. We get heavily censored real-world television, so I know it's more challenging outside than here. The real world is dangerous: vampires, demons, the fae, and all manner of scary creatures roam outside the ward, living their lives and killing each other. Still, I'd love to see it all.

I continue with my nervous tapping and sympathetic queue smiling. "Not long now," I say brightly.

It feels like forever until the gum-chewing runner

returns with the packet of jellied eels. She shoves them at me and then hurries away, leaving me with the bag of funk that I slide under the till. I'll have a break soon and will throw it into the damaged-item area myself.

I keep eye contact with the sweet eater as I scan the new eel packet barcode, give her another smile, and tell her the total.

She pays with her card.

"Thank you for shopping with us. Have a lovely evening." I hand over the receipt, and the fake smile slips as the seconds tick and she doesn't move.

Come on, lady, please move.

Sweet Eater meticulously checks the receipt.

Out of the corner of my eye, I can see the duty manager making her way down the row of tills. Her eyes are fixed on me.

Uh-oh.

I clear my throat and ensure my voice is extra monotone, without a shred of irritation or panic. "Excuse me, um, there's a line of people waiting behind you. Would you please step aside? If there's a mistake with your order, the customer service desk will be happy to rectify it." I point helpfully to the customer service desk and the employee staring into space while biting her nails.

Please leave. Please, please, please.

Sweet Eater lowers the receipt and lifts her chin. "I'm going to report you, Karen." She spits out the name, huffs, snatches hold of her trolley, and—

Outside, a loud *boom!* makes the entire store shake.

Chapter
Three

My knees sting as they impact the floor with a crack. I shove the till's rolling chair out of my way and duck under the solid frame of the bagging area. The lights go out, and the ambient everyday noise of the supermarket—the torturous store music—cuts off.

It feels eerie.

The silence is broken only by customers' obligatory whimpers and rasps of my breath. Seconds later, a massive blast of magic rolls through, heating the air and making my ears pop. The windows along the front wall rattle, and the entire building trembles.

The taste of ozone burns my throat, and the wave of energy brings a ripple of sound. Outside in the car park, car alarms blare, and the *thud, thud, thud* of presumably pieces of blown-up stuff rain down. I flop on my bottom, knees to my chest, and cover my head with my arms.

Oh fate.

What the heck was that?

My entire body trembles, and for about sixty seconds, I keep my head down; when nothing further happens, I push off the ground and peek around the back of the till.

The sensible people huddle for cover, and the bold ones stand and stare through the wall of windows, unconcerned, as if explosions happen every day.

I notice one guy at the end of the row of checkouts twitch. He's the closest person to the main doors. *Don't do it.* His feet jiggle, and he rocks a bit. *Please give it a little longer.* In the next second, he must decide as suddenly he takes off running. His frantic bolt to the doors seems to knock everyone out of their stupor, and a mass exodus ensues.

A flood of customers and *staff*, some dumping their trolleys, others taking the chaos and lack of power and cameras as an opportunity to steal stuff.

The store goes wild.

The hold that binds them to decency has snapped.

My mouth pops open as I watch, keeping low, tucked into the till's bulky side. I shake my head. They're behaving like animals. There's nothing I can do, and I don't get paid enough to deal with this shit. After another few seconds, the store's emergency lights flicker on, and I can't help but sag a little in relief.

Then the sweet eater's legs wobble into view.

Her once precious receipt flutters, discarded to the floor. Her hands grip the green handle of her trolley, making her knuckles turn white and her pink nails dig into her palms. The sweet eater hunches over as if she is going into a rugby scrum, and with a growl, she barrels off with her shopping. The customers in front of her who don't move out of her way fast enough get rammed.

Shit.

I watch people go flying. Wow. When the shit hits the fan, everyone is out for themselves.

"Oh, come on! Come on!" yells the three-items guy.

His sudden scream makes me jump. I wince when I knock my head. He throws a tenner on the till, and clutching the precious three items to his chest, he's off, joining the melee to get outside.

Stay or go, Kricket? Stay or go?

What I can't do is stay hiding next to the till all night.

Shock and fear pulse through me, and my heart pounds. I brave it, get to my feet, glance around at the madness and brush my trousers off with trembling hands. I avoid looking anywhere near the windows. What if there's carnage outside? I'm unwilling to look in case I see something that I can't unsee.

I have enough nightmares as it is.

Does anyone need any help? The time of night means at least most of our older customers are tucked in bed. I nibble on my lip as I take in the mess the shoppers have left and realise it's going to be me who will have to clean it up...

There's another explosion. This one feels closer, and perhaps it was in the other direction. It's hard to tell as I'm back on the floor, hiding behind the till.

Feet move past me as more terrified customers leave.

One explosion could be an accident.

Two explosions in different directions are a pattern.

I shiver, peek out, and this time force myself to look through the windows. There is thick, fog-like smoke. Without streetlights cutting through it, I can't see a thing.

Are we under attack? *Could the supermarket be next?*

I gnaw on my lip. "Does anyone know what's going on?" I yell. "Does anyone need any help?" No one bothers to answer. Those explosions sounded severe, like war-level bad.

Where are the peacekeepers?

The smoke outside is getting denser and is pooling through the store's open doors. I need to do something. *I need to move.* The shaky duty manager—who was after me a few minutes ago—fiddles with the main automatic door, which is unwilling to close.

I was working when the doors were serviced, and I know there's a keyhole at the bottom of the door on the left that switches the automatic function off and on. In case of a power outage, it allows someone to manipulate the doors by hand.

She needs to close those doors for safety. I've already

seen people stealing and keeping them open only exacerbates the problem.

There hasn't been an explosion for a few minutes. I don't think it's safe to move, but I must. I know how to help, and it's the least I can do. I glance to the left at the far-off staff area and my locker and look right at the trembling manager.

Bloody hell, Kricket.

Heart pounding, I grab the edge of the till and drag myself to my feet.

My head is on a swivel. I don't want to be rammed by a trolley or some idiot to see me as a target. I huff out a disgusted breath. I watch way too much TV. This entire situation is not helping my overactive imagination. I move my feet and creep to the manager's side. It might be my imagination, but the smoky wind off the car park still has heat and moves strangely, like a river of dry ice.

Magic.

It makes the little hairs on my neck rise.

"Here, let me." I take the manager's keys out of her sweaty hand, and she stares at me with big, round eyes. "There's a feature in these doors so you can manually open and close them if the power goes out." I crouch next to the door, my back hugging the window, and nerves skitter up and down my spine. I don't like being next to the glass.

The freaky magic smoke billows through the open doors. It smells mildly sweet and tickles my throat. I swallow a cough and cover my mouth with my arm, not wanting my lungs to filter any more of it.

"The doors should have their own electric supply, perhaps a battery, so things like this don't happen, but what do I know? I'm not a door technician," I mumble, half to myself and half to the manager.

With some wrangling, I get the key into the slot, and as it turns, the door mechanism clicks. I give the door an experimental shove, and it moves easily on its tracks. I push against the black frame, and it slides. As one side closes, the other follows, and they meet in the middle.

My thighs burn as I push from the floor, wobbling to my feet, and slide the key into the lock, turning it until there's a reassuring click.

I close my eyes in relief.

The duty manager nudges me out of the way and takes control of the keys. "Thank you. I'll stand here to help the customers leave if you can gather the staff and return any meat and cold products where they belong. We will need to save every perishable before anyone goes home. Leave any ambient." She means tins and long-dated stuff. "We can do that when we have full power."

I blink at her. "Sure."

I don't have the heart to tell her if we don't get the power soon, things will unfreeze anyway. Also, is it really a priority with what's happening outside? Most of the staff ran out the door. I even saw the security guard jog out with a couple of whiskey bottles.

I rub my neck and stare out at the swirling smoke.

Goosebumps rise on my bare arms. Standing so close to a wall of glass, I feel a tad freaked out and vulnerable, as glass and random explosions aren't a good mix. I do not want a glass facial.

"Shouldn't we... um... move away from the windows?" My voice squeaks at the end with stress, and I can't help hunching my shoulders.

Yeah, standing here isn't the best idea.

The duty manager gives me a funny look, as if I'm the one being stupid. "What? Why? This safety glass will be fine." She taps the door to highlight her point.

Safety glass? It's not even magical, and things are exploding.

"Do you want me to grab a ward from the office?" We have an emergency stash, and nothing will be if this isn't counted as an emergency.

"No, I can't authorise that. Now look—" Her eyes drop to my stolen name badge. "Karen," she says the name with a sneer. Now that the doors are closed, she is growing bolder and has slipped back into her bossy persona. Her hand flaps to encompass all the abandoned trolleys. "You've been accommodating with the doors, but can you do as you're told and go and sort out the frozen and the meat products?" She drops her voice and narrows her eyes. "Don't make me write you up, Kricket."

Yeah, and now I'm not going to argue. I back away from her with my hands up. "Okay," I whisper and scuttle. Heading for a safer area, I move to the wide centre aisle—away from the windows—and instead of doing what she asked, I hustle to get my stuff from my locker.

Bye-bye, I'm out of here.

I pass a few determined customers still hanging around, although they look just as shell-shocked as I feel. I keep my head down and power past. I'm a horrible person for not asking if they need help, but I've got to get to my phone and check in with my family—the urge to check that they're okay drives my fast steps. I move too fast to change directions when I see a familiar figure.

My nemesis, Anton Hill, shouts at a young cashier, "Why can't you check me out? I've got my card." He waves his card in Rich's face.

Ugh. I keep walking; if I dart away, it will look like I'm running away from *him*. I'd never live it down. Trust him to be between me and the staff room.

"I'm sorry, but we have no power. The till can't work, and no till equals no card reader," Rich explains.

But Anton Hill isn't listening. He continues to talk over the top of Rich, his voice smarmy and condescending. "You stupid kid," he continues to rant.

Okay, that's it. I'm not a confrontational person. Well, I'm confrontational in my head, but I try to keep my mouth shut. Life taught me that much. I try to be a bubbly, friendly girl. But seeing horrible Anton Hill behaving rudely to a teenager after what is going on outside—people could be hurt or dead—makes something inside me snap, and entirely out of character, I yell.

"Oi, Anton Hill, get out!" My voice carries

over and above his shouty rant, and both guys turn to watch me approach.

Rich's mouth hangs open.

Oh heck, I've done it now. Oh well, in for a penny, as Nan always says.

I can't abide rudeness; it's on the level of chewing with your mouth open. "The store is closed," I snarl.

"You."

"Me."

I went to school with this guy. He was a dick then, and he's a dickhead now. I like people. I consider myself a people person. Yet I really dislike one person in this world, and it's Anton Bloody Hill. He's a caricature of a bully. It's like the man has a checklist in his head of all the cruel things he can get away with, and he daily ticks them off one by one.

The number of times he has made me cry... and he hasn't changed, not one bit.

"Kricket." He gives me a big, wide, toothy smile.

His teeth are so fake white they remind me of square pieces of chewing gum. It takes everything inside me to remain professional. I swallow down my retort and do my best to get hold of this situation. "Sir—"

He lets out a lecherous laugh and leans forward into my space. "*Sir*, I like that." He raises his eyebrows, licks his fleshy lips, and rocks his pelvis towards me.

Ew. Just ew.

I shuffle a few steps away from his thrusting. "Anton

Hill, whatever's happening out there is an emergency. We. Are. Closed."

To highlight my point, there's another explosion.

I throw myself next to a roof support post and drop to my hands and knees. The building creaks ominously and the emergency lights flicker. Whatever is happening is getting closer.

Both guys stare down at me as if there's something wrong with me being on the floor and covering my head. I don't care if I'm on the floor, but what is more concerning is that they aren't.

"While you're down there, Kricket, love." Anton Hill holds his hand out like he's miming, holding the back of my head, and he does another pelvis shimmer.

Blarg. I think I threw up a little in my mouth. Oh boy, it's a close call as I curb the almost overwhelming urge to dick-punch him. I don't even need to touch him. I can swipe a can off the shelf and throw it.

Stuff being professional; I'm level with his basket. I lean up with one hand and tip it towards me with the other. I peer inside. "Hot date with your hand?" I ask with a sweep of my lashes and a coy smile.

Did I really say that?

Rich lets out a gasp snort.

Oh yes, I did. I mentally fist pump. I'm on a roll and far from finished. "Surely you don't need hand cream, frozen pizza, and a six-pack of Coke this badly, eh, Ant?" I smile sweetly.

"Bitch," Anton snarls. He moves his foot, and I snap my hand off the floor before he can tread on my fingers.

I scramble to my feet and narrow my eyes. "Out, or I'll put you out." He knows I can kick his arse.

Like gunfighters in the Wild West, we eye each other, and Anton Hill must see something in me as, with a roar, he launches his basket into the nearest shelf. Items clatter to the floor as he stomps away, heading for the main door.

I can't help puffing a sigh of relief when he walks past the manager.

"That was stupid," I mumble, scratching my head. He'll make my life even more difficult. And worse, this incident will get right back to my mother.

"Thanks, Kricket."

"You're welcome, Rich."

"What do we do now?" he whispers, rubbing his arms as he stares at the mess surrounding us.

"I have no idea. I'm sure the peacekeepers will sort this all out in no time. Avoid whatever is happening out there, I guess, and when you get home, hide. You only live across the road, right?"

He nods.

"The duty manager is on the warpath. I'd avoid the front door and slip out the rear fire exit. That's what I'm going to do."

"What? Now? You're going home? What about your shift?"

"Rich, almost everyone has left, and they do not pay me enough to stick around. I need to check in with home." I give him a small, worried smile and hurry to grab my phone.

CHAPTER
FOUR

THE BACK AREA of the store is darker. "Typical that the emergency lighting isn't as bright in the staff area," I grumble. On the way past the manager's office, I throw the borrowed badge back on the desk and rush into the staff room.

I make quick work of opening my locker, grab my phone, and while waiting for the old handset to load—it will take an age, and I'm now regretting that I'd turned the damn thing off in the first place—I zip my coat to cover the garish bright green polo.

The left pocket of my coat bulges with a dark green woolly hat that I wear when the walk to work is windy or raining; it gives an extra protective layer. Having wet shoes, legs, and hair while working in a supermarket is not pleasant, and you can guarantee some manager will observe your drowned-rat aesthetic and make you do a stock take in the freezer or give you a till close to a row of open fridges.

The monsters.

I pull the hat out and stuff it on my head. It's too warm to wear, but my bright red hair is attention-grabbing enough on an average day. Now weird and dangerous things are happening. I'm not going to question my overwhelming urge to blend. I'm feeling a tad vulnerable, and I'm not going to make the mistake of not carrying a pocket full of spells ever again. I'll have to think of a way to disguise them, but that's a problem for future Kricket.

At this point, I don't care anymore if I'm caught with my specialist spells.

My hand trembles as I tuck my hair under the brim. My entire body finds movement rough, and the strands bunch around my ears, muffling ambient sounds. I don't bother fixing it because my fingers aren't dextrous enough. They are like lumps of Plasticine. I'll be liable to tear my hair right off instead of tucking it around my ears.

I think I'm in shock.

I know I'm in shock.

Just breathe. I take a shaky breath in, hold it, and breathe out. My chest feels tight, but I continue to take big gulping breaths, and it gets easier, even if my thoughts remain fuzzy with my panic. I need to calm the fuck down and think logically about this mess. I'm being dramatic. Right?

The world isn't ending.

This hidden town is a glorified dragon blood protection scheme, but they won't leave us to die, and there must be a simple explanation for those explosions: a gas leak. We haven't had new people for at least eighteen months. Perhaps there has been a new intake, and something has gone wrong. *Yeah, it might be a gas leak.*

A small, strangled laugh comes out with my next breath. I've always had an overactive imagination that overrides all my common sense, and I tend to jump to the wrong conclusions. My gut feeling has always been off base.

Yeah, I'm being dramatic and need to get a grip.

There hasn't been another explosion for a while, and I bet everything is now under control. *Everything is fine.* I can't let fear rule me. I watch movies and read books, and I've seen it myself. When people panic, they do stupid stuff. Like the sweet eater ramming her trolley into the backs of people's legs, hurting others so she can get her *shopping* out the door faster.

How silly is she going to feel when she gets home?

I check my phone. It's still loading. The bright white logo on the screen burns uncomfortably into the back of my eyes. I wince as it imprints on my retinas and remains when I blink a few times.

Bloody thing. There is no need for that. I don't know what the manufacturer was thinking. I bought the crappy thing, so it's not like I need the symbol superimposed on my eyeball. I scowl and turn the mobile so the screen rests face down on my thigh.

Added to the stress I'm already feeling, I'm beginning to get a pounding headache. I rub my thumb and forefinger on either side of my nose and do more deep-breathing exercises.

In the past, new people have come into town and freaked out. Who can blame them? About ten years ago, while trying to escape, an entire family ran into the buzzing, flashing killer ward encompassing the town.

Horrific. It was horrific.

I lift the corner of my phone and peek—it's still loading. "Come on," I grumble, bouncing on my toes. "Come on." I want to check in with my family.

I turned the stupid thing off before my shift 'cause I was jealous of my friends arranging a night out and the flashing notifications drove me mad.

I shuffle out of the small staff area and into the massive stock room. I check the phone and sigh in relief. The main screen is on, and the local network is still live—that's a good sign. My heart skips a beat when I see a text from my dad. I thumb the message open.

Are you safe? Please let us know if you are safe. We are hiding in the basement. Unless you have to move, sit tight, and as soon as I can, I'll come for you. We love you so much, pumpkin xx.

So it's not just me overthinking things.

I prop my bum against the rough warehouse wall and quickly tap a reply.

I'm safe. Please do not come! It's madness here... I pause, groan, and delete those last few words. I don't want him to read that and feel obligated to come and get me. He has Mum, Nan, and my two younger brothers to think about. *There's thick smoke, so it's not safe to drive. I'll wait here instead of going to my flat. I'll come to you when I can. Do you know what's going on?*

He immediately calls my phone, and the sound echoes in the dark, silent space. I wince. *Shit, shit, shit.* I dash behind a row of shelves. "Dad?"

"Kricket, okay, we trust you to be smart. But if you need us, if you need me, I'll come and get you. I don't care about smoke."

"No, Dad, I'm fine." I can take care of myself.

"Why are you whispering?"

I roll my eyes. "The duty manager is mad." Dad clucks his tongue, and I head him off before he starts on a rant. "Do we know what's happening? Is it an attack?"

"We don't know. There's no news, but you know how paranoid your mum can get." Mum is like me—an overthinker. I smirk when I hear her in the background. "Oi," my dad dramatically yelps.

I imagine she's giving him a dig in the side.

I close my eyes at the sound of my mum's voice. "It's not paranoia if things are getting blown up. I don't like this, Kricket. I have a bad feeling; be smart. We love you, sweetheart."

"I will. I love you too."

"Oi, give me that. Let me talk. Can I talk to our daughter without you assaulting me?" The phone rustles. "We'd prefer you to come here rather than go home, but only if it's safe. We are in the basement, and we've used one of your wards. Keep in contact and keep your head down."

"I will. Love you all." I get mumbled replies of love in return. "I need to save the battery. Talk to you soon. Bye-bye." I flick the phone on silent and shove it back into my pocket.

Thank fate, they're all safe.

I puff out my cheeks. I lied when I said I'd keep my head down. If I wait much longer, my dad's going to come and get me, and it will be my fault if he gets hurt. There's no way he will leave his little girl stranded at work, and like my mum, I can't help the niggling feeling that things have gone horribly wrong.

Sometimes you must keep moving, as staying in one place can be a mistake.

I need to get home.

I adjust the hat, pushing loose strands of escaped hair back under, and stare out into the warehouse. It's empty of life. The staff back here have long since cleared out, which is what I need to do once I get up-to-date information on what's going on outside. My hand drifts to my phone, but I shake my head and let my arm drop uselessly to my side.

The phone is out because the town council strictly

controls all our information online. They wouldn't want any of this known. They've always gone the gaslighting denial route. It's hard to cover stuff up when there's a record.

My eyes drift up to the mezzanine area containing the pricing office. It's where they print off all the barcodes, offers, labels, and merchandising designs. I narrow my eyes, and it takes me a second to determine why I'm staring up there. The frightened, lizard part of my brain catches up with my intelligent, logical side.

There's an access door to the roof.

The roof! That's it. My stomach flips, and I don't waste another moment.

As I clatter up the metal stairs two treads at a time, a plan forms in my mind. The supermarket is high up or higher than the other surrounding residential buildings, and from what I remember, the creepy magic smoke seemed to cling to the ground. If I can get above the smoke, I might be able to see what's going on and find a way to get to my family. It's usually a twenty-minute walk to my parents' house, but perhaps I can knock that in half to ten if I run, and if I'm lucky, I'll see which route to take and which streets to avoid.

And find out what the hell is going on.

I fling the office door open and dash towards the handy compact kitchen. This is step one in my plan. I dig through the fridge and cupboard, sighing in relief when I find salt and water bottles. I pour a huge amount of salt into the water of each bottle, shake them, and stuff two of the bottles into my coat pockets. The third I keep ready on the side. Magic and salt aren't friends. Salt breaks down the structure of most common spells, and depending on the magic's strength, it can take minutes, days, or years.

It doesn't break down my spells.

The bottled solution should work with the smoke magic outside. I find a clean tea towel in the bottom drawer, drop it into the sink, and pour the saltwater solution over it until it's soaked. When I leave, I need to get through the streets fast. The acrid air blowing through the store's front doors was almost unbearable. If I stop every thirty seconds to hack up a lung, that won't be good. I might as well protect my airway now if I'm going anywhere outside.

I fold the tea towel into a layered triangle and tie it around the lower half of my face, covering my mouth and nose.

There, that's step one down.

I weave around the desks and slap the metal bar on the burgundy fire door with both hands, shoving it open with my shoulder when it sticks a bit. It swings open, and I'm about to sneak out.

I stop.

What are you doing? Sloppy, Kricket. Sloppy. I can't leave the roof door wide-open. If there is another explosion, the building shakes, the door closes, and I'll be locked out.

Stuck on the roof isn't a good time.

I eye the fire extinguisher on the wall and dismiss the idea of using it to wedge the heavy door; the weight might knock it out of the way.

Instead, I search the nearest desk, grab a thick piece of cardboard, and wedge it into the door-locking mechanism. The cardboard will stop the latch from clicking closed. As an extra precaution, I snag some brown tape and scissors, cut two strips to make an *X*, and stick the cardboard and tape ensemble down on the doorframe.

With a worried flutter in my stomach, I check to see if it works. It closes almost flush, but the lock doesn't engage. Great. It works. My hands shake as I bury my nerves and the horrid, nagging feeling I'm wasting time and could already be halfway home.

I step onto the wide, flat roof.

CHAPTER
FIVE

THE BITUMEN SURFACE is rough underneath my trainers, and the moon is full and bright. With no streetlights and the power out, in the distance, I can see swirling plumes of smoke and twinkling stars. The smoke has a reddish tinge. It twists into the night sky to the left, right, and back of the building.

Water from the soaked tea towel drips onto the front of my coat and dribbles down my neck, making me shiver. I ignore it in favour of being able to breathe. I was right—the magic smoke isn't as bad up here, but the scent is still cloying, and even through the layers of wet tea towel, it tickles the back of my throat.

At least the fabric, for now, does its job.

Then there are the screams... My heart misses a beat.

That isn't my overactive imagination playing tricks. I swallow and for a second close my eyes. Let's just say I'm so glad my thick hair and woolly hat cover my ears. The muffled collective sound of terror below makes me feel sick and once again doubt why I'm up here.

I dislike heights. My legs wobble as I take short, shuffling steps away from the door's safety. At least my dark brown coat blends into the night, so I'm unlikely to be caught and get into trouble. I scuttle, stooping for a low profile, and move to the roof's edge. When I get close, I drop and the rough surface bites at my knees.

Grabbing the roof's raised edge, I peek into the night.

"Oh fate." A moan that ends as a whine slips from my lips. Down the street to the left, twisted metal reaches into the sky like macabre fingers as the remains of the Peacekeeper Station and the attached Courthouse burn.

No one has come to put the fires out.

I swallow and tear my eyes from the devastation, not wanting to imprint that sight into my mind. To the right —my heart races—the Gargoyle Academy is also gone. It's a black smudge and a crater in the ground. Bile burns my throat, and the rancid taste of it floods my mouth.

The gargoyles. The young gargoyles. The handsome gargoyle. All I can hope is that they had a warning and cleared the buildings. That he's safe. I shiver and rub my arms. *This is a nightmare. This is a bloody nightmare.*

Yet if I pinch myself, it will be all too real.

Come on, Kricket. You can freak out later when you get home. Bad things happen, and sometimes all you can do is push forward and put the horrid stuff to the back of your mind until it's safe to deal with. I came up here with a job to do: check the roads and plot a path home. I need to do that.

I stare back at the Peacekeeper Station and take in the surrounding streets with a critical eye. It's not just the Station that was hit. That way is out, although it might be the best way to go if I can get past the piles of debris littering the ground. The buildings around it are in tatters, so whoever is attacking us will unlikely hit the same area twice.

But they might go after survivors.

Oh heck, my inner voice scares me sometimes.

I rub my arms and adjust the tea towel on my face. When I've stopped faffing, a flash of anger, born from long, festering frustration, hits me right in the chest. This town should be safe. It's supposed to be bloody safe. The creatures that forced us to move here are supposed to keep us safe.

They can't do that if they're all dead.

Whoever is doing this attacked the gargoyles—super-strong creatures with impenetrable skin. If they can hit the strongest of us so fast, the rest of the town—we are all practically human—have no chance.

If they come after us now, we are as good as dead.

Trapped within the wards of this bloody town, lumped together, it will be like shooting dragon bloods in a barrel.

I tip my head back briefly for just a second to stare

into the night sky. *I don't know what to do.* I sigh. Keeping as low as I can, I creep to the other side of the roof and the car park view. If I go this way, it will be a longer way home.

In the air, I trace the hazy streets with my index finger. I can loop around Midland Road and go up Gate Lane. *Yeah, that might work.*

My eyes scan the thick, swirling smoke below, and I make out odd shapes. Disbelief hits me hard as my fried brain tries to make sense of what I'm seeing.

My thoughts freeze.

There are *dead people* in the car park.

If I survive, when I relive this nightmare, I'll lament why my eyes are drawn to her first, of all people. I shake my head at the overturned trolley with familiar grotty bags. The food she purchased is spread around her, along with blood that pools around her head like a halo.

Sweet Eater is dead.

I blink to clear my eyes, and no, I'm not seeing things. The trolley's frame is dented as if she has been hit by a car or went up against a car in her ramming frenzy—which could be more likely. And she ended up dead. That shouldn't happen. Everyone knows mean, nasty people never die. They live forever just to torture others. It's their job to re-create hell on earth.

I hope Mr Three Items Guy got out okay.

Practical. I need to be practical. I robotically turn away, ignoring the bodies, the bodies of people I know, and continue to search for a way home.

That way is clear, but it might also be the next place to be hit. There are no high-value targets, just homes, but I've got to presume anything can happen. My vision blurs. I do my best to wipe the torrent of tears from my eyes, but I can't wipe them fast enough, and they just keep coming.

I gulp. There's this lump in my throat that I can't swallow past.

A sob rips out of my mouth, and I drop to the roof like a sack of spuds. The rough surface bites into my bottom and the backs of my thighs. My trainers drag against the black surface as I pull my legs up and hug them tightly.

I can't do this.

I can't.

This is all too much.

If you don't do this, you are going to die.

These are all people I know. Horror and frustration mix to make me feel numb. I rock, drop my head, and cry into my hands. *I want my mum.* I'm nineteen, an adult, yet for the first time in years, I want my mum and everything inside me wants a cuddle from my dad.

I need to get a grip, but my feelings are too big not to come out. *In a minute. I'll get up in a minute.*

Grief and fear are riding me hard, so I don't notice the ripple of music until it grabs my mind and my body moves of its own volition, jerking me forward.

If I wasn't sitting down, if I didn't have on the thick woolly hat and the copious amount of hair covering my ears, I think... I know I'd have walked off the roof.

A spell.

A musical spell has attempted to grab hold of my brain, and my innate power slaps the danger away. It's the worst kind of magic. It's a Pied Piper spell—illegal and dangerous.

My sorrow flees with a heavy dose of fear and adrenaline.

The explosions, the dead, it was just the beginning. My heart hammers against my ribs as I plant my arse firmly down and, fighting the urge to cover my ears, keep on rocking. I grab my phone to message my dad. I need to warn them.

Cover everyone's ears! I quickly type.

With my music-loving brothers, headphones are in abundance in my family home. Nan is as deaf as a post, so all she needs to do is turn her hearing spell off.

Whoever they are, they're using a Pied Piper spell.

Please let them be okay. Please. Please. My illegal wards are excellent, and if Dad did use one of my charms, even with the strong Pied Piper spell, it shouldn't reach them in the basement.

While I wait for a reply, even though I know it might already be too late, I copy and send the warning to my friends' chat group.

When I get a message back from my dad, I sag with relief. *We are safe. The spell hasn't reached us. What about you? Are you safe?*

I look away from the screen and stare at the roof's edge, at how close I came to going splat. Safe? Ah, well, that's the question.

I've got the store's sensory headphones. I text back, and then I add another big whopping lie. *I'm okay.*

I'm far from okay.

I feel like I'm going mad.

CHAPTER
SIX

I PUT the phone away and get to my feet while I avoid glancing down at the bodies in the car park. My eyes scan the road. "Ah, crap." Of course, they've been caught in the spell. The baddies are using it to zombie people out of their houses. They hit our strongest, and now they are rounding the dragon bloods up like rats.

People are leaving their homes in droves and joining together to wobble down the street towards the source of the magic.

Hopeless.

I never knew what true hopelessness felt like until this very moment. I'm powerless. I have no magic on me and can't do anything to help; there are too many people

—hundreds of people. I have nothing to counteract such a potent spell.

Instead of debilitating tears, righteous anger burns in my chest and licks up my collarbone. A tiny mercy, they seem to be stumbling away from my parents' house and towards the centre of town. *Wow, and there we have it.* I huff out a self-deprecating laugh. My selfishness astounds me.

You really see what you're made of when things go awry.

As long as my family is all right, fuck everyone else. Right? Right? *Bloody hell, Kricket, you are a twat.* I rub my neck. That lump is back, grinding, clawing against the soft tissues of my throat.

It's something else I'll need to contemplate later. Bury everything. Forget what I've seen, and stuff everything away to deal with later. That's probably where PTSD comes from—when people hide things and get on with it, and then later the memories sneak up and attack.

As if I can stare through the roof, I wonder if the supermarket is better insulated from sound. If I act quickly, I can warn my colleagues and remaining customers. They might not believe me and won't be able to see with all the smoke. If they are caught in the spell, there's also a good chance that they won't be able to get out if the doors are locked. I might be able to help. Do something to prove I'm not a total loss of a human being.

I move to go back inside, turning my head for one

last glimpse at the shuffling horde, and it's then that I see them.

They move down the road in what I can only describe as a creepy half-shifted form, their bodies overly large. *That's not right.* I don't know massive amounts about shifters, but I do know they don't have a half form —not like that.

Yet these creatures stalk down the street, their faces distorted and grotesque. They move in an arrow formation: one takes point, and the other five are spread out behind like a wedding train.

A strike team.

A kill squad.

I don't know why I'm so sure, but fear of what they represent grabs hold of my insides and almost brings me to my knees. I've never seen creatures move like that— like murderous dancers. These six creatures ooze menace as they drift across the car park. Even the freaky rolling magic smoke parts out of their way.

Under the tea towel, my mouth hangs open. I realise then that I'm standing, staring. I drop down so my silhouette doesn't stand out against the night.

The creature at the rear on the far right cants his head in a weird, birdlike motion. The scary man's attention is caught on something within the swirling smoke. I narrow my eyes, and the smoke rolls and shifts.

I see what has got his attention: a crawling woman. She's caught in the sound spell, and she's dragging herself along the tarmac; her legs appear to be broken. I bite my tongue so I don't cry out a warning that she wouldn't be able to understand as the spell has taken hold of her mind.

The creature at the back flicks his wrist, casually tossing a spell, and it hits the centre of her back. There's a flash of red, and she isn't crawling anymore. I jerk back. *I've never seen that medical technique.* The tone of my inner voice is now bordering on manic. Madness bites at my brain, and only the shock of the sick comment keeps me from wetting myself.

They're closer to the supermarket now, and the big one at the front of the pack stops and lifts his hand. From his palm comes a bolt of something, almost like a lightning flash.

The bolt of magic hits the front of the building, and the same glass windows I was so worried about before shatter. The building shudders. The lack of blowback suggests all the glass debris has blown inside the store. I lean forward as far as I dare, trying to see what they're doing, but the angle is all wrong. I can't see. They don't stop advancing. Boots must crunch on the glass as they enter the store.

Shit. I'm trapped—or will be trapped if I stay here for a second longer. I can't go down there, and I can't stay here. I force myself to move. I haven't got time to think. I run for the roof door and scramble through the office to the stairs. I slow before I hit the metal. I don't need to break my neck. On my toes, I move down the steps as quietly as possible—no need to rattle them.

Just as my trainers hit the stock room floor, Rich staggers into the back area. His eyes are wide and glazed with fear. "Kricket." Even with the tea towel covering half my face, he recognises me.

Rich is alive!

I wave him into silence. Grabbing his wrist, I drag him away from the wide-open doorway and deeper into the shelves, holding the flat of my hand out in a universal sign for him to wait.

He nods.

I haven't got much time. I dash to the office and grab two noise-cancelling sensory headphones hanging by the door. We only have the two; they're for our autistic customers.

"Outside, they are using a Pied Piper spell." My lips barely move, but my words must make it through the tea towel as Rich nods his understanding. I can't believe he hasn't already been caught up in the magic. Whatever the kill squad are doing must be louder than the spell.

The freckles across his cheekbones stand out stark against his sickly pale face. I plop the set of expensive headphones over his ears while donning my own.

I don't remove my hat or the hair stuffing my ears. I'm scared to let any sound in. Instead, I tug the hood of my coat up for added security and to wedge them in place.

Now I can't hear, and the hood has reduced my visibility, but it can't be helped. I can't be caught in that spell.

I mime keys. Rich pats his pocket and gives a jerky nod. I take his damp hand and pull him across the stock room and through the rear fire door. Rich is gangly and easy enough to tow behind me. He's talking, mumbling to himself. Before we hit the smoke, I read his lips. "They killed them. They killed them all."

My stomach sinks. I squeeze his hand, the only comfort I can give him.

I know where he lives. It's a mid-terrace house directly across the street. Thank fate, it's not opposite the front of the store, where the kill team went.

Rich's house is so close, but entering the thick magic smoke is disorienting. The smoke burns my eyes. Rich covers his mouth with his arm the best he can, and his shoulders shake. He's coughing. I have to fight down the urge to join him.

I should have wet the bottom of his polo with the saltwater solution so he could have held the fabric up to cover his face. It's too late now, and it's best to keep moving.

The trip across the road feels like miles. I make sure to keep us straight as best I can. Stumbling on the kerb, I almost go down but retain my balance with a weird shuffle hop. I begin to doubt my navigational skills, and then suddenly Rich's peeling blue front door is there.

We made it.

It takes Rich a few tries to insert the key into the

lock. His hands shake so much that I'm about to help him when the door swings open.

"Come inside," he mouths.

I shake my head, pat him on the arm, and step back, disappearing into the smoke.

CHAPTER
SEVEN

Magic particles cling to my eyelashes, making them feel weighed down. My trainers pound against the tarmac as I run down the middle of the street. The damage cast off from the blown-up buildings makes every step uneven, and it's hard to see with the smoke. I jump over some undefinable rubble, and the balls of my feet sting.

Perhaps I should have stayed with Rich and attempted to do this when visibility improved. But if I can't see the baddies, I'm betting my life on their inability to see me.

I've always watched apocalyptic or action films with a kind of smug demeanour, thinking if I were ever in that position, there'd be no way, no way in hell I'd run towards danger. Safe on my sofa, tutting at the plot and people doing stupid things. I was the first to shout at the screen for the characters to run and hide.

I'd hide out, I told myself, avoid groups, and get enough food and water to survive. Wait it out. Yet here I am, running across town to my family like a proper numpty.

Out in the open where the baddies prowl.

As I continually scan the ground for hazards, it's hard to tell if I'm getting used to the smoke or if it's slowly dissipating. Paranoia and fear sing a twisted song in my mind.

I'm so bloody scared.

The kill squad murdered that woman and attacked everyone in the supermarket. *No, get it right, Kricket, they killed them.* Why would they kill them? Surely they'd wait for the spell to work unless... unless anyone caught in it is dead anyway.

I don't understand what the heck is going on. But why would I? This is above any frame of reference. People do bad things, and trying to understand their motives without all the facts will drive you mad.

When they killed everyone, I deviated from the plan to go straight to my family. Instead, I need to detour to my place to arm myself with spells. I mentally go over my charms. I haven't got enough—I didn't plan for a fucking invasion.

The council wants us to be passive little dragon bloods. Having magic of any kind other than their crappy spells is illegal, and if caught with unsanctioned spells, the repercussions wouldn't be pleasant.

Producing any magic can lead to a death sentence.

That's why I have everything stashed at my bedsit. If I do something stupid and get caught, I don't want to implicate my mum or dad. Plus, if my brothers get hold of my charms, there's no end to the pranks and mischief they'd get up to.

I sidestep a smouldering car. The magic I create is a passion project. It includes silly items like a carrot-shaped charm that allows you to see in the dark—an excellent idea for sneaking into the kitchen to grab a snack without turning on the light.

My wards are a little different; they are serious spells. If I can make powerful wards, perhaps I can make more hazardous magic. What's that proverb? Necessity is the mother of invention. I'm pissed enough to invent some dangerous spells.

I hate it in this stupid glass prison of a place, but I don't hate the people, and these invaders who have come here and are killing us have messed with the wrong bloody town.

Despite the bulky hood of my coat restricting my vision, my heart jumps as I glimpse something white out of the corner of my eye. *Don't look.* I fix my gaze on the road. I don't want to see the doors to the houses lining the streets eerily wide-open.

I wouldn't have thought it possible, but the Pied Piper spell is intricate, produced by a talented witch, and strong enough that the people caught in its grip can open doors. I don't want to see the bodies of the spelled move within the smoke. As they trudge to fate knows where.

My hood does an excellent job of blocking out the stumbling masses. I can't hear them, and... I'm in a real-life alien invasion and cannot help anyone. No matter how often I tell myself there is nothing I can do without the right magical tools, the light inside me dies, and guilt chips away at me.

Another part of me wants to think *fuck it* and follow, find out where the spell is leading them, and save the day. Blow the baddie's shit to kingdom come and rescue everyone. It's a ridiculous thought. I'm ridiculous. What am I going to do against professional killers? Unknown creatures that are armed to the teeth and can explode lightning from their palms?

Nothing, that's what. I can't do shit. My ego isn't so big that I'll fool myself into thinking I can deal with them.

A big piece of smouldering metal is stabbed into the tarmac like a freaky art installation. I slow and move onto the pavement to get around and squeal in fright as a woman slithers over a gate.

The tops of her bare feet drag against the pavement as she rocks onto her hands and knees and then stumbles to her feet. Her blonde hair covers her face as if she's auditioning for *The Ring*.

Dressed in cartoon duck pyjamas and taking odd lurching steps, she heads down the road. Underneath the swirls of smoke, I can see bloody footprints. She's hurt herself in her desperate attempt to get out of her house and over the padlocked gate—that damn spell.

Now she's moving, her hair falls back, and I see her face. "Chloe?" *Oh no, I'm going to be sick.* I swallow the bitter stomach acid back down my throat and hurry to catch up. I block her path, and her sightless eyes stare through me and into the smoke. "Chloe? Hey, Chloe, it's me, Kricket. Kricket, from school." I wave my hand in front of her face, and when that doesn't work, I reach out, gently grab her wrist, and give the limb a little shake. She twitches, jerks her arm, slips out of my grip and takes determined, shuddering steps past me.

I run to get in front of her again. *What the heck am I doing? You're wasting time.* Desperate, I reach for one of the saltwater bottles, spin off the cap, and pour the liquid over her head.

I wait.

The water drips from her nose, and her wet pyjama top sticks to her chest. She does not respond; her shuffling steps do not pause. *Of course not. I can't salt-dip her brain.* She keeps on walking.

I hurry to catch her and grab her again. I hold her more firmly this time, and she reacts more strongly to being restrained. Her other arm sweeps out, cracking me across the face and into the neighbouring hedge. The prickly bush digs into my back, and I must let her go to prevent the headphones from falling, but I'm not quick enough to stop the tea towel from dislodging and sliding down my face. It splats onto the ground. I pull down my hood and secure it back around my face, all the while holding my breath.

When I glance back, Chloe has gone.

My heart sinks. "I'm sorry, Chloe." *I'm so bloody sorry.* I sniff and turn back. I refuse to wipe my weepy eyes. I need to keep going. With hunched shoulders, I drift back into the road and jog again.

My face is now sore beneath the wet tea towel. As I move, the rough saltwater fabric, now peppered with dirt from the pavement, rubs my cheekbones. It feels like it's digging a hole in my face, and my eye where she caught it is throbbing.

Woman up, Kricket. Think of Chloe and her bloody footprints. At least I'm able to feel pain, able to feel my face.

I narrow my eyes. *That's strange.* The smoke ahead is oddly moving, parting like a wave. My eyes widen, and with a horrified gasp, I react in an instant, dropping to my knees.

Oh no.

A kill team is coming around the corner.

If I hadn't noticed the change in the smoke... or spent the time trying to save Chloe, I might have met them further up the street, head on.

Fate has a funny way of keeping you safe.

I frantically hunt around for a place to hide. By luck, the vehicle I'm crouching next to has high ground clearance, and there's enough room to get underneath.

In my head, I roll under like they do in films. Instead, I flop onto my back and use my legs to push, shunting myself under the car while one hand holds the bulky headphones and tea towel in place. My puffy coat makes the entire move an ordeal.

I cringe. I'm making way too much noise.

When I'm finally under the vehicle, I reluctantly turn my head and see shuffling, zombie-style feet. The spelled are giving me cover.

A stone or piece of rubbish digs into my shoulder as the kill team's boots prowl closer. They're on the other side of the rear tyre, close to my head. Then two pairs of feet from the group separate. I close my eyes. I brace myself to be dragged out.

Any second now...

My heart is beating so fast it's going to burst from my chest and splat against the car's undercarriage. A spicy wave of magic gives me goosebumps and tingles my nose. I grit my teeth and...

And I'm not dead.

Reluctantly, I peek. Their boots are facing away from me. Thank fate; they must not have seen me. With my limited vision and hearing, I try to make sense of what they are doing, and I think they've forced their way into someone's home.

Why did they choose that house? Why not any of the others on the street? The answer burns into my brain, and my fingers twitch. I want to grab my phone and send a warning text, but my coat has shifted, and the handset is trapped under my lower back.

The front door was closed.

They're clearing the closed-door houses; either the people inside are trapped—I swallow and instantly become sweaty and hot with the direction my thoughts are heading—or people are hiding. The space around me narrows, and the car's non-existent weight crushes my chest.

People hiding like my family.

CHAPTER
EIGHT

They aren't wannabe terrorists. No, these invaders are professional killers. It's not even been an hour since the explosions, and it must only be around fifteen minutes or so since the Pied Piper spell almost walked me off the roof. They're already organised, already clearing houses and killing people.

My entire body trembles. I pin my hands to my sides and push my thighs into the rough tarmac so my limbs don't flop around as my imagination runs riot. Different scenarios run across my mind like an old movie reel, and I see another team of invaders kicking my parents' front door down.

Fear is a horrible thing.

I've never felt genuine fear before today, never felt

horror on this scale, and it's frying my brain. How do other people cope with this? My nerves are on fire and my heart is pounding.

I need to get a grip on myself.

I slam my eyes closed. If I can just block the world out, perhaps I'll wake up and everything will be back to normal, and all this will be a bad dream. That's not going to happen, right? I'm stuck. This is hell and we are all stuck here. I need to grab hold of waning sanity, shove it down inside myself, and somehow use the fear.

The invaders are too close for me to continue to panic, to make a mistake, and if I get myself killed, it will only be a matter of time before my mum and dad come searching for me and they'll die too.

This is hard. I worry I'm breathing loudly as I can't hear myself with the headphones on. I force myself to breathe in a natural rhythm as much as possible.

Dad said he used one of my charms. The only comfort I have is my confidence in my magic. The ward will keep them safe—it has to. Yet I worry that they are already dead.

I have an idea. It's as if a bolt of lightning strikes my brain. I know what I need to do. I have all this power locked inside me, and I've used my magic secretly. But now is the time to use it. To let go of my tight control.

With my eyes still closed, I wait until my heart rate calms. It sounds daft, but I use the power of my mind. Cautiously, I touch the magic within me with metaphysical fingers. The power is tucked behind my breastbone, swirling in my chest. With the precision of a surgeon, I tug out a thin strand of magic, and like threading a needle, I use the strand to reach out into the world.

It pulses. I'm careful to skirt around and not brush against anyone else's senses. I don't know how other people perceive magic. I've always presumed I'm extra sensitive and don't know the strengths of these creatures. It would be silly to make a mistake by sounding an alarm.

I push more, and the magic eagerly responds. It crests into a wave. The wave spreads and then returns. Instantly, I feel it. As if tugging on seaweed, it drags information of all the magic I have put into the world. It connects me to all my charms. I see them. They are like dots in a vast ocean.

Whoa, that's cool. I search and find the right pulse, the right little dot.

The ward my parents are using is fine. I can feel it hum happily in my head, and on a whim, I tie the ward magic off, wrapping it around my little finger and connecting it to me so it will give a tug of warning if anything happens.

Okay, the ward is there. They are safe. Come on now, Kricket. You can't lie here blocking the world out all day. Yeah, I need to see when the kill team leave so I can go.

I open my eyes and carefully turn my head; the bulky headphones dig into my temple and ear just as the spicy invader magic dissipates. It seems the team has completed its nefarious task. I hold my breath as their bloodstained boots march past the car, heading down the street.

Away from me.

I force myself to wait another painful five minutes, counting the seconds in my head until I deem it safe enough to move. Still under the car, I twist and roll, sliding my phone out. The network is dead. No, no, no, this is bad. I want to warn them about the doors, but now I can't. I want to say screw going to my place as I need to get to them now.

But the ward wrapped around my little finger gives me confidence; it will warn me if the house is attacked, and if the worst should happen, I'll need magic to fight them.

Fight or die trying, right?

I don't want to die.

I stuff the useless phone away, dig my heels into the tarmac, and shimmy out from under the car and back onto the street. I drop the hood of my coat and adjust the headphones. I no longer have the luxury of ignoring the world—I never did. *Stupid, Kricket. It's so stupid to hide behind my coat like a little kid.* I kick at a shard of glass. I didn't want to see the spelled, but obstructing my vision could have been a deadly mistake, a mistake I can't make.

I double-check that the coast is clear before patting the car bonnet in thanks. This time, as I jump over the debris, most of my attention is on the smoke, which is an invaluable early warning system for baddies.

With no more interruptions, it isn't long before my feet hit the correct road. I slow my strides, and behind the towel, my breaths are an unhealthy rasp.

The large white converted house looms out of the smoke. It's split into a dozen small flats, all single occupancy. I'm the youngest resident, and I've been here for around three years.

Mum and Dad didn't chuck me out of their house or anything. I left without a fuss 'cause of my magic dabbling. Also, a stupid council rule says if you aren't in full-time education as soon as you turn sixteen, you're encouraged to move to allocated accommodations subsidised by your assigned job.

Full-time education. I roll my eyes and huff under the wet tea towel. It's a cruel joke. There is no full-time education. They just want us to learn enough to be busy worker bees. Kids aren't being born, and we don't even have a full-time school anymore. There are not enough children to sustain one. Babies are rare and only come to town when poor sods are dragged here from the outside world.

It's a ridiculous way of controlling the populace, unbalancing entire families. Sixteen. Most teenagers are still babies at that age. I cringe when I think about my thirteen-year-old brothers. I can't imagine them being out on their own in three short years. They'll never shower again. I felt guilty for moving out, and my mum was so upset.

But that's what you do; rules are rules.

I ignore the wide, sad, flapping front door and hurry around the back of the building. We aren't allowed to own homes, and accommodations are allocated for the size of the family. Nan moved in and took my bedroom so my parents didn't lose the house. Once someone reaches a certain age, they are encouraged to live with family, and Nan pretends she needs extra help.

The woman is a marvel and still works part-time at the library. Librarians are the smartest people in the world, and I wish I'd inherited her patience and grace.

The stairs to my place have rusty black railings leading into the ground and a small square concrete surround with a black flowerpot—my crappy attempt at gardening—full of stinky, dark brown, stagnant water.

I'm in the basement, which is excellent as I have my own private entrance and a window. My mum hates this place. I can admit it's creepy, hidden out of sight around the back of the house. Dad replaced the rickety wooden door that was here when I moved in, and he got George, the welder, to install bars on the only window. He also got me a motion security light. Usually, the beam is so bright that when it turns on, it lights up the entire street and the street behind.

You can bet my neighbours love that. I smile as I carefully traverse the stairs and open the door.

CHAPTER NINE

The one-room bedsit—well, one room and a tiny bathroom—smells musty and has the tang of ammonia. Yep, it stinks of cat pee, a smell I've been unable to shake no matter how I clean. I get used to it when I'm home, and after a while, I become nose blind, but when I return from work, the smell hits me in the face all over again. It's gross.

I worry it'll rub off on me, onto my clothing. The cat-pee girl. It's ridiculous, as this flat has never seen fur. Not in over twenty years. Another cruel thing is that the council disallows us from having pets.

The small place is in darkness. It's hard to see with the power out and billowing smoke blocking any ambient moonlight from the tiny window. There's a bed

—a small single tucked into the corner, a wardrobe, a cupboard, a mini fridge, and a counter with enough room for a box of tea bags and a kettle.

I get everything I need with touch alone, grabbing a bag quickly enough. I wear mostly black clothes, so it's no issue to throw in random combinations. I could use my phone, but nothing says someone is sneaking around more than the glow of a torch.

I hurry to the bathroom, close the door, and drop a towel on the floor to block residual light. In the pitch darkness, the backs of my legs brush the toilet as I shuffle sideways to the oversized mirror. Muscle memory helps my fingers reach the hidden catch on the side.

This is why I'm glad I got the creepy, stinky flat.

The hidden room.

I don't know why the builders sealed it up. Perhaps they ran out of money? I found it when I attempted to replace an old mirror and, in a DIY frenzy, made a massive hole by mistake.

I flick the knobbly switch and the mirror swings open. I quickly figured out the hole led to a sealed-off room, so of course I made the gap wider between the joists and bought a bigger mirror.

What sixteen-year-old doesn't want a hidden lair to do her illicit spells in?

The tension in my muscles eases as the ward protecting my workshop glows bright. The comforting red light from the magic allows me to see what I'm doing. I stand on the boxed-in pipework, and with a grunt, careful not to knock off the headphones, I throw my leg over the wall and duck into the gap.

Into my workshop.

The wooden stool on the other side of the wall makes things more accessible even if the damn thing wobbles under my weight.

The ward protecting the room licks at me as if welcoming me home. My magic is a little unusual. I'm not going to say the magical items I create are sentient, but to me they feel like it sometimes. I know it sounds daft, and I'll never say it out loud, but they have their own personalities. Perhaps that's me putting human emotions onto magical objects—like a weirdo. I really do need a pet.

And it's not like I have any help or guidance with this magical stuff. Sometimes it feels like if I don't get the spells out of my mind, I'll explode. I'm winging it most of the time. It's magic, it works, and that's what counts, I guess.

Unlike witches who train for years, what I do isn't as simple as following a recipe and throwing items into a cauldron. It's like I place a tiny part of myself inside every spell. That's why I had the idea to reach out and touch them, and now I have a feeling I'll always know where each of my charms are.

I can only seep power into particular wood, stone, and metal—for example, I can't push magic into a Coke can—and it takes a while to prep the materials I use. I must handle them. Skin-to-skin contact is best.

Thinking of handling them, I wiggle out of my coat and wrap a string of uncut, rough-shaped obsidian stones tightly around my left arm and a string of wooden pieces around my right. The metal pieces I loop around my stomach. It all needs skin contact, but I'm not putting anything around my neck. With what's going on outside, I don't need the extra risk of getting strangled by my supplies.

That'd be a horrible way to go.

Nobody knows I get all the supplies from the outside world. I invented a magic that can open a gap in the town's ward without setting off any alarms. It was a silly and dangerous thing to do. I was fourteen at the time. Hormones played a significant role.

At first, I made the gap to see if I could, like an air hole, just to breathe easier and dream of leaving, then later, when I got older, to plan our escape and make it a reality, as I've always been determined we would leave this forsaken place.

The gap isn't big enough for a person but plenty big enough for a box of stuff. Besides, I've not tried it with living tissue. My magic keeps it open, and I'm not stupid enough to stick my hand in. I need my hands attached.

Once I opened the gap, I got a signal and used my mum's ancient mobile SIM card to talk to the outside world. The old thing worked with a bit of magic, and now I have an outside contact—an old friend of Mum's from her school days—who helps sell my magic and procure the materials I need to make more.

With my jacket back on, I methodically move from left to right, holding the bag open to sweep all my treasures from the shelves. I feel bad for treating them so rudely. I love these charms, and selling my magical horde has been hard. To let even one charm go is traumatising. But I had to for my family's sake. You can't make a clean getaway without money.

Once I clear all the shelves, I stuff the bag back through the hole, holding its strap until it lands softly on the bathroom's tiles. Then clinging to two of the charms —one shaped like an ear and the other like an umbrella— I climb back into the bathroom.

I glance at the ear charm with a smile and rub the lobe. I made the charms for my nan. I have several. When I asked her what she missed the most about losing her hearing, Nan said she missed the susurrus whispering of a page and birds singing.

Beautiful, simple things. I promised myself that when we got out of this town, Nan would be able to hear better than anyone. A shifter, a vampire, will have nothing on my nan. She will be able to listen to a mouse fart if she chooses.

We only tested the charm, as it isn't safe for her to use even at home. Gosh, I hate her current authorised shitty spell. If she can't hear the frequency of birds, what's the point? It's cruel. But someday… someday might be now. Butterflies flutter in my tummy.

I'm not ready.

I roll my shoulders and smile down at the little ear.

"Ello," I whisper; in response, the ear in my mind makes a delighted sound and warms my hand. The wood I used for this charm is Gabon ebony, which takes my magic well.

With a tweak, the charm will filter the magic from the air, blocking that bloody Pied Piper spell and allowing me to ditch the bulky headphones. If I do my job right, I can listen for baddie sounds.

I rub the ear between my fingers, and with a gentle magic push, we—the ear and I—have a conversation. I feel it when the new magic sound filter locks into place, and I slip the charm into the inside pocket of my work trousers. The thin cotton pocket won't be much of a barrier, and anyway, my magic is strong enough that it doesn't need skin contact once a charm is activated.

Trusting I've done my job, I tremble, take a deep breath and tug the headphones off. Alert, I wait a few seconds, and when nothing bad happens, I relax. My ears are tiny, and headphones never sit well. I vigorously rub my throbbing lobes, which are so sore that they thrum with the beat of my heart.

I then use the umbrella to unravel the ward. The red light dims and darkness takes over as the ward gets sucked back into the charm to be used again. My lips twitch. That's the magic that freaks my mum out the most.

Witches are powerful, yet they have limits to their magic. They can set the most potent wards; there's lots of chanting, and the ward will be strong but only be set in an area. If they're removed, they are gone forever.

That's what makes my magic so unusual: my charms can be used again and again. If all the magic is used, they use the residual magic in the air to recharge themselves. A user who isn't me just needs a simple chant to invoke them. I don't have to chant, and I've been working on an intent trigger for customers, but it's ridiculously complicated.

Five minutes down, and I'm ready to go. I kick the towel out of the way, slip the backpack over my shoulders, and leave my bedsit with the front door wide-open.

Might as well not invite trouble.

CHAPTER
TEN

THE BAG on my back bounces with every stride as the Peacekeeper Station's twisted, destroyed mess gets closer. The impact of what happened here is worse on street level. The remains of the building's frame stab into the night sky as if magic has taken a bite out of it. The image lingers, searing my brain—a poignant moment I will remember for the rest of my life.

It's life-changing, and I can't get my head around it.

One second, everything is unchangeable, unfair, and frustrating but predictable, and the next second, everything is gone. You don't know what you've got until you lose it.

The closer I get to the Station, the worse it is, and the

ground rapidly changes under my feet. Whenever my trainers land, puffs of grey ash join the swirling smoke.

The heat here must have gotten so bad that the glass and metals from the surrounding buildings have turned to sand. Even the tarmac has a sand-like consistency, and the granular particles make running hard work. The burn in my Achilles tendons attests to that.

The spell or weapon they used was a devastating one. Evil.

I don't know what the invaders want or what they think we've done to warrant this level of destruction, but this is so wrong.

I hunch my shoulders, and as I place my left foot down, the sandy surface moves. I squeak as my foot lands on something squishy. "What the hell!" I don't know what I'm thinking when I grind to a stop to stare at the ground. I almost swallow my tongue when I see the squishy thing is a *hand*. Grey skin. *A gargoyle*. I freeze, and my breaths puff like a racehorse.

He's dead. He must be dead, right?

I step back, carefully removing my foot, and the buried fingers twitch.

Oh fate, they moved!

My eyes almost pop out of my head. It must be 'cause I stood on them. I snap my gaze from left to right, checking that the coast is clear, and then drop to my knees to dig the gargoyle out.

What are you doing? My inner voice screams.

I hunch and dig faster.

Leaving him without checking if he's alive would be wrong, and it won't take a moment. Gargoyles are powerful creatures, but they still need to breathe.

As I scoop the ash away from the area around where his head should be, my hands burn and itch. The sand stuff is made up of tiny shards. The gargoyle with his tough, impenetrable skin will be okay—if he's alive—my skin, not so much. Unless a healing spell can fix this, I'll be picking micro particle shards out for weeks.

No good deed goes unpunished and all that.

Still, I dig. I uncover a sharp-angled face. Breathing heavily, I sit back on my heels. He appears like a fallen statue with his square jaw and full lips. His grey skin is an unhealthy pale shade. He doesn't look like a local gargoyle, not that I'm observant. I'm terrible with faces and names and try to avoid them.

The guilt of making illegal charms makes me awkward. I don't know if they can sniff my magic out. The council keeps us ignorant of other creatures. It's another bugbear of mine. I go to the library when I can and read—raiding the forbidden reference section. Forewarned is forearmed and all that jazz.

He looks dead.

I lean closer, and it's then I recognise his beautiful face. I've seen him before. He was the gargoyle at work tonight—the one who made me blush.

Oh.

I hover my now red, splinter-covered hand over his

nose and mouth and try to catch any of his breaths on my skin. If I had a mirror... Under the ash, his chest isn't moving.

He's dead.

My heart hurts for him. It's such a waste.

A piece of red hair that has escaped from my hat tickles the side of my temple and sticks to my sweat-covered cheek.

The smoke around us swirls, and the time I'm wasting ticks. I know I need to get going. The ward attached to my pinkie finger is happily buzzing away. For now, my family is safe.

I can take the time.

I don't know what possesses me. I groan and dig the sand stuff from around his neck and broad shoulders, uncovering the top half of his torso. He feels warm, but that doesn't say much as the area has been boiling.

My hands flutter again in front of his face. I have no idea what I'm doing. I rub them on my trousers, and tugging off the rucksack, I open the bag and grab a healing charm. It's a mixture of yellow, white, and rose gold, and it has a cute gold pin badge shaped like a potion bottle with the words HEAL ME in a swirly font.

The magic sings in my fist. It's a good, potent spell.

I slap it onto his forehead, and the charm activates with a spark of my internal magic. The surrounding air ripples, and like rising heat, the spell glows.

"Well now, it's doing something. It wouldn't react if you were dead."

I wait, hunched over him, worried we'll be captured any minute. If he's alive and does wake up, will he be caught up in the Pied Piper spell? Gargoyles are much stronger than humans, but I'm unsure if he'll naturally be protected from that awful magic.

The smoke drops and parts. Within a beat of my heart, I have the glowing healing charm off the gargoyle's forehead and back in my pocket, and another charm in the shape of a ghost activates.

I activate the magic just in time as another kill team strolls out of the smoke. They come from around the right side of the building. The Don't See Me Now magic hides us. It will continue to do so if we don't move or make a sound. It's not true invisibility—no one can do that—but it's strong enough that their eyes should brush right over us.

The gargoyle's eyes snap open.

Shit!

I slap my hand across his mouth and widen my eyes in the shut-up expression I cultivated for my brothers.

He tenses.

Oh no. I wait for him to be caught in the spell and stagger to his feet, but the angry light in his pale green eyes never changes. With my thumb, I tap him on the nose, and his eyes narrow.

He must see my panic, and as if a switch has been flicked, his training kicks in, and he stills. Deadly eyes watch me.

Oh, this is bad.

This is fucking scary.

He must deem me an easily rectified non-threat. One twist of those shovel hands of his and he can break my neck. The gargoyle turns his attention to the magic bubble surrounding us, the destruction, and finally, the invaders across the street.

His chin dips with understanding, and with the kill team facing away from us, I slowly slide my hand from his lips.

It seems to take forever for the kill team to move on. When they get out of sight, neither of us twitches a muscle for another few more minutes. It looks as if he can lie there all day. My patience runs out, and I do my best not to slap him in the face with my salty, wet tea towel as I lean forward to whisper in his ear.

"I don't know how long you've been out. But they hit the Station and the Academy about an hour ago. They have a Pied Piper spell—a strong one. Everyone caught up in it is heading towards the centre of town. They have teams of six going house to house, hitting the homes with closed doors, killing any dragon bloods who are not caught up in the spell. You need to get off the street."

His hands take hold of my shoulders, and I shiver as I'm gently moved back out of his space. I cringe. I'm glad the tea towel hides my no-doubt-red cheeks. I was a tad too close. After everything that's happened, I might be feeling a little clingy.

"Where is everyone?" His voice is a rumble of rocks being shifted.

By everyone, he means the other gargoyles. "I don't know." I don't say it, but everything inside me screams that they're dead. I can't help but reach out and pat his bare shoulder and shake my head. I flip my hand to indicate the ground. "I dug you out." I turn away from his intense, searching gaze and check for any changes in the smoke. "I don't want to be here when baddies come around again."

With an overwhelming need to get going, I drop the Don't See Me Now magic and wobble to my feet.

His eyes narrow as the spell rebounds back into the ghost charm.

You saw that, did you? I mentally grumble as I stuff it into my pocket and take a second to heal my hands. The pain relief is instant, and I can almost imagine the *plink, plink, plink* sound of micro shards being pushed out of my fingertips and palms.

The gargoyle's veiny forearms tense as he effortlessly pulls himself from his ashy tomb. He unfolds, and his massive body keeps going and going until he stands, towering above me. He must be a couple of feet taller than my five-foot-six frame.

I blink.

The gargoyle is missing his clothing.

Oh, bloody hell.

I can only imagine that it got blown off in the explosion. He stretches his wings, his lips move, and it takes me a second to tune in to what he is saying.

"Where are you going?"

"Home." I keep my eyes purposely on his face as I'm no Pervy MacPervson. I feel sorry for him. We are at war, and he's naked—running into battle with his meat and two veg flapping in the wind. He doesn't seem too bothered about his state of undress, but how can I leave him with nothing?

You can't fight invaders with your bits flapping.

I've already used two charms in front of him. What's one more? Shit, we are all going to die anyway. I dig in my bag, hold out my hand, and drop a charm onto his palm. "The chant is simple. You just say *clothe me*."

His expression goes from deadly to confused as he rolls the obsidian stone in the shape of a sock between his fingers.

"Here, let me." I place my hand on top of his, and between us, the charm glows blue. It takes a single sweep of my lashes and the gargoyle is dressed in a simple black jumper and jogging bottoms.

Huh. Not bad.

He tugs at the top, which has even made space for his wings.

Get in. I'm mightily impressed with myself and mentally pat myself on the back. I was worried about the fit because he's so big, but now I'm sure the charm can put sweats on a whale.

"What the hell are you?" He's back to looking angry.

"Ah, and that's gratitude for you." I adjust the tea towel and tuck the wayward strand of hair under my hat. "I'm nobody. I'm nothing, just a girl."

I need to go. I give him a friendly nod, then spin on my toes. My magic is odd, and now I'm paranoid that he'll think I've got something to do with the attacks and attempt to arrest me. Or kill me.

CHAPTER
ELEVEN

The gargoyle doesn't tackle me to the ground, and I take off. *He let me go. Phew.* He has a lot more going on than dealing with me, and maybe with my face covered, I'll be unidentifiable.

The explosion was centred around those buildings. The sandy surface of the road quickly changes, and returning to the tarmac, I increase my speed and head for home.

Will Dad be gone? Did I miss him? Did he leave in the car to go get me? I turn the corner to my parents' house—and stumble.

An odd little whine rattles in my throat like I'm some wounded animal.

My hand shakes as I open the front door. The old

Victorian has seen better days. The single-glazed windows rattle with lousy weather, and the wind whistles through the gaps. In winter, it gets so cold in the house that frost covers the inside of the glass.

My parents do what they can; Dad paints the wooden window frames every summer, and the house is so clean that even with my nightmare brothers, you could eat your dinner off the mustard tiles in the hall.

The fear bouncing around inside me dims just a little. I pull off the hat—strands of my hair crackle with static—and I remove the tea towel, stuffing them both into my pocket.

The front door creaks, and I make sure to leave it open, nice and wide.

Like a beacon, the ward surrounds the entire house. I pull it back to shield only the basement area and the bottom stairs. I then pour magic into a prepped chunk of obsidian. The illusion charm forms quickly; it shapes itself into a simple spell to make the basement appear empty and dark. For effect, I add a few things: creepy, unbroken cobwebs, a thick layer of dust coating the stairs, and a few haphazard boxes. At a glance, the basement door will appear like it hasn't been opened for years.

The stairs creak under my weight. When my coat moves, I get a whiff of my body odour—the stink of fright clings to me. My ankles throb and my calves ache. This night feels never ending, and my emotions are all over the place, flickering from fear to despair to relief.

My adrenaline level is so high I feel like I'm still running.

I'm home. I shuffle through the door, my eyes flitting around the space.

Tears prick, and a lump forms in my throat. *They're all safe.*

The homely basement glows with warmth. Mum is rooting around in a cupboard and Dad is reading a book. Nan is asleep on the chair.

My two brothers seem entirely unconcerned. They're taking full advantage of staying up late, sitting on beanbags in the corner, each with a handheld game console—some Nintendo thing; I'm not sure without looking at the logo. They're both whisper arguing. They're identical except for the hair. Aleric's red hair is a little longer than Ledger's, and he keeps stealing my dad's hair-care products.

Fate, the two of them are spoiled. They'll be disappointed when the battery runs out of those things, but I guess it's keeping them quiet. A lot of the tech we have is pre-locked up. Though we still have new stuff, it's just tricky to get, and it's not like we're flush with money—or we wouldn't be if it weren't for me selling my magic.

We cannot use the cash here in town; that would be raising a red flag. The money is for when we get out. Life is hard here.

"Kricket, I thought that was you. Were you born in a barn? Why didn't you close the front door?" Mum meets me, her hands on her ample hips, and she looks me up and down with a critical eye. Her strawberry blonde hair sticks up like she's been running her fingers through it all night. Mum leans forward and kisses my cheek; the move instantly softens her harsh words. "I'm glad you're home." She pokes me. "Now go and close the front door."

I have no idea how she can tell the door upstairs is wide-open—it must be some strange internal mum sense, I guess. I clear my throat. "I have a good excuse for why it needs to remain open."

Mum's gaze narrows as I go to shuffle around her. "Shoes, Kricket." She tuts. "Honestly, girl, you are a mess." If she could get away with stripping me down to my underwear like she did when I was little, I'm sure she would. She points at my legs.

I glance down at my ash-covered feet and legs. My toes wiggle within my dirty trainers. I don't want to remove them in case we have to leave in a hurry, but the stink eye my mum is throwing wins the battle.

Deal with the most significant danger first.

I huff out a weird, manic chuckle and drift back to the bottom of the stairs, toe off the trainers, and hang up my coat. Behind me, Mum moans to my dad about the front door and shoes being left on. I hear *born in a barn* more than once. I don't know whether to laugh or cry. This normalcy is jarring. My head dips as I tamp down the urge to cry.

Yeah, this is all so normal. They are the exact same

people they were when I left for work, and I've irreparably changed. We didn't just live the same hour.

And now I must explain what it's like outside.

They know about the explosions and the Pied Piper spell, but bad things are easy enough to dismiss if you haven't seen them yourself.

Ignorance is bliss.

Keeping a death grip on my bag, I head for the sofa, stopping to kiss Nan on her soft, papery cheek when she smiles at me sleepily. I perch on the edge. My fingers play with the bag's strap, and my left knee jiggles. I don't know where to begin. I'll have to start at the beginning and tell them everything.

Mum returns, holding a loaf of bread in one hand and a jar of peanut butter in the other. She smiles. "Do you want something to eat?" She has this smug light shining in her eyes, and I can read her like a book.

She's excited. Mum is so bloody chuffed she was right about things going wrong. She huffs about the room. Tidying little things here and there. She'd planned and waited for this very moment, and now, with her stores of peanut butter and the secret basement refurb—it used to be only useful for coal storage—all the nagging at my dad has been worth it. Her foresight is coming to fruition, and she's so bloody happy. I bet she didn't think it would turn out like this.

I wish I could sink into the settee. I don't want to do this. Crap, she's going to feel so bad. I rub my face. It's gritty with ash.

Mum tilts her head to the side. "Your face is all red." She smacks my hand away from my face. "Did you use that horrid cream again?" She leans in close.

"No." My voice is a husky whisper. "The smoke outside is heavy with magic. I used a towel covered with salt water to protect my airways. I'll heal it in a minute if it's so bad. I have something important to tell you."

"Something important to say? More important than closing the front door? You can't leave it open like that, Kricket. I hope you don't do that at your flat—" Mum loses track of what she's saying as her eyes drop, and she stares at my wrapped arms. "When did you get so many spell ingredients? You shouldn't be wearing them outside like that."

"I had my coat on. I was covered. I have to wear them, and at this point, it doesn't matter who sees me." Raising my voice to get everyone's attention. "Please come and sit. I need to tell you some things about what's going on outside."

"I can't talk to you when you're like this. Does anyone want tea?" Mum huffs and drifts off to fiddle with a camping kettle.

"Yes please," I croak while everyone else shakes their heads.

With tea, everything will be all right.

My feet curl into the rug that covers the bare concrete. The rug's old. It's probably from the '70s, pink with little splodges of white. You can even see bits of paint where my brothers have played down here and caused a mess.

My brothers stop their games, and Dad marks his page and slumps next to me. The old sofa dips and I roll slightly into his side. He throws his arm across my shoulders and kisses the top of my head.

"I thought you were waiting for me. You said you'd hide and keep safe."

Nowhere is safe. I wince. "It became too dangerous to wait."

Dad nods, accepting my explanation and giving me a side hug.

How do you tell your family that things have gone from bad to horrendous? How do you put it into words? I worry they won't believe me. If they don't believe me, will they get themselves hurt checking out what I've told them? They tend to be pragmatic.

"Mary, leave the girl alone and come and sit down," Nan scolds from her chair.

Mum is still complaining to herself about my face and the wide-open front door as she heats the hot water on a small camping stove. We all wait until she returns with a mug for me and one for herself.

"Thanks, Mum."

"I added sugar. You're looking a little red and washed out." She's not going to let my red face go, is she?

Dad leans forward. "Tell us, pumpkin, what's going on."

I swallow, eyeing my thirteen-year-old brothers, who

flop on the rug. My parents aren't going to like it, but I'm not pussyfooting around. They need to know. "The Peacekeeper Station and the Academy have been attacked." I stare at the steaming mug I grip in both hands. "I'm sure most of the gargoyles are dead."

There is a click of lips as my mum opens her mouth, and Nan makes a noise of censure in her throat.

I lift my eyes to see Mum snap her mouth closed.

I start from the beginning and explain what I've seen and what I've done. When I describe what happened with Chloe, my voice cracks. But I keep going. Dad stops me to ask the odd question, and Nan watches me with an intense, sad expression.

Watching the fear rise within my family is taking its toll.

"So you showed the gargoyle your magic and then ran off?" Mum asks. Is that what she got from that entire monologue? I shrug.

Her face goes red.

I appeal to my dad for backup. I know she wants me to keep my magic a secret, and I'm all for that too, but sometimes you must break promises when it's the right thing to do. I can see she's worried. At this point, I don't know if she's angry at me or over what's happening outside.

At least they believe me. I could have come home, and everyone could have said I was exaggerating or making things up, but I'm covered in ash and exhausted. I haven't looked in a mirror, but I bet my expression is haunted. If you take the time to look, you can see when someone has been through hell.

"Can't we save everyone?" Aleric asks.

Ledger scoffs.

Aleric scowls at him and then turns back to me. "Kricket, you're strong enough to save people, right? You saved the gargoyle. You can save everyone from these invaders if you just try." He stares at me as if he has every faith that I can fix this, and wow, it hurts.

My dad comes to the rescue. "Yeah, bud. Your sister is an incredible magic user, but all this is different. She's only one person, and we don't know anything about the creatures attacking the town."

"If you think you're so tough, why don't you go rescue everyone?" Ledger says, digging his elbow into Aleric's side. "No? You'd piss yourself, that's why. You'd never have come down from the roof. Hell, you'd have continued stocking shelves and got yourself blown up. As if Kricket can take on pros, nobhead."

"Ledger! Don't speak to your brother like that," Mum growls. "And Aleric, contrary to popular belief, Kricket is a nineteen-year-old girl. To you, nineteen might be ancient, but in the real world, your sister is barely an adult and isn't a Marvel character. Yes, she is smart and brave, and yes, she can do a very nice ward, but putting ideas in her head will only end up getting her killed. In this family, we do not encourage others to throw their lives away."

"We don't live in the real world," Aleric grumbles,

picking at a loose thread on his hoodie. "We live here in this shithole town."

"Aleric!" Mum's pointy finger comes out, and before this can evolve into a fully-fledged argument, I interrupt.

"I have a plan."

"A plan?" Doubt flashes across my mum's face.

"Kricket, that's our job. It's our job to look after you. We will deal with any planning. You need to get cleaned up and get some sleep," Dad says, rubbing his face with his palm.

It's late, and everybody is exhausted.

I twist my fingers around the mug. My eyes drift to Nan, who gives me an encouraging nod.

Okay, how do I say the next bit without getting into trouble? "I can get us through the ward."

There is a beat of silence.

And then everyone talks at once.

"What do you mean?"

"What?"

"Why the hell are we still here? If you can get out!"

"Kricket, that ward kills people. There's no getting past that barrier; hundreds of people have tried and paid the price with their lives," Dad says.

"I can get us through the ward and into the real world. I have a charm that makes a hole." I hold up my hand when Mum opens her mouth to explode. I'd never dream of doing the talk-to-the-hand gesture in normal circumstances; she's my mother. But these aren't normal times.

Mum gives me her classic wait-till-I-get-you-alone expression, aka the look of death. I've triggered her you-are-my-child mode.

"It's a small hole, but if I don't need to be cautious, I can pump more power into the charm and make the gap bigger, stabilising it enough for us to leave."

"Kricket, have you been leaving—"

"No, Dad. Never. I didn't think it was possible to use it like that. I made the charm because I could. It was a challenge, and I was very careful. Mum always goes on about how we lived before. I wasn't so young that I don't remember much of our lives before we came here. I wanted to be prepared for when we left and to make sure we had choices. Good choices. You know they'll freeze our bank accounts, if the town bank works outside. You know they'll make it impossible for us to survive. I can do it. I know I can get us safely through the ward, and in preparation, I have money set aside."

Mum slams her tea down. "You have money? Kricket, you work in a supermarket. The kind of money we would need would be too much for your piggy bank."

I gulp and hit them with it. All the secrets are coming out tonight. "I've been selling my spells under a pseudonym for years."

"You have? Since when?" Mum snarls.

"Five years," I croak.

"Five years? So that's how you got so many raw materials." Mum's pointy finger is out again. "Who have you been selling your spells to?"

"I... might have borrowed your old number and been in contact with Ava, a friend of yours from school."

Mum is a witch, but she can't practice. She says she doesn't enjoy stirring spells, but she isn't allowed to anyway, and I think that's something she says. Her dad, my grandfather and Nan's late husband, was a talented witch. Mum had to go to an expensive school—the Witch Academy—to train. When you have a fancy education and a purpose and can't use it, it must be like cutting off a limb.

Of course Ava doesn't know about our prison of a town. I keep that information hidden. And she doesn't know she's been dealing with a girl, let alone a teenager, this entire time.

"That phone is over thirteen years old. How can it possibly work?"

Well, there's magic for that. I can mix magic and technology, and the SIM works better than when it was new. I don't say anything; I fidget as Mum glares.

"You said you trade under a pseudonym? What name do you use?" Dad asks as he rubs a point between his eye socket and nose.

"Ah, well. I used your nan's maiden name and Grandad's first name."

"Gary. Chappell?" Dad says softly.

I nod. "Yeah, Gary Chappell."

CHAPTER
TWELVE

Mum wants to stay, Dad wants to go, and Nan has the deciding vote. After an hour of deliberation—aka arguing—they finally agree that we will leave. Rather than wait for the invaders to do something else, we'll attempt to cross the ward tonight while it's dark and the wisps of smoke still linger. By tomorrow, it might be too late.

Dad does a quick perimeter check with a recalibrated ear charm—Nan always loses her glasses, so I made spares. I'm glad I did, as we're lucky there are enough for everyone. Dad returns to tell us the coast is clear and the street is silent for now.

"Okay, kids, you have ten minutes to pack a bag. Make sure to re-check your ear protection charms before you go upstairs." Mum then hustles everyone through the ward, out of her precious basement, and up the stairs.

My brothers clatter upstairs like a herd of elephants running to their room.

Already packed, I wait by the open front door, eyes on the street. The spelled fog has lifted. If the ear charms fail or anyone in my family gets caught in the spell and attempts to zombie walk out the door, I have a sleep charm in my coat pocket, ready to go.

I can tell Mum is sad and angry we are leaving from the way she's stomping around. It must be a bit of an anticlimax. Her pride-and-joy basement only gave shelter for a few short hours. It's been my brothers' game room and storage area for years, so it isn't a complete waste of time and money. I do not doubt that the basement, combined with the strong ward, saved their lives.

I slump against the doorframe. If she wanted my opinion, which she doesn't, under normal circumstances, I'd agree the basement would be a fine place to hide out. This is not normal circumstances. Those invaders aren't following any villain's playbook. They're killing indiscriminately, and women and kids aren't safe. My mind instantly goes to the crawling woman, and my eyes fill with tears.

Mum might not be vocal about it, and she might pretend not to have faith in my magic, but she's been silently cheering me on all my life, even if she spends all her spare time telling me off. I wouldn't be the person I am without her. She's made me strong.

Strong enough to do this.

Twenty minutes later, we pile out of the back door and into the garden, each carrying a bag with personal items that we can't live without, some food, and a change of clothing.

One thing we have going for us is the location of this house. It's on the edge of town. At the bottom of the sixty-foot garden running along the rotten rear fence is the humming, flashing barrier of the ward.

Dad holds his elbow out to Nan, and she smiles and gracefully accepts his help. Mum herds my brothers towards the back of the garden. They look freaked out and pale. I follow behind, my feet dragging. I'm so tired. It's hard to navigate the paving stones and then the grass. My body will crash soon.

I can feel the ward as we march silently towards it. It makes the little hairs on my neck stand up, and goosebumps rise all over my arms. I grit my teeth and lift my feet higher. I'm determined to use every drop of energy and power to get my family out of here.

Mum keeps looking back to check that I'm okay.

Dad gingerly removes one of the wooden panels when we reach the fence and waves me over. "Are you sure about this, pumpkin? I can easily put this old panel back, and we can go back inside."

"I'm sure." My voice cracks a little. I hope he doesn't notice, but I catch his wince. I take a deep breath, drift past him, and stand before the spitting, rolling ward.

This is just like I'd practised.

The magic crackles across the boundary, and sparks fly. One burns my cheek. I lock my knees. This close, I can read the magical signatures of the dozens of witches who created and now maintain the ward. It's like a patched jigsaw puzzle.

The charm, delicate metal shaped like a bridge, sits cradled in my palm. I can do this. I can make a hole big and safe enough for everyone to cross. The bridge charm is excited; it can't wait to do its job. "Wait until I tell you to move." I rub the bridge with my thumb, opening myself to the magic.

"No, shit," Aleric grumbles behind me.

I close my eyes to centre myself and steady my breathing. *Okay, little charm, just like we've done before. Slow and steady.* The ball of power in my chest unravels. Carefully, it slides down my arm and pools into my palm, all warm and tingly. I feed the magic to the bridge, and its power seeps out, creeping into the air and wiggling its way into the ward.

Nothing happens.

I'm being too careful, and the ward is more substantial than usual. I feed the charm more power, and a hole opens up. It's not big enough. It's not going to work if I don't... I sigh and do something I've promised never to do. With the charm within my fist, I thrust my hand into the gap in the barrier.

Please don't melt my hand off.

The direct contact with the charm sends a magic

pulse, and I shove out more power—more than I've ever used before.

The ward parts.

The gap is so wide that I can see the other side, a field, a copse of trees, and a road beyond. The real world looks safe and quiet. I grit my teeth. Using this amount of magic is painful, and my chest is burning.

"Okay, move."

Dad steps through first. Once he's on the other side, my brothers and Nan follow. I feel like I'm holding a considerable weight and, any second now, the magic will hammer me into the ground like a nail.

Mum turns when she's on the other side and holds out her hand. "Come on, sweetheart. The ward is flickering." Her voice is far from calm; it's edged with panic.

"One second. I must time this right. Will you please grab my bag?" Sweat beads on my brow and my teeth chatter as I pass the bag full of spells and my mobile with her old number.

The gap is beginning to close.

Mum takes them, drops the bag at her feet and holds out her hand once again. "Kricket, come on now."

"The charms in the bag are worth a lot of money. There's a datapad with the full inventory and their retail prices," I say through my teeth as my entire body shakes from the strain. "The funny thing is nobody can do what I can, which makes my spells luxuries people are willing to pay a fortune for."

Mum's eyes widen as she realises what's happening.

"Kricket, don't you dare." Her hand shakes as she points to the floor. "Come here right now. This isn't a game. This is not funny."

"I'm the bridge, Mum. The gap in the ward won't work if I don't hold it open. Banking details and an address for the new house are in the bag. It's in a lovely town and owned outright. It's also fully furnished." I groan and drop to my knees.

"Kricket!"

"Don't be in a rush to sell the spells. They're in high demand, so get the right price." The gap in the ward is almost gone. Dad wraps his arms around Mum's waist to stop her from getting closer to the angry, sparking ward. "I love you all so very much. Please remember I didn't have a choice. The bridge charm wouldn't work if I weren't on this side holding it steady. Be safe. Be happy, and I'll see you very soon."

"No." Mum moans.

Everyone is crying.

A tear rolls down the side of my nose. "Ring Ava, and she'll send a car to come and get you. Get the word out about what's happening here. I'll do my best—"

The barrier snaps closed, and the poor little charm in my hand is silent. Dead. All its power has gone, and it'll take days to recharge.

"—to save as many as I can." I'm talking to thin air, but it's something I need to say.

Even if I'm the only one to hear my words.

Exhausted, it takes three attempts to get to my feet. I

turn and stumble back to the house. I need to get clean and changed. My clothing wasn't in the bag I handed to Mum; I'd hidden it before we came outside.

I have no plan and no idea what I'll do now that I've got my family out. I should feel elated that they're safe, but my only emotion is fear.

I guess I'll see what the invaders are up to.

CHAPTER THIRTEEN

It didn't take long to get to the town centre and onto another roof—a multi-storey car park this time. It was once part of a thriving shopping centre but has been empty for over ten years. It's an old, cheaply made building in desperate need of demolition—the concrete is crumbling. Not giving a shit about public safety, the council settled for half-heartedly closing it off.

From my vantage point, I peek around the chipped concrete pillar and through the open-air window covered in mesh to thwart jumpers. It provides the perfect view of what's happening below. The town square sprawls beneath me like a stage set for a play no one knows they're in.

I found them.

They are alive and still caught in the spell. Standing shoulder to shoulder in tightly packed rows are my friends and neighbours. Thousands of people. They remind me of blades of grass swaying in a non-existent breeze and waiting for... What? I've no idea.

Tugging my coat tighter around me, I cross my arms to retain some body heat. Under my hat, my hair is still wet. Taking a shower was worth the risk. Even without power, the hot water tank was still full. I desperately needed to wash the night away and change into fresh clothes. I binned my dirty uniform. I don't want to see another green polo ever again.

It's five in the morning, and with my circadian rhythm out of whack, my body is in that weird, trembly, need-sleep state. I can't stop shaking, and my vision around the edges is hazy. How could I sleep with all this going on? After last night, I don't think I'll sleep for a week. When I first started at the supermarket, I dreamt of working on the tills and endlessly stacking never-ending shelves. I don't want to think about what I would dream after all this.

My memories flick back to my mum's expression, the fear and heartbreak in her eyes. I know I broke her trust, but I don't regret lying. I'd do it again without question to get them away from this cursed town and the mess happening in the town square.

It's a horrible thing to make your entire family cry.

I pray they're safe. I should have made them promise

to leave the area. If they don't and get themselves killed, I'll be so bloody mad.

They'll go.

They have no choice but to keep my brothers and Nan safe.

I huff out a soft breath and stuff my fear down deep inside. I can't have negativity on my mind. I have things to do and must believe they're safe outside this wretched prison. I've been working hard for the past five years so they will have long, comfortable lives.

Five years.

I've always been different and a bit weird, and I grew up faster than my peers. But I've never been the hero type. I'm selfish. I did everything for me so I could be with them in our new life. I certainly didn't see myself on this fool's journey, watching them leave while I was left behind.

I'm under no illusions. Things are going to go wrong, and as I watch the spelled swaying, I make my peace with that. Dying will be easier than living with myself if I do nothing. Guilt will eat at me until there's nothing left.

Fate, the gods, magic, or Nature... whatever. The higher calling that puppeteers us all has given me a gift, and soon I'll see what I'm made of—and if my magic is strong enough.

Shit, that makes me sound like a narcissist.

If there is a higher power, will you give me a sign? I need a nudge in the right direction.

I don't know what I'm doing.

What do I do? How do I go about fixing this mess? It seems an impossible task. Maybe I shouldn't have sent my family away with all my charms. I groan and press my forehead into the pillar. I was panicking and I didn't think. I guess I never do.

Kricket, you're an absolute fool.

The kill team guys are easy to spot as they stand to attention on the edges of the silent crowd, still shifted in their strange warrior forms... unless they aren't shifters at all and just look like that.

Aliens.

It's all hush-hush, but everyone knows there are gateways and ley lines to other worlds. It wouldn't take much for them to come here. So the theory is not far-fetched; the invaders could be aliens.

But why would aliens attack a town full of dragon bloods? It doesn't make sense.

I stand and stare. The sky lightens, and the first light of dawn casts long shadows, but the eerie stillness makes the air feel heavy.

Nothing has happened for hours until I notice a change within the stoic guards—they get a little bit livelier and stand straighter.

Others arrive, increasing the enemy count to over forty. After an animated conversation, they begin to set something up—pieces of curved metal. The pieces quickly slot together, creating a strange circle. The circle is then raised from the floor and attached to a stand, a platform.

What is that? A portal gate? Nah, ley lines don't work like that; the gateways must be fixed.

I step back when the dark grey metal circles within the frame spin. They move in opposite directions, like something from a sci-fi movie. Within minutes, the movement is so fast that it appears not to be turning. A few seconds later, a ripple of glowing blue blooms outward from within the centre like a stone dropped in a pond.

"What is that thing? What is going on?" I murmur, shuffling forward and curling my fingertips into the mesh. The bite of the old metal grounds me.

The new arrivals—who are bigger and better dressed and look like Generals—drift through the ranks of the spelled, perhaps searching for someone. Then they roughly pull random people out of the line-up.

Get off them, I want to shout.

My uneasiness makes me shake harder. There's no rhyme or reason someone is pulled out and others are left behind, but then I notice the pattern. They bypass the witches and the fae. They're going for people with strong dragon blood DNA.

Once they've picked out about fifty people, they cluster the chosen together away from the others. I see a familiar blonde head and suck in a breath. It's Chloe. Chloe and a few other people I know. I scowl. Hateful Anton Hill has made the cut.

The baddies talk and point a lot, and then the kill teams split up. They herd the spelled—the ones not in the special group—towards the gate.

At the front of the first line, an older man shuffles, and my heart misses a beat when I recognise him. It's George, the welder who did my security bars. He's a friend of my nan's, and he's always been kind.

Poor George is oblivious to what's happening around him as he zombie walks towards the gate. His body touches the blue centre, and he disappears. *What?* A dozen more people follow George through the gate, and I watch, growing more confused as person after person disappears.

Have I got this all wrong? Is this a rescue? And then I see it. I notice something, a build-up of ash. Ash particles flutter and settle on the ground each time someone steps through.

Ash.

Huh, whatever it is, it must create a lot of heat. I don't understand why there is... My brain is slow to connect the dots, and when it does, I gasp.

It's not some otherworldly portal. I pull away from the mesh to clutch at my stomach, and bending forward, I moan. Bile rushes up my throat. I'm going to be sick. There's no rescuing George. He's dead. Everyone that goes into that thing is dead.

It's killing them—vaporising them!

Oh fate, what have I done? I've stood here watching, doing nothing, while the invading baddies kill people.

I need to destroy that machine now!

I let my mind roll, opening myself to the magic inside me. *There must be a spell.* I focus on the raw materials pressing into my skin and ask them for help.

Before the magic can form, I'm grabbed from behind. I squeak in surprise as a massive arm wraps around my waist and jerks me against a solid chest.

"What the—"

A giant grey hand slaps over my mouth, cutting off my words. "Shush."

They've found me.

"Don't throw your life away for people that are already dead," says a rumbly voice—a voice like rocks falling, a voice that I've heard before.

The gargoyle.

"You can't do anything for them, nothing girl. Or should I call you by your name, Kricket Jones?"

How does he know my name?

"They were already gone as soon as the spell got into their heads. They're brain-dead."

I moan, and his heavy palm presses harder, muffling the sound. We are still facing the same direction, and they've started with another line of people. I don't believe they're brain-dead. I don't believe him. I need to do something. The gargoyle needs to do something. *Why is he just standing here? Why isn't he helping?*

The gargoyle drops his voice and menacingly whispers against my ear. His hot breath tickles. "The stunt you pulled with your family finally pushed them over the edge, using ancient magic to get them through the ward." He tuts. "What were you thinking? What did you think would happen? You should have left with your family when you had the chance. Did you think they couldn't feel the power? Stupid, selfish girl. They knew you weren't with the people down there the second you tapped the ward."

His fingers curl, digging into my face. He grips my chin, forcing me to watch the people below. He's a fool, and the move is pointless 'cause I've not once looked away.

"That's why they're killing every dragon blood in this town, because of you. Did you know that?"

Me? *That's not true. He's lying.*

The gargoyle tightens his hold; he's now hurting me. I whine in pain. I attempt to throw my leg back and kick his shin. He lifts me until my feet dangle, and then for good measure he traps my flailing legs between his thighs and bends me like a pretzel.

"They came here because of you. They killed hundreds of gargoyles, and soon thousands of innocent people will die, and it's all your fault." His biceps tighten, my bones groan at the pressure, and to drive his point home further, he viciously shakes me like a rag doll till my teeth clack together.

The gargoyle adjusts his hold and then thrusts a hand in front of my face. I cringe, tense, and close my eyes. When he doesn't hit me, I blink a few times to refocus on the object between his fingers—the sock charm.

Oh. *Where's he going with this?* I helped him, so shouldn't he be grateful?

"What we don't know is where you found the charms. Did you really think selling dragon artefacts would slip their notice?"

My head goes fuzzy.

Dragon artefacts? No, no way. That can't be right.

They're my charms, mine. My power has absolutely nothing to do with dragons. I'm part witch, that's all. All the books say that dragon bloods have inert DNA, and it doesn't do anything; we don't do anything.

The building falling on him has damaged his mind, and being buried alive has done him severe mental harm. The gargoyle is confused and not right in the head. You can't argue with crazy.

I take a deep breath through my nose, pushing down the panic bubbling inside me. I force myself to focus on what he's saying—it's hard when someone spits such vitriolic words. Rage oozes off him. I've never met anybody so angry.

I focus, rolling his words in my mind. All this talk about dragon artefacts leads me to believe he doesn't know. He must not know that the magic is mine. He thinks I'm using a stash of ancient charms.

Shit, this is bad. Really bad.

"The dragons are hunting you, Kricket. It's only a matter of time till they find you. You've already seen what they can do; they will make you hurt until you tell them everything they want to know. I promise to keep you safe if you tell me where the rest of the charms are. I'll ensure your prison sentence is light and let your family go as a favour."

Oh, that's good of him.

What the hell, prison? And hang on a second. What did he mean about the invaders? This just keeps getting better and better.

"Dragons?" The word comes out garbled 'cause of the massive hand covering half my face. Ugh, he needs to get that big paw off me. I don't want him touching me. I've no idea where that hand has been.

I try to think of a spell that'll put him down. A Taser comes to mind, and I have the sleep charm in my pocket. As soon as the thought forms, my coat sleeve is roughly shoved up—along with the string of obsidian stones wrapped around that arm. My skin burns as the little hairs are ripped away.

Something slaps against my bare wrist.

Oh look, the gargoyle has brought a friend.

The other gargoyle grins at me with narrow, serrated teeth. Nice. Where the first gargoyle has a face like a magnificent statue, all angles and male beauty, this guy looks like any local gargoyle. Big, hard, and scary. The thing he slapped on my arm unravels and then tightens.

Everything that I am stops as if the entire world has held its breath.

I gasp.

I can't get enough air into my lungs. I've never seen

one, but I have heard of them. It's a null band, a magic-stealing bracelet.

"Why is she not out?" the friend grumbles. "Even pure humans are out like a light."

"I don't know."

"Strange."

Another band slaps down, joining the first. Uh-oh, they put on two. I'm getting weaker, but I can still feel the charm in my pocket, and if I can just... before I can ask the little pillow for its help, another band slaps into place.

Three.

"Yeah, she's strong." The gargoyle holding me aims for confidence, but even to my numb ears, he sounds confused. "That's why we've been watching her."

My head flops. I can't seem to hold it up, so I sag back against the gargoyle's chest. *Dickhead.* I can't believe they've been watching me. "I should have left you buried in the sand."

CHAPTER
FOURTEEN

To keep compos mentis, I let my gaze drift out the window. My eyes land on a familiar green shirt. The person is in the middle of a line of spelled stumbling their way towards the spinning machine. My eyes widen, and adrenaline sloshes through me, chasing away the lethargy of the bands.

Rich! It's Rich from work.

My heart misses a beat, and something inside me snaps.

Red-hot anger heats my blood.

How dare these gargoyles try to control me! How dare they steal my magic, attempt to knock me out, threaten me, and accuse me of theft! And how dare they do nothing to help the innocent people down there, people like Rich.

The gargoyle is wrong if he thinks I'm easily controlled. I'm my mother's daughter and, to no avail, she's been trying to control me for years.

The null bands might lock my power down and keep me from accessing my internal magic. But my magic isn't just internal. It's also on the outside, stored within all my charms.

I can't use my magic with the null bands on, but the little pillow charm in my pocket can.

I grin and let go.

I allow the charm to access my magic. Pain cracks in my chest—it's nothing like I've ever felt before. My insides feel like they are on the outside, and my intestines are spilling out.

Boom.

The power in the charm explodes, and the energy blasts in all directions, hitting the two gargoyles, throwing them off their feet and sending me flying. *Ouch.* I crunch against a pillar, and for a few terrifying moments, I can't hear, see, or sense anything.

My head swims, but rage gets me moving. *I need to get rid of these bloody null bands.* I roll onto my hands and knees. "Fuck you, gargoyle. You're a lying turd," I mutter as I half crawl, half drag myself across the dirty car park floor towards his unconscious body. "That's it, you twat. Stay down."

Blood from a stinging cut on my forehead dribbles

into my left eye. I rapidly blink, and when that doesn't work, I wipe it away on my sleeve. I feel dizzy and want to stop and lie down, perhaps have a meltdown and cry. But the gargoyle's words from before rattle around my mind. *They came here because of you. This is your fault.*

No, fuck that. This is their mistake. Not mine.

"I'm not about to be a martyr or a scapegoat," I huff, pulling myself forward an inch at a time. "I know, I bloody *know*, this isn't my fault. The council thought it was fabulous to lock us all up without giving us the lowdown on our powers. When in creature history has ignoring anything worked out? This mess is on the council. It's on the weird-looking fake dragons outside who are right now committing genocide." A sob wrenches from my throat. I drop my head, and blood drips on the floor and onto my hand.

My fingers dig into the dirty concrete, and I keep crawling.

"I'm just the convenient person to blame—if that's even the truth. I don't trust you." I drop my voice to imitate his rock-like rumble. "Spill your guts, Kricket. Give us the charms, Kricket, and we will only lock you up and not cut off your toes. Dickhead, do people fall for that crap?"

I flop against him. Huh, he's as hard as the concrete digging into my knees. When the sleeping spell hit, he'd turned to stone. Handy trick. I can't stop myself from poking his cheek. Yeah, the handsome bastard is solid.

At least his clothing is normal, and I don't think

twice before I rifle through his pockets. There should be... Aha! I find the tool I need to unlock the null bands, or it should. I hope.

I bite my lip, wince, and press it to the first one.

There is pressure, and five seconds later, the band unravels from my wrist, and the other two quickly follow. Three null bands—what were they thinking? They could have killed me.

There's a ping of familiar magic coming from his trousers. In an inside pocket, I find the sock charm. "Hi, little sock." I pop it in with the others and keep digging.

There are lots of weapons. Whenever I find one, I throw them into the dank corner by the stairs. I hope they get scratched or that the gargoyle never finds them.

I also discover his stash of spells. The gargoyle has many nasty ones, some bordering on illegal. I hold a marble-sized red ball to the light streaming through the far windows. *Great, I'll be able to blow shit up.*

I then pop the top off a vial of healing potion, unzip my coat, pull my jumper away from my neck and pour the gloopy liquid onto my chest. He owes me one. The magic isn't as good as mine, but it will fix my head, cuts, and scrapes.

Feeling better, I wobble to my feet and stare down at him. "Here, have a cookie." I'm a tad vindictive, and instead of kicking him in the head, I slap two of the null bands on the gargoyle's thick wrist and pop the third one on his friend. "Let's see how you like that, arseholes." A vicious smile pulls at my lips when I think of their colleagues coming to collect them and finding them sleeping on the job with their null bands on.

I flick my wrist and chuck the removal tool, satisfied when it bounces into the dark depths of the car park and disappears against the dirty floor.

Then I remember Rich.

The sound from outside has stilled; everything is quiet, and that's odd. Before, the invaders were vocal, their voices carrying and echoing around the empty car park. I shuffle back to the windows and see— *Oh!*

Oh, oh heck.

My eyes are wide enough that there's a risk my eyeballs will roll out of my head. Everyone is flat on their backs, asleep. *Everyone.* I laugh a little manically—no wonder the sleep charm's blast felt so strong.

The magic wave wasn't just confined to the car park. No, it's knocked everyone in the area out. Adrenaline hits me, and I dash for the stairs. I clumsily take them two at a time. I don't know how long the fake dragons will stay down.

CHAPTER
FIFTEEN

My trainers hit the street, and I step over and around sleeping bodies as I anxiously search the crowd near the machine and notice a splash of bright green. Rich is still alive. He's safe—or as safe as someone supposedly brain-dead can be.

The invaders—the dragons—are still in their warrior forms. The closer I get, the more I want to poke and prod their faces as they don't seem real. They're distorted like they're using quality illusion spells, like movie prosthetic magic. Like a Scooby-Doo villain mask.

Do dragons really look like that? Surely not. My gut tells me it's magic.

I pull off my hat, my still-damp hair tumbles around my shoulders, and I rub the sweat and blood from my brow. We were told that there were only a handful of dragons left. Was that another lie? These creatures can't be true dragons. If they were, why haven't I seen any of them fly? Why haven't they shifted into dragon form? If things don't make sense, usually they aren't true.

The wind ruffles my hair as I stand in the middle of the bodies. I turn in a circle, trying to think of a way to restrain the invaders. I could create a feather charm to make them light as feathers and stuff the baddies into the still-revolving gateway.

Add their ashes to the pile.

Now that would be poetic justice.

The thing hums innocently enough like it's not a giant body-ashing machine. I groan and rub my head. I have this pesky moral compass that screams that it's a horrible thing to do, and when I really think about it, the idea makes me want to hurl.

Dad wouldn't want me to do that, and Mum wouldn't think twice. She'd kill them all.

The invaders are all out cold. It would be murder. I'm not ready to kill people no matter how bad they are. No matter if they deserve it.

A feather charm though... is a good idea.

I check my magic to see if I have enough juice to make a new charm and find my power is no longer a ball in my chest.

What now? I mentally whine. What if the null bands have done some serious damage?

I prod a little more. No, the magic is not contained at

all; it's free-flowing from the top of my head to the tips of my toes. I'm flooded with power.

Well, now that is weird.

The magic I used to knock all these creatures out should have put me on my knees and made me sleep for a week. But I feel like I've had a full eight hours, and my skin—what I can see on my hands—is glowing.

Shit, what the heck is going on?

Okay, I can freak out about this later. These invaders might wake up any second.

First, I need a feather charm and something to contain the invaders. I flick my fingers when it comes to me: a simple ward will do the trick. Thank fate I'm full of power—making two potent charms, one right after another, is no mean feat.

I send a pulse of magic at the raw ingredients and request help. A few respond and feel capable, and there's a bright spark somewhere near my feet. I drop my gaze to the ground, and there's a glint of something heeding my call. A piece of glass, an old bottle shard hidden against the kerb. Its response to me is bright, clear, and full of confidence.

What the hell? That's new.

My magic doesn't work like that. A random piece of rubbish off the street can't be used as a charm.

The shard disagrees with that hypothesis.

I guess things are changing and changing fast.

My stomach flips. I bury my anxiety, squat down, and extract the glass from something slimy, wrinkling my nose as I stand. "Ew, that's gross. Why did you have to get wedged down there? You think you're special and don't need to make skin contact with me, huh?"

I hold the spiky shard carefully in the centre of my palm, then close my fist and pour magic into it. I might as well go for it; there's no time to waste.

After thirty seconds, it's done—it should have taken hours to power this level of charm, but I'm not going to think too hard about that. I carefully peel back my fingers to see the most delicate, arty-looking feather in the centre of my hand.

It's beautiful.

It still looks like glass, but I can tell it'll be super strong. I close my eyes, and my anxiety about the baddies waking up falls away. Using the charm, I focus on the fake dragons, send out a pulse of magic, and... lift them with my mind.

I have to peek—and about thirty sleeping bodies are hovering in the air. "Okay." I blink a few times. "Well, that's great."

I pick my way through my sleeping neighbours, and the floating fake dragons follow me like weird balloons.

I search the ground for an empty spot with no pipes or electric lines. Usually that isn't a problem, but if these invaders are strong magic users, fake dragons or not, I don't want the risk of them breaking the ward.

I direct the feather to dump them unceremoniously into a baddie pile.

Then using an angry piece of wood that's been

digging into my wrist all night, I turn it into a new umbrella charm. The ward springs up, crackling and spitting with power, neatly locking the invaders inside.

I sag. The relief is instant. Of course I've no idea if any more are hiding or a team of gargoyles will come out of the woodwork and capture me. This is the age-old thing of being careful what you wish for. I always wanted to be popular. I roll my eyes. Dragons and gargoyles, oh my, aren't I popular.

Fuck my life.

I move towards the spinning machine and, without touching it, gingerly place a few of the gargoyle's red spells around its base. I could make a charm, but why deplete my power when I can use this ready-made magic? I set the charges and shuffle away.

I can't help imagining the spells going wrong and the machine being launched from where it's being held up, and suddenly in my mind, it's doing an Indiana Jones roll of doom and sucking up everybody it passes.

Ah, shit.

Just to be safe, I throw up a ward to protect against flying debris. It's just in time, and I cover my ears as the gate blows. The explosion is contained. The worst of it is a puff of smoke and pieces of metal hitting the ward, then dropping harmlessly to the ground.

I shuffle forward to check, and I'm confident it can't be resurrected. I drop the ward, and it rebounds and settles back into the umbrella charm.

It's done. I rub my arms, feeling cold and lost. Now

that I'm still, the silence gives me the creeps. I drift over to Rich's side and kneel down. His chest gently rises and falls. "Why did you remove the headphones, Rich?"

Perhaps a kill team found him—at least he doesn't look hurt. None of them look seriously hurt. I turn my head, and a shudder ripples through me as I take in the thousands of bodies surrounding us.

I can't make myself look at their faces. If I start to truly recognise people, recognise friends, I'm going to be rocking in a corner, having a meltdown.

People are half-dressed; even with no awareness, they must be freezing. I'm cold with a coat on. In my pocket, the sock charm sings, wanting to help. Like me, the bridge, the pillow, and the obsidian-stone sock are all brimming with power. It doesn't make sense. The bridge charm should be dead for several more days, but whatever I did before has made us stronger.

"Can I do it again?" I swallow my unease and let the sock directly access my power. One second, the people around me are in various stages of undress; the next, they're dressed in the same black outfit, jogging bottoms and a jumper, that I clothed the gargoyle in.

"That's so much better," I mumble, patting my pocket. "Thank you, little sock."

My brain can't even contemplate the scale of magic—thousands of people dressed within seconds. And it might be all for nothing. *What if they don't wake up?* Surely there must be someone coming to clear this mess up. What if they die, and I'm the only one alive when the cavalry arrives? Will the Creature Council blame me if these people die covered in my magical signature from the sleep spell, the sock charm?

Of course they will.

The gargoyles already think this is my fault.

These people need medical attention and specialist help. Would a healing charm be strong enough?

Healing is entirely different and way more complicated than stuffing clothes on. Do I have enough magic to heal *and* wake everyone up? Can I fix the damage done by the Pied Piper spell?

Whop, whop, whop... At the sound, I tilt my head. Is that...? Is that an incoming helicopter? I frown in the direction I think it's coming from.

The sound resonates off the surrounding buildings, so it's hard to tell, but I'm sure it's coming from where the ward should be—and that's not possible unless the ward has fallen. The bridge charm lets out a smug ping, and I stare at my pocket in horror.

No. My eyes flit about. Oh *nooo*.

What the hell is going on with my magic? Fear flips my stomach; what else have I inadvertently done?

The *whop, whop, whop* of helicopter blades is getting closer, and all I can think about is the out-of-contact gargoyles. An entire group of them might be on that helicopter, coming to chop my head off. Or it could be more invaders.

I can't do anything if I get caught.

I go with my gut and bolt for the nearest building,

automatically darting for the library, a good choice. Not only do I know the layout but also the staff-only areas like the back of my hand, thanks to my nan working there for years.

I run, dodging the spelled people on the ground. Their sleeping forms make me feel guilty. What'll happen to them nags at me. They need help now, but there's no time. If I had another few hours...

Come on, Kricket. Who else is going to help them? "The government?" I scoff. The world has already decided that dragon bloods aren't worth protecting—no, they shove us behind a ward and pretend we don't exist.

My magic has levelled up; before this weird phenomenon stops and I return to normal, perhaps I can heal everyone?

I don't stop running. On the fly, instead of making a single charm, I desperately throw my magic out and search for things to use. Anything. I find jewellery. The gold in people's ears and wrists, the delicate jewellery around necks and fingers, and even a few plastic watches answer my call. Each one should fix a cluster of people.

I throw my magic out wider, like a net, to capture anyone left behind, the poor spelled trapped behind those closed doors.

Then I focus on my memory of the Pied Piper spell. It touched me, reached out, and tried to take control of my mind. I know the spell intimately; while it was in my head for those few seconds, along with the panic and fear, I got a good look at its makeup.

If you know something intimately, you can destroy it. Right?

My feet hit the stairs and I hurry inside. At the library's entrance, I brace myself against the oak door and turn to look out onto the square at the thousands of sleeping people.

I remember at the last minute to block the magic from interfering with the two gargoyles and invaders sleeping within the ward. No need to wake up trouble. Those creatures need to remain asleep.

I glance at the sky, scared the helicopter will land any second. I open my arms and throw everything I have into the temporary charms. "Heal," I demand as I let them take what they need. It feels like they're sucking at my soul.

The charms use me like a battery, and the strain on my body makes my heart miss a few beats. Hundreds of odd, weird, and wonderful charms scream in my mind. I can feel the spell's structure warp and melt as they dismantle it.

They remove all traces.

A big, black helicopter comes into sight.

I can't wait to see if what I'm doing works. Like a drunk, I turn and stagger into the library, swaying past the front desk and through the stacks.

The charms have done all they can, and I have no idea if it'll be enough. I don't have a connection with people like I do with the magic.

I take a deep breath, and then—I've never done

anything like this before—I rip the power out of the temporary charms. The rush of the returning magic sends me to my knees. There's a horrific pain in my mind, and my heart feels like it's limping in my chest. A *pop* of sound and a flood of hot liquid comes from my eyes, nose, and ears. I swipe at my face, and my fingers come away bloody.

I'm bleeding. Again.

Some blood vessels must have burst. The only plus point is that my heart is still beating. I drag myself to my feet—barely, but I'll take it—and stumble towards the staff room, aiming for the tunnels in the basement. The tunnels lead to the council offices, and the council has a ley line gateway—a portal.

It's my magical getaway car.

Usually it's guarded. But with the entire town outside on the square, I'm betting no one's there to stop me from using it.

With blood dripping down my face and my vision going grey at the edges, a paranoid thought flits to life. *Blood.* With blood, they can track me, and I'm leaking like a sieve. I've also left droplets on the car park floor, plus my magic signature is everywhere. I need a charm to cleanse my blood and magical presence from everything.

Have I got another spell in me? Can I make a brand-new charm? I enter the code to open the staff room door and shuffle through, closing it firmly behind me. I use the power remaining in the umbrella charm to ward off the door.

It's now or never, Kricket.

I'm gasping. Each breath is impossibly hard. I pass through the door on the left and take the stairs down, clinging to the railing as I stumble forward. My vision is fading to a pinprick. Damn it, I'll fall down these bloody stairs if I don't get to the bottom soon. I keep going. I trip over the lack of a step when the floor evens out and drop to my knees.

Everything has gone dark as if my eyes are closed.

The tiled floor in the basement is cold and smells faintly of lemon cleaner.

If I push a little more, my survival rate might drop to nil. But if the two sets of baddies hunt me... I'm dead either way. Ha, I'm not quite the superhero then. Here's me thinking I'm a magical bigwig, and instead about to kill myself by over-taxing my magic.

With the last of my strength, I make the charm.

Oh fate, it hurts. It won't wipe away any active magic —my spells will remain—but the charm *will* wipe away any trace of me. It'll scramble the evidence.

My power understands my intention, but for this, I speak. "Please." I grit my teeth. It's like someone is stabbing my brain through my ear. "Please cleanse all traces of me." The words spill from my lips, and the new charm forms and immediately takes what it needs.

A big, rattling cough shakes my chest, and blood bubbles up my throat and from between my lips and dribbles down my chin. Everything fades, and my breaths slow—

CHAPTER SIXTEEN

I WAKE. I'm warm, and the duvet against my cheek smells clean. *Do I have to get up, or am I on late today?* I try to remember my shift pattern, but instead of work, memories flood my mind, and I groan with disbelief before I can keep my mouth shut.

"It's okay, you are safe," says a voice from my left.

I freeze. Oh heck, I won't be able to keep playing dead. Although dead people don't get fresh sheets. Neither do prisoners.

"You are safe and with a friend. My name is Emma, and I'm a friend of Ava's. You can open your eyes; I've dimmed the lights. I know what it's like to wake up in a strange room. A glass of water, a packaged sandwich, and snacks are on the bedside table. I didn't know what you'd like, but I bet you're starving." Her voice is sweet and full of understanding. Full of empathy.

I want to wiggle; her kindness makes me uncomfortable.

I take a deep breath and crack an eye open to see who I'm dealing with. Bright, multi-shade-blue eyes meet mine.

Emma smiles at me. She is beautiful and ageless, with pale skin and thick silver hair plaited away from her face.

"Hi," I croak.

"Hi." She smiles wider, and her eyes sparkle.

I reach over, grab the glass of water, and take a sip. "You know Ava?"

"After your parents contacted her, she asked for my help to get you out." Emma tilts her head to the side and her nose scrunches up. "Although I didn't do much. If I hadn't been able to get to you, you would have been just fine. Instead of waking up in bed, you'd still be on the basement floor, but seeing your charms at work..." She shudders. "Yeah, I have a feeling you would be fine."

I lick my lips; they feel soft, so I'm hydrated.

I go over her words. I put a ward up, and it would've protected the entire staff room and basement. If the basement was warded, how did she get inside?

"How did you get me out?"

"Magic." Emma wiggles her fingers and grins. She doesn't elaborate.

"Oh okay." I rub my face. That's erm... helpful? "If you speak to Ava before me, can you tell her thank you?"

"Of course."

I put the glass down and stare at her more closely. Emma has secrets—don't we all? I don't think she's lying. She sits demurely in a chair, and I notice the baby bump when she adjusts her arms.

I blink.

Pregnant women aren't usually sent in to be the baddies, right? I continue to gawp at her belly. I have no idea how to communicate with a pregnant lady, and I can't remember the last time I saw one in person. Perhaps as a child, when mum was carrying my brothers. Emma is growing another human, and it's all kinds of miraculous.

Then it hits me: I'm out. I made it out of the glass prison.

It's like my head is too heavy for my neck. I sink into the covers. I'm in the real world, and I'll encounter more pregnant women, babies, children, and animals! I can go anywhere. Wow, the sense of freedom is shocking.

It's shocking and unbelievable, and it will take me a long time not to feel trapped unless they gather us all like they did before and lock us up again.

Perhaps they'll make sure we disappear permanently.

Ah, there goes my overactive imagination. With everything that's happened, it's on overdrive.

"Did it work?" My voice is barely above a whisper. I pick at the edge of the duvet and dread her answer. "I healed everyone, or at least I tried to. Did it work? Are they okay?" I brace myself for her answer.

"Yes, they are. People are going nuts over the hidden

town and the dragon bloods. We didn't even know having dragon DNA was a thing. Everything is up in the air, and speculation and conspiracy theories are rife. The Creature Council wants to question you, but you seem at the bottom of their priority list. The gargoyles are very angry and will be even more upset when they break through the ward you set and find you gone." Emma's lips twist. "They are going to be pissed."

"My family?"

"All safe and where they should be."

"Thank you. Thank you so much for getting me out and looking after me." I tug on the sleeve of the black jumper, and as tears obscure my vision, I glance down to control my bubbling emotions. I did it. I saved them. I tuck my hands into the long sleeves and huff out an amused breath when I take in what I'm wearing. I'm dressed in my very own sock outfit, and I'm clean and healed.

Emma must notice the direction in which my mind has gone. "The feather helped me get you out. You floated right to the portal. The mop insisted on cleaning you up."

Floated? Mop? Ah, the quickly thrown-together cleaning charm.

"One charm healed you and kept you hydrated and I presume did all the bathroom stuff. Another dressed you. I've got to say, Kricket, your magic freaked me out. It's wicked scary—and very weird." She shrugs her shoulders in an apology.

I don't take offence. The charms were working independently without direction. That's new, cool, and yes, very freaky. They shouldn't be able to do that—take care of me.

The umbrella charm has also been busy doing its own thing. I can't miss the crackling ward around the room; its power sings in my mind. Frowning, I stare at Emma and then back at the ward. Has she been here the entire time or...

"How did you get through the wards?"

Emma makes an awkward sound in her throat. "Ah, well, magic doesn't work on me. I'm sort of a null." Her secret rolls off her tongue.

Sort of a null.

"Nothing works for me." Emma continues, her hands flopping onto her lap, and absentmindedly rubs her baby bump while the corner of her eyes crinkle with worry.

"Oh, that must be hard. I'm so sorry." I can't imagine not being able to use a healing potion, especially with the baby.

"Yeah, it's not great. You play the hand you've been dealt. I can walk through wards, and"—she counts the magic she can use on her fingers—"use gateways and pocket realms. The big world-building magic is fine. But every other magic treats me like I'm not there. Apart from your freaky charms." She holds her hands up. "Before you ask, I didn't invoke them, I didn't touch them, I didn't know they were there, but I worked it out quickly when you started floating."

She shakes her head and switches the topic. "We have hidden cameras at the library, and Ava thinks the gargoyles will get through the ward you set today." Emma leans forward. "They brought in a big hitter—a witch who has thoroughly embarrassed herself over the past few days. When they get in, then the fun will begin. Once they've checked the building, the tunnels, and realise you're long gone, the shit will hit the fan."

"Few days?"

"You've been unconscious for three days."

"Whoa, I've been out for three days?" She said about the gargoyle's attempt to get to me before, but I didn't know they'd been at it for three days. *Three days.* Blimey, that's impressive for a quick ward. The new umbrella charm is a keeper. *What a good ward.*

"You really got yourself into a mess. When I found you, you barely had a heartbeat and you were covered in blood."

I wince, remembering the pain.

"You said people are going nuts?"

"Yeah, pretty much. But the biggest news story overshadowing everything is your town's existence. Here, let me just..." She grabs a remote and clicks on a few buttons. The television turns on and she turns up the volume. "You don't have to pick a channel; it's everywhere. Kricket, you saved the entire town. From the early investigations, over a hundred gargoyles died. The news is calling you a saviour. You single-handedly saved around five thousand people and caught the perpetrators. Well, not you. Your magic name, Gary Chappell. He is the hero. Single-handedly taking on a group of magic-welding *humans*."

She pauses to let all that sink in, but I must have misheard her.

My eyes flick from her to the yelling reporters on the TV. "Humans? Who is going to believe that? The magic they used, how they moved, and how big they were—they don't grow humans that big."

"Well, they aren't going to say a murderous group of creatures pretending to be dragons while wearing bad Halloween masks."

I snort. "You noticed that too?"

"Yeah. So a powerful witch saved the day, and a group of extremists were caught. It's amazing. The Creature Council made a statement, and the humans had identification on them corroborating their identity." Emma rolls her big blue eyes. "Handy."

"Ah, yes, so handy. That's precisely what trained soldiers do; they keep their pockets full of personal information. So when their bodies are found, they can be easily identified and their enemies can go in and give condolences to the families."

Emma hums in agreement.

"Do you think I can join my family?"

"No, the Creature Council and the gargoyles are

watching them. I have safe houses you're welcome to use."

I don't need a safe house. I have money... *Uh-oh,* I sent my mum away with all the bank details, and I bet they're watching that too. What a nightmare. Luckily, I don't need money; I can make charms.

Yeah, and how did that go? I messed up. I'm not responsible for what those people did, but I've been playing with magic I don't understand—dragon magic. I shiver. There's a reason they locked us up in the first place. Perhaps we *are* dangerous.

Not we, *me.*

I'm dangerous.

The magic I've been playing with might be why dragons are almost extinct, and I've sent my family out in the world with millions of pounds worth of charms. Charms they can no longer sell as it's unsafe, and if I've got a target on my head, so do they.

My stomach flips. People will kill for that kind of magic.

They already have.

Now that I've seen what I can do and what my magic is capable of, I'm worried about the potential consequences if it falls into the wrong hands. With a snap of magic, I can pinpoint a charm anywhere and maybe remove its magic. I bet I could do it to every one of them right now. But they protect people, and I took their money. Gary has a reputation, and I don't want to shoot myself in the foot.

Instead, for my peace of mind, I'll place little magic tags on my charms, a little moral indicator if someone is up to no good or if the charms are in trouble. A morality clause.

Emma sits silently, half watching the news and half watching me.

"What do you want for the rescue and the help?" Nothing is for free.

"Ah." Emma leans back in the chair, twiddling her thumbs like a villain. "One day soon, I'll ask for your help. It'll be nothing illegal, nothing that you won't be able to give, but one day soon, I'll need your help to help somebody else. All I ask is you pay it forward."

I think about it for a moment.

Nah, there's no way she's doing this out of the goodness of her heart. But her bright blue eyes stare back at me earnestly. She means what she says. "You genuinely help people?"

"Yes."

Emma is like some creature superhero. A pregnant superhero. "Okay. But I want in. If you and Ava are going to help me, I want to help you back, not just on one occasion. You might need me to help you with my magic."

"The freaky magic?"

I wince. "Yeah, about that. I might need help in getting it under control." It would be great if Emma or Ava could find somebody to guide me. "And I need to get a message to Ava and my family not to sell charms for a while."

If at all. The magic is too unpredictable, and I don't know enough. If I've learned anything dealing with this nightmare, my charms are dangerous.

"I can get a message to your parents, and I know a family of witches. Between them, they might have some idea of how to help you. But it might be a while as we can't put them at risk."

"No, of course not. I don't want to put anyone else at risk. Thank you for your help. So I need to wait for the Council to forget about me and avoid the gargoyles until they hulk smash someone else." I sigh and rub my face. "Then everything will be okay."

Whoa, that was easier than I thought it would be.

"Okay? Well, not really."

"Oh?"

"I think you're the most wanted person in the country. There will be a public inquiry, and nobody in power will want you to give your side of the story. Add that to the fame of your alter ego, Gary Chappell, and everyone wants a piece of you."

"So I can't hide and wait for them to forget about me? I thought now the invaders were caught, everything would be over."

Emma snorts. "Over? No, Kricket, this isn't over. I have a feeling your story is just beginning."

That doesn't sound ominous. Not at all. A shiver of premonition shoots down my spine.

CHAPTER
SEVENTEEN

Now that I'm awake and moving around, Emma goes home. With nothing to do, I take the sandwich and snacks and eat them in a hot bath. To my dismay, when I take the first bite, a rogue tomato escapes and plops into the water. I growl and do a half-hearted search to no avail. I guess I'll find it later.

The sound from the television echoes around the tiled walls. The news is still going on and on, skimming a torturous edge of speculation and getting everything wrong. I don't know why I didn't turn it off. The Creature Council doesn't help. They keep popping in to roll out the tried-and-tested propaganda script: the town was warded to keep the dragon bloods safe.

Safe.

When the reporter asks why creature hybrids aren't given the same status, as they're persecuted and murdered all the time, the Council representative changes the subject.

The Council lying isn't what has made my mood plummet. It's them, my friends and neighbours, who have pissed me off the most. I'd thought—wrongly—given the chance, most of the residents would have gotten out. Surely the newly trapped or the people from different counties would have left and sought asylum.

I thought they would do something, but no, it's worse than that. The news says the ward has been reinstated mainly to prevent the press and the overzealous public from entering the town, which is still an active crime scene. The barrier has been resurrected, and most, if not all, the residents are back behind it.

They stayed after everything that had happened, and everyone is trapped again. Why would they do that? Why did they not run when they had the chance? To me, it doesn't make sense, and it makes me feel sick to my stomach. It's hard to listen to.

I guess everyone is frightened of change. It doesn't help that the spelled woke up in strange clothes and, frightened, did what frightened people do: they went back home.

They went back home 'cause that's all they knew to do, and I have to remember that people have lost loved ones and friends, and believing what they're told, they've returned to the lives they know.

We've spent years being told where to live, where to go, and when to turn up to the assigned job. They have no idea how to think for themselves. If the Creature Council wanted to neuter a supposedly powerful race, they've done that.

It all plays out on the news, and the way they talk makes everything seem so logical while I feel like I'm going mad. Like I'm a failure and let everyone down. I press the heel of my palms into my eye sockets, cutting off my vision.

Maybe if I press hard enough, I'll forget.

I had a waking nightmare that nobody else was a part of, and I don't have anybody I can commiserate with. Only I can corroborate what happened. Without me, they can all pretend that nothing happened. Emma is right. I'm a serious loose end. I might be the only person who truly saw what the invaders did. Everyone else is either dead, hidden, or spelled.

I understand all this, yet I can't help being mad.

I want to shake them awake, shout and scream for them to go, to live, while also being aware that they have nowhere to go. They haven't got an Emma or Ava to watch their backs. But it fundamentally comes down to wanting to help and knowing if I emptied my bank account and handed over the cash, it would not change a thing.

They are all so happy in their cages.

They're caged birds who have never learned to fly.

What a mess.

A new live segment begins, and the reporter's excited voice announces they're interviewing survivors. I groan when I hear Anton Hill's whiny voice. "The attack happened while I was in the supermarket. I attempted to save everyone I could, but the staff threw us out the door, leaving us at the mercy of those humans."

Humans? Even Anton Hill is spouting the council's propaganda. I can't believe he's bringing up the store.

"Kricket Jones." I squeak and almost drown myself. A wave of water splashes the black-and-white tiles. "The girl who's wanted for questioning was the one who forced me out of the supermarket, physically pushing me into the clutches of the enemy."

What the eff... "He named me? The little shit. Bloody Anton Hill named me." Gosh, how I hate him. I. Hate. Him. He named me, and I didn't bloody touch him! Gah, I feel sick. This interview is on every channel. *My mum is going to kill me.*

"Mr Hill, can you tell us about the spell and the magic saviour?" the vampire reporter asks excitedly.

"I fought the spell valiantly," he says with a dramatic sigh, "but of course I was trapped like everybody else, and I woke up in the town square thanks to Gary Chappell and his magic. The humans were apprehended..."

I groan and add some more hot water to the bathtub, drowning out his stupid voice.

What a load of codswallop. The news has now named me a few times. I'm wanted for questioning, and they're concerned for my welfare. Blah, blah, blah. The appeal for information has been nicely topped off with a ghastly work photo of me.

That bloody green polo is going to haunt me forever.

At least Gary Chappell is faring well—much better than me. There's a campaign to have the Saviour Witch knighted. "Good luck finding him," I grumble, dunking my head under the bubbles. I hope the rogue tomato doesn't find its way into my hair.

I stay in the bath until the water runs cold and find the waterlogged tomato caught in a whirlpool by the plughole. I get dressed by encouraging the sock charm to clothe me in something other than the black outfit, and I get leggings and a lovely green jumper.

Emma said my family is being watched and that *they* are monitoring their movements and phone calls. *They* must be the government and the gargoyles. I bite my lip as I think. I need to talk to my parents. Emma is nice, but she's still a stranger. I must let them know myself about not selling the charms. I'll worry if I don't.

I have an idea for a new charm. It isn't something I've tried before, but I might as well give it a go. One wall in the bedroom is taken up by a narrow wardrobe with mirrored sliding doors. The only limit to my magic so far has been my lack of imagination. I huff. It's a scary thought. If I can make a feather charm from a random piece of glass, I can do this. They won't think of tracking a mirror—why would they?

How can you realistically track that?

I can do this.

My hand shakes as I place it onto the wardrobe's frame and press my fingertips lightly on the glass. *I'm scared.* After passing out for days, I'm frightened to do any type of magic. What if my brains leak out of my ears?

I take in a big, shuddering breath. Yeah, I'm feeling a little squirrelly. I push a tiny bit of power into the mirror and something happens: the surface distorts. *Okay, that's good.* The mirror's surface becomes a liquid, and as the magic builds, I can let go. I focus on my parents—on Mum's scowling face and Dad's hugs.

Keeping them both at the forefront of my mind, I also focus on the charms in their possession. Ah, the magic in the charms does the trick. It leads me and makes it easier to locate them.

The power does all the hard work, and when everything is ready, like picking a charm to use, I hunt for the closest mirror to them in the house and repeatedly send a pulse of magic into it. As if I'm knocking.

I jump and almost drop the connection when there's a screech. "Kricket!" Mum yells. "Are you dead? Did they kill you? Ava said you were safe. Our daughter is a ghost!" She screams for my dad. "No, I'm not making it up! Look, she's in the mirror!"

My dad hurries into the room and does a double-take when he sees me in the mirror. I wave, and his face pales. "I'm not dead. I wanted to talk to you, and I've been told it's not safe to use the phone. I thought I'd try some new magic."

"You thought the best way to contact us was to

emulate the evil queen from *Snow White*?" Dad rubs the stubble on his chin.

I snort. I knew I borrowed the idea from somewhere.

"Mirror, mirror on the wall," he says in a high falsetto.

I giggle.

Mum snaps out of her shock. "Oi, you two, this isn't funny. Be serious. Kricket Hera Jones, you're in so much trouble. We've seen the news. What were you thinking? Why—"

"We are very proud of you," Dad says.

Mum gives him a sneaky dig in his ribs with her pointy elbow. Dad winces. "Yes, we are very proud of you," she snarls. "You put yourself in danger, and Gary Chappell gets all the credit while you are labelled a common criminal. We are sooo proud."

As usual, her sarcasm game is impressive.

Dad clears his throat. "We said we wouldn't make judgments until we spoke to Kricket." He turns back to me with a soft smile. "We want to hear about what happened from your prospective, pumpkin."

"But perhaps it is best to wait till we are all face-to-face." Mum leans heavily against the wall and glares into the mirror.

"The invaders—"

"You saved everyone, including Anton Hill?" Mum's lips twitch as she interrupts me.

Ah, so she's watched the news. My eyes roll to the back of my head, and I growl. Mum knows I dislike him from my consistent moaning about him over the years. "I couldn't leave him out," I grumble.

"Yeah, so we've seen. Kricket, why did you have to pick such a terrible photo? There are so many better ones to choose."

I wrinkle my nose. "Mum, I didn't pick the photo. The news people did that." As if I'd give them a photo.

"It's an awful one. You look spotty and red."

I throw my hands up into the air and groan. "Mum, I was sixteen."

She narrows her eyes and peers at me. "You didn't look that bad at sixteen surely."

I huff. "Are you okay, Dad? You're looking a little pale?"

It's Dad's turn to nudge Mum out of the way. "I'm fine, pumpkin. I've been worried about you and everything that's been happening. It has been a long week."

Tell me about it. "I called for a reason. There is a spelled safe in the main bedroom. Can you lock all the charms away? Oh, and don't sell any please. Ignore what I said when we last saw each other. Selling them isn't safe."

"We can do that of course. That's no problem. It didn't feel right anyway, as you've given us plenty of money." Mum sneers.

Why does money sound like a dirty word?

"Have you had any issues?"

"What, apart from a team of gargoyles and some

council stooges watching the house? No, nothing. I can't believe you bought this place," Mum says.

"Why? Is it bad?" I try to peer behind her. It looks nice. I even had it fully furnished. "It was beautiful in the photos and videos."

"Yes, yes, it's a beautiful house. But how could you make such a massive purchase without our input? I'm your mother, and I've been worried sick that you spent too much." She drops her voice. "It's overlooking the park."

"Why? Does the park have rogue teenagers?" She pulls a face, and this time I grin. "You know I couldn't tell you, Mum. It wouldn't be much of a secret if I blabbed about it."

"Well, now I'm concerned about that. You are a very secretive young lady and very sneaky. I don't like it. It makes me wonder what else you've been hiding." She narrows her eyes and looks behind me. "Have you got a boyfriend or a husband hidden somewhere we don't know about? When you were younger, we talked about protection. Do we need to talk about that subject again?"

Her eyes twinkle at my expression of utter horror.

"But I'll say again, I'm too young to be a grandmother." She talks about protection when she knows I haven't got a boyfriend, and there was no point when we were living in a town where nobody got pregnant. Still, I feel my cheeks go pink as they radiate embarrassed heat.

"I'm an adult, Mum."

"Barely. Your brothers miss you, and your nan has been worried sick."

"I miss you all too. Well, I'm glad you're all okay. The magic is pulling on me, so I need to go." It's only a tiny white lie.

"I know I'm hard on you. I'm sorry. It's because I'm frightened." Her eyes widen, and I can see her fear below her snark and anger.

"Everything will be fine. I'll be fine."

"Perhaps..." She bites her lip. "Perhaps you should turn yourself in?"

Turn myself in? "Mum, you know I can't do that. I haven't given you details about what happened after you left, but it was bad. Are you using the ward?" I know she is. I can feel it. But I need her to focus on something else.

"Yes, and don't change the subject. It's my job to worry about you, not the other way around. We are all okay. Your nan walked into the local library yesterday and came out with a book and a job." Mum shakes her head and a rueful smile tugs at her lips.

I grin. Nan would find work in the desert. Libraries are her sanctuary.

"I don't know how she does it. Anyway, we are all fine. We shall keep the spies busy. Just don't do anything more heroic or silly, Kricket. Please keep your head down. We love you."

"I will. I love you. I love you all."

"Love you," Dad says.

They wave, and the magic fades as my dad folds Mum into an embrace and she sniffles into his chest.

Oh, Mum.

CHAPTER
EIGHTEEN

A phone Emma left me rings, and I answer. "What did you do?" she asks, direct and straight to the point.

My attention is still clinging to the now regular mirror. I'm so pale. The dark circles under my eyes make me look awful. "Huh?"

Eloquent of me, I know.

I also know what I did. Contacting my parents was a massive risk, and I feel guilty.

"You got in touch with your parents. Really, Kricket? What were you— You know what? Never mind, it's my fault. I thought I was clear when I said they were watching your parents."

"I used a charm," I say softly, sinking down on the bed.

"Used or made?"

Gosh, she's worse than my mum. "Made."

"You made a communication charm?"

"Something like that." I rub my face.

"They have cameras inside the house."

"What? Why? How?" I bolt to my feet. "Can we remove them? You said they were safe."

"They are safe. I have friends in high places that will continue to keep them safe. Nothing will happen to your family, but what you did has made things so much harder."

"I'm sorry." I sit back down. "Can we remove the cameras?"

"We decided it was better not to."

They decided. That's nice to know.

I wish Emma would have told me at some point that they have cameras inside the house. I can't help but wonder what else she's keeping from me. I wouldn't have made such a mistake if I'd known. I groan. That's me again, being cocky with my magic and making a mess of everything. I've only been awake for a few hours; it's like I'm cursed or something. I pull my knees to my chest and hug them. To be sure, I better clarify things, such as, "My parents, do they know?"

"Yes."

Ah, that's good to know. It's why Mum kept interrupting me, going on about the stupid photo. It was her way of protecting me, winding me up so I'd forget my train of thought and cut the conversation short.

Well played, Mum.

I don't think I said anything to reveal my location, and I know I didn't say anything about who is helping me. But I did talk about the charms, and now whoever is listening knows there's a stash in the house. *Nice one, Kricket.* I groan. "I'm a bloody idiot."

"You're not an idiot. I should have said something. Although I didn't think you'd magic up a communication charm just after waking from a magically induced coma." Her sweet voice is full of censure. "Please don't do that again. No magic for a while as we still don't know if they can track you when you make a new charm."

"Track me? Who? The Creature Council?"

Emma is silent.

"The gargoyles?"

Nothing.

It must be the baddies. It seems she's keeping everything close to her chest. It also seems I'm not allowed to know about my life or the danger I'm in.

I don't know if that's a blessing, but the saying *forewarned is forearmed* isn't famous for nothing. "Emma, I need to know these things."

"Yes, I guess you do. I'll talk to you tonight and tell you everything; keeping someone in the dark about this stuff usually works for other people, but you—" She groans. "We've never dealt with anyone who can make magic out of thin air. Even the fae with their rune magic need parchment paper, and the ones that don't would never in a million years need our help. Okay, I'll tell you everything tonight."

"Thank you."

"Oh, and before I forget, around midday, expect a delivery of food from the local supermarket. The driver can be trusted."

When the bell rings, I hustle to the front door and swing it open. The delivery driver is tall, broad, and green—a troll. He grins, revealing sharp, yellowed teeth with prominent lower tusks. "Delivery for you," he says in a gravelly voice, holding out a digital device for me to sign.

"Uh, thanks." I quickly scribble a random signature as I can't very well use mine.

He nods, seemingly satisfied, and starts to unload the crates from the back of his van. Despite his hulking frame, each movement is precise and efficient. He carries my groceries to the doorstep with ease.

"Been a busy day?" I ask, trying to break the awkward silence.

He chuckles, amusement flickering in his eyes. "You could say that. Trolls don't get much downtime. The supermarket gig isn't so bad. Better than living under a bridge."

I laugh, unsure if he's joking or serious. "I guess that

makes sense," I say to be safe. I shove the bags through the door and pile them in the narrow hallway.

After setting down the last load, the troll waits for me to grab the last of the shopping, then stacks the blue delivery crates together and tucks them under his arm. "Have a good rest of your day." He turns to leave.

"Thanks for bringing the shopping all the way to the door."

"No problem," he says. "I'm just doing my job." He gives me a friendly wave and climbs back into his van. I watch him leave.

As I go to close the door, a woman getting out of her car across the street stares at me. I give her a small smile as our eyes meet, and she narrows hers.

"You," she mouths.

Me? Shit. *Me.* An instinctive alarm goes off in my head. I think I've been made.

It's only confirmed when she pulls her phone out, smashing the buttons on the keypad as she hurries away.

Great.

Why did I think opening the door without a disguise charm was a good idea? *Because I haven't got one and Emma said I can't make one.* I've messed up again, and it looks as if this safe house is blown.

While I think of what to do, on autopilot, I put away all the essentials that need the fridge or freezer. *The tip line must be inundated with false calls.* I lean against the kitchen counter and strum my fingers. I'm probably overreacting, but sometimes you have to go with your gut, and my gut is screaming at me.

I might have lost it with everything happening, but it's best to get out of here for now, even if it's just a few hours. Decision made. I use the sock charm to change my clothes into jeans and an oversized hoodie. Granted, my gut has had a workout lately, and I'm paranoid and anxious.

It's not paranoia if people are out to get you.

When I go to grab the phone, I catch my bright red hair in the mirror. I need to cobble together a charm to disguise myself. I didn't promise not to make a new charm. I just agreed it wasn't the best idea. Things have changed, and this time, it's an emergency.

I send a pulse of magic out, requesting help from my materials, with a focus on changing my appearance. I'd prefer a nice piece of stone or wood, but that would be way too easy. "Not again." I groan when I find the old lager bottle cap pinging excitedly to my call. It's wedged behind the pedal bin in a cupboard, and the scent of hops still clings to it.

Ew.

When I open the front door, my bright red hair is gone, replaced by a short dark brown pixie cut. My skin tone is darker, my nose is narrow, and my eyes are closer together. Little changes are easier to maintain than trying something flashy that could go horribly wrong.

With my hands in my pockets, I set off. I'm halfway

down the street when four cars screech past me to a halt outside the safe house. I turn my head to watch. The car doors open simultaneously as if choreographed, and massive dark grey men emerge.

Gargoyles.

Is asking for one hulking killing machine in each vehicle too much? No? No. It's a team of gargoyles—at least a dozen of them. Heart pounding, I turn my head and keep walking. One foot in front of the other, all nice and casual. When people around me hurry, I match their pace—there is no need to stand out.

"You, stop," bellows a familiar voice behind me.

No one else stops, so I keep moving.

Nothing to see here, guys.

"It's her. I can smell her." Ew. Gargoyles have super sniffers. Who knew? I sure as hell didn't. "Nothing girl! Kricket Jones, you're wanted for questioning."

I turn the corner and run.

Crap. That was my *gargoyle back there.*

"Why am I always running?" I huff out. Talking to myself somehow settles my nerves and tricks my body into thinking I'm not running for my life. If I've enough oxygen to speak, everything is okay. "This is so unfair. Why can't I leisurely stroll away from the baddies?"

Being so massive, I hope they can't run fast. "When this is all over, and if I make it out alive, I'm going to take up running—proper running with fancy trainers and everything, with leggings that don't chafe," I add as the jeans burn my inner thighs.

I don't know where I am, and I have no idea where I'm going. I turn onto another street and sprint down an alleyway as fast as possible. I'll need to stop soon and alter my face, scent, and clothes. I dash around a bend and risk a look behind me.

I think I've lost them, lost him.

And I bolt straight into someone.

I hit them hard, bouncing off their solid frame. I crash to the pavement and wince as I jar my bottom. "I'm so sorry," I say as I gasp for air.

The man I ploughed into stares down at me. His face is all sharp angles, his blond hair is floppy, and his eyes are so pale there's barely any pigment. He reaches down, grabs my wrist, and hauls me up.

I let out a sound of dismay. I don't need any help. But I ran into him, and it's rude to snatch my hand away, so I allow him to guide me to my feet—panicking a little when he doesn't immediately release me.

"I'm okay. You can let go." I attempt to pull away, but his hold gets tighter. So tight the bones in my wrist grind together. "Ow." I hiss. "I said I was sorry. Please let go. You are hurting me."

"Ah, my missing witness, the dragon blood." His voice has a strange ascent. "Don't struggle. You'll only hurt yourself." He drags me towards the road just as a car pulls up.

The car's tyres *thud, thud, thud* against the kerb, and the rear door is flung open. I dig my heels into the pavement, but that doesn't stop the stranger from effortlessly dragging me towards the gaping door. I look about wildly and open my mouth to scream for help, and he cuffs me across the back of my head.

Black dots and wiggly worms fill my vision, and before I can shake off the blow, I'm in the car and the door slams closed.

CHAPTER
NINETEEN

"I'm one of many. We've been killing all kinds of creatures to meet you, Kricket Jones," he says with a smile as he adjusts his seat belt and clicks it into place.

Good to know, and that explains everything.

One of many. I should have gone with the gargoyles.

He seems a bit disgusted that I don't comment. Perhaps he wants fear or fake awe. My poor head is throbbing, and all I can do is blink at him. I'm going to keep my mouth shut. I don't want to be smacked around again.

No, thank you. I'll keep my mouth closed. I'm sure he wants me to do the victim thing and ask lots of questions: *Why have you taken me? What are you going to do?*

And don't forget the serial killer's favourite: *Please don't hurt me.*

I've never been one to beg.

I'm too stubborn. And I'm used to making mistakes, saying the wrong things, and shoving my foot in my mouth.

Sometimes it's better to say nothing—nothing at all.

He's kidnapped me, after all. This is his game. Being caught is not what I envisioned. I've been wholly outmatched since the first explosion, and sitting in this car with him, I've never felt so overwhelmingly young. I'm sick of being deathly afraid.

"We are the Claw Brotherhood."

Claw Brotherhood. I'd snort a laugh if I weren't shitting myself. It's obvious he's an invader, a wannabe dragon, one without a stupid mask to disguise his foolish face. I don't know what he expects from me, but he continues his mini tirade. I have a feeling he's just warming up.

"I'm here to make sure that nature's faults are corrected."

Nature's faults, I take it that's me and every other dragon blood?

"My name is Damien Hass. You can call me by my title, Grand Claw."

Erm... I'd rather not. I peek at his face, and he's serious. That's his title. *Wow.*

"It's my job to find out where you got the charms and to recover them."

I can barely stop myself from rolling my eyes. The charms again. Everybody wants that information. I wonder when they'll connect the dots and see me. I don't know what's better, people thinking I'm a thief or knowing I'm the creator.

I twist slightly in the seat. I had enough foresight to nudge the phone from my hoodie pocket with my elbow. It dropped in the gutter just as I was shoved into the car. My charms are still in the inside pocket of my jeans. I immediately signal them to be quiet and hide, and their magic signatures disappear from my senses. I send an approval down our link with an added command to protect themselves.

"I had to come myself as it seems my brethren are incapable of dealing with one little girl. You weren't hard to catch, not at all, and this entire trip has been a waste of my time. I need to be hunting this Gary Chappell, not a thief."

The car jerks forward into traffic, and the momentum pushes me back into my seat. I wiggle closer to the door.

Damien Hass—even in my head, I can't call him the Grand Claw—gives me a nasty smile and flicks a finger. I'm frozen.

It's like he's Medusa and I've been turned to stone.

He frowns at my face and then waves the same hand, and my red hair tumbles around my shoulders as he removes the disguise spell. "There we are. That's much better." He leans closer and tilts my chin, pinching it between his thumb and forefinger. "I'll have to kill you soon, and you know what? It's such a shame. It's a total waste as you're a pretty little thing. I can see why Gary wants to spend time with you. But we can't allow you to live. You know too much." Creepily, he sighs.

I want to wrinkle my nose as his breath smells tangy, a gross combination of rotten tomatoes and coffee. He needs to quit breathing on me and maybe brush his teeth.

"You're beautiful, but you shouldn't exist. None of you should. The Creature Council promised to keep you all under control, but that promise was broken. We have now ratified the problem by culling everyone."

Culling. Killing. Is he trying to say he's killed everyone? I don't believe him. It's a trick. It must be.

He. Is. Lying.

Damien Hass and his Claw Brotherhood friends can't have gone that far, not with the entire world watching. I saw Anton Hill's smarmy face live on the news this morning, and he looked fine—more than fine. The man is too much of a slimy coward for it not to show on his face. He didn't look stressed or frightened.

"Everyone in that fate-forsaken town is dead, and you will join them soon enough. But first, I'll need you to tell me where you found the charms." Then he smiles. It's not a nice smile. "I need to know about Gary Chappell and how to find him. According to our sources, you're his main contact. Is he your boyfriend?"

Does he expect me to answer? Spoiler alert: He's frozen my fucking face. I'm lucky that I can still breathe.

"No? Are you not going to confess the nature of your relationship? Ah, Miss Jones, you're in a terrible mess. The old adage of follow the money, and the money leads to you. Has your witch boyfriend set you up?"

Does he want a pat on the head? It doesn't take a financial genius to see that my family has moved into a new house, a house which I own outright.

"He must care about you. That's why he came into town and destroyed my spell. You're the key to getting him out from the rock he's disappeared under. If you cooperate, I won't kill you. I'll let you and your family go if you confess two things: where you found the charms, and where I can find your boyfriend."

He sits back, and the leather seat squeaks as he jiggles his knees and taps a weird tune on his thigh. A familiar tune.

And then it comes to me. That's the tune from the Pied Piper spell. My heart jumps and sinks like a rock to my boots. He's the witch, the magic user, who cast it. He was the one who spelled everyone.

Shit. I'm in seriously over my head.

If he's waiting for a reaction, he has made a mistake in freezing my face because I'd be unable to stop my response from hearing the rhythm of that awful spell. He's testing me. Only the person who made or unravelled the spell would recognise it.

"I don't know what stolen charm Gary Chappell

used to remove my spell, but he won't be doing that again. He won't be able to save you this time, but you can save yourself." His voice rings with arrogance. He's seriously pissed, and that's why he came to collect me himself. He's livid.

That doesn't bode well for me.

"That Pied Piper magic was a work of art. It was the best spell I had ever cast. I had an entire town in the palm of my hand." He stops jiggling long enough to stare down at the said hand. "I haven't had someone interfere with my work. I was surprised he could. He used another charm to circumvent and unravel it." He shakes his head. "He repaired all those minds. I didn't think that was possible. It was an act of cruelty, you know, such cruelty in saving them. They all knew they were going to die when the time came. You don't owe him any loyalty."

He grunts when I remain silent. "You're more than you appear to be, and I'm excited about picking *your* mind apart. What I'm going to do to you, girl. By the time I'm through, death will be a mercy, and you will be begging. Begging me to end your pitiful life. With a few words, you can save yourself."

His jiggling and *tap, tap, tapping* is driving me mad. He doesn't need to think up any elaborate torture, as he's doing perfectly fine.

"The mighty dragons are our gods. The brotherhood serves them, and you will regret ever touching their magic, charm thief."

Bingo. Religious fanatics. Is it strange that I'm disappointed? I thought they were professional soldiers, not a bunch of dragon-worshipping weirdos. And I'm back to being a thief. I'd rather he believed I have sticky fingers than him knowing I can create dragon magic.

"They're ours to worship and protect while we rid the world of their unworthy offspring. The Creature Council believes in our righteousness."

Yeah, it seems they let you get away with attacking our town and murdering innocent people and all those gargoyles.

That's what I don't get. The gargoyles are chasing me. Instead, they should be hunting this guy. It's like everyone has lost their minds and all their common sense.

"You and your people are freaks of nature, daring to carry such mighty blood in your veins. Keeping you alive risks an all-out war. Everyone wants to eliminate the problem just as much as we do. Once the rest of the stragglers are hunted down, this blip on the dragons' name will be gone."

Stragglers hunted down, like my family?

I want to rip his head off.

He must be baiting me. I can't believe his lies, as he must be lying. His nervous body language doesn't connect with his words. He's talking about genocide and mass murder and yet fidgeting like a child. No, I don't believe him.

The man has power beyond my comprehension, and yet to look at him, he seems like an average guy, like he'd help you with your taxes. I just don't get it. I don't get him. Perhaps I haven't been alive long enough to understand that evil people have many guises, and his is one of them.

If I could give him what he wants, this guy would never let me go, even if I could produce my alter ego. I can see it in his eyes. Leaving one dragon blood alive would be too much.

His expression is fanatical as he continues, waxing lyrical about dragons. The man is a dragon zealot. I've seen that look on alcoholics at the supermarket. No matter what he believes, dragons aren't going to start popping out of the woodwork, and if there are more of them around, I can't see them being happy these idiots are killing in their name.

No wonder the general, the silver dragon, the only known dragon left in this world, doesn't advertise his whereabouts or personal details. He's impossible to track or these guys would no doubt be camping outside his house.

That dragon is a war hero. There are books written about him. No, he wouldn't be happy to hear what these men are up to.

They wear masks and pretend to be dragons, even convincing the gargoyles. I hate to say it, but they're a bunch of weirdos, granted trained, professional, killing weirdos with one guy who can work excellent, scary magic.

I can't move my head but can move my eyes to gaze outside. I'm done with him. The motorway's blue signs whip past, highlighting roads and towns that have zero meaning to me. I don't know where we are or where we're going. We could be in a foreign country.

I've also never had to sit so still before, and being unable to move is excruciating. My skin and muscles feel on fire, and my left ankle throbs. Pins and needles stab at me, and my entire left foot feels like it's going to drop off.

This is great.

I need a plan to save myself. I have time while we are driving and Damien has finally stopped talking. I need to do something with this spell, do something rather than sit here and think about how much I hurt.

I take a gander at the magic crushing me into my seat and can confirm that the magical signature is the same as the Pied Piper spell. At least he's telling the truth about that.

Unlike the Pied Piper spell, the magic that has frozen me isn't as intricate or as carefully woven. It's basic and sloppy. My metaphysical fingers give it a prod, pick at it, and manage to unravel a corner. I pause to check if he's noticed. He hasn't, so I unravel some more, loosening and weakening it.

I make the spell mine and wait for the perfect time to use it.

CHAPTER
TWENTY

WE MUST TRAVEL three miles down a quiet road when the road finally turns abruptly to reveal a guardhouse and gate. Behind the gate is a familiar-looking ward. If I could move, I'd sink to the floor with despair. We are back where it started.

After days of this cat-and-mouse game, three of which I spent asleep, I find myself back in the glass prison.

We drive up to a barrier and pull up next to a group of official-looking men guarding the gate. The guards wear uniforms with the large Creature Council patch on their arms and don't ask for any identification.

They speak to the driver, nod at Damien, and take note that I'm in the back seat. My face is all over the news

—and they don't even blink. Then the car is let through. The ward doesn't impede the vehicle, and that tells me everything I need to know.

The Creature Council are aware of everything.

We drive through familiar streets, and the car stops at the town square.

Damien removes the spell—or attempts to—and exits the car. The door on my side opens, and I'm left with a single burly guard. I'll never get a better chance. The guard moves to grab my upper arm, and before he can make contact, I get ready to flick the spell from around me to him and...

This is too easy.

What am I doing? The spell is ready to go, but I can't use it. They'll know I can use magic without a charm if I do. He'll know it was me who twisted his magic and that Gary is fake. It's a test. The sloppy, put-together spell must be a test.

It's so hard to let the spell go, and as it harmlessly disperses, I want to kick myself for my paranoia.

The burly guard pulls me out of the car. This will be unpleasant; my body is stiff as a board. I wobble, and he fists my hoodie and slams me against the car frame. My spine and legs creak into the new shape.

Six massive men, three in front and three behind, surround the car, stepping between me and freedom. I did the right thing; I never would have gotten away. I recognise all the guards' magical signatures. It wasn't so apparent when I was in the square surrounded by bodies and on the edge of exhausted panic. But now I see they're all tainted with the same magic as the Pied Piper spell—Damien's magic.

The last time I saw these men, they were asleep and trapped behind my ward, wearing their Scooby-Doo villain masks. The realisation makes my insides tremble as I take them in, and angry tears fill my eyes. That's another thing Damien Hass was right about. The Creature Council had to be aware of this, and they let them go.

I never thought I'd regret not killing someone. I never thought murder the best choice, but now I regret not stuffing these bastards into that ash-making machine. It was a mistake. My mistake.

I stare out into the square. I wish I could go back to that day.

Slow clapping comes from the left.

"Bravo. Well done," Damien coos as he strolls to my side. "You, Kricket Jones, are very entertaining. I have never seen anyone not try to run away. They fall over, and it's so hilarious. It gets me in the feels every time." He thumps his chest and then taps my nose. "You're one to watch. Tricky, tricky little girl. What are you looking at?" He bends, presses his face to mine, and stares at the building-packed street and the rows of homes in the distance.

"Ah, your town. I see it from your point of view, all these places to hide, all these buildings and houses. If only you could get your stiff legs to work." Damien waves his hand to encompass the town, then turns and strolls away.

"Come, let's fix the temptation. I have an inkling to do some powerful magic. Bring our guest."

The men surrounding me close in, and I'm led—more like dragged—into the street and to the square, where not long ago the entire town was asleep.

After a minute of shuffling, the stiffness leaves my limbs, and I no longer hurt.

"Excellent." He waves the guards to step back and grabs my upper arms and positions me slightly to the right. "There," he says with a smile and a painful squeeze. "Here will give you a perfect view. Don't move now."

I couldn't if I wanted to, as with a flick of his fingers, I'm once again stuck to the floor, frozen. This spell is much better than the last, and it'll take me a few hours to unravel—another test?

He flicks his fingers, and two of his minions hurry to opposite sides of the street and begin to draw a massive chalk circle. It must be a potent spell if it requires one.

The two guys must have done this a lot; as the circle takes shape, it looks perfect.

Another man brings out a table, places it in the centre, and carefully lays out a tablecloth and a plethora of dangerous-looking magical items. He backs away with a respectful bow as Damien steps forward and, after making a big deal of rolling his left sleeve, he selects a curved ceremonial knife.

He holds it up, and the blade winks in the sun. It

looks sharp. It is sharp, as with one movement from left to right, he slashes open his forearm and then places the wet blade back onto the table. With blood dripping between his fingers, he begins to walk clockwise around the circle.

Blood magic is not necessarily evil. But sacrificial magic does tend to scare people. Anyone with a lick of common sense and magic knowledge knows magic itself isn't inherently good or bad. It's the intentions of the magic user you have to watch out for.

He lines the circle with his blood and then, unconcerned that his arm is still leaking, does nothing to stanch the flow as he moves to the centre and begins to chant. His arms thrust into the sky, one palm open, and the other, the left one, the one covered in blood, is gripping an object tightly in his palm. Something about the thing in his hand resonates with me. I narrow my eyes, catch black peeking through his fingers, and realise with shock it's a *charm*.

With the chalk and blood circle simultaneously blocking and amplifying the spell, I should not be able to feel it, but I can.

I realise something quite profound: the magic that Damien Hass uses has never been his. The charm is the source of his magic—the only source of his magic. That's the signature that oozes darkness over everything; it has its claws into him and the guards, and it created the Pied Piper spell.

No, the magic has always been that ancient charm,

and this is the reason everyone's freaking out about my magic. Unlike my charms, which have a single job to do, this thing's magic is vast and endless.

That charm is incredibly dangerous.

It whispers inside my mind, telling me it likes the blood, pain, and sacrifice. It's a horrible, bloodthirsty thing, and it likes to destroy things. I was wrong when I thought that magic couldn't be inherently bad. I was wrong; this thing, this charm, is evil. The Dragon's Eye wants to destroy everything.

The Dragon's Eye—the charm, has a name.

My power and charms are nothing like that. They are an extension of myself and my magic. Most are jokey, bubbly, and light yet strong enough to heal and protect.

That thing in his hand is dark and corrupted. Everything inside me screams its wrongness. I block my mind and push away its whispers. I want to run away as fast and far as I possibly can. I would have been long gone if he hadn't stuck my feet to the floor.

Damien throws his head back, and the tempo of the chant increases. I feel it when the Dragon's Eye takes over. It doesn't connect with him on the level my charms do. Instead of working with him and using his internal power to feed the spell, there is no internal power, so it tugs at his life force.

I can see the magic, and I can see the minutes, the hours of his life being sucked away.

It's horrifying.

The power grows, crackling in the air. The magic

builds until the chanting finishes on a crescendo, and then he opens his jaw impossibly wide. The spell blasts out of his mouth and shoots blackness into the air, spreading across the sky like nothing I've ever seen.

At first, I think the black is millions of insects, like he has unleashed a plague. But that's not right. It's not smoke either; it's thicker than that. It keeps coming and spreading, and the fear—oh my gosh, the fear and terror that magic produces hits something primal inside me. The urge to flee makes me feel feral, and if given the chance, I would fight the guards and hurt myself to get away.

My heart is pounding so hard that pain shoots down my jaw and neck, and the still sane, sensible part of me worries that I'm going to have a heart attack. I don't know what is happening as I watch the black stuff drift. Then the buildings around us crumble. Cracks appear and break off, but they don't fall. They don't get to touch the ground.

The magic *eats* them.

It's hungry and eats everything in its path, everything it touches: concrete, metal, brick, and glass.

Is it going to eat me?

His guards shuffle with anxiety. Now the fear isn't just affecting me. A few of them hack as if they can taste the horror of the magic, like something noxious at the backs of their throats.

A whine slips from my frozen lips as I watch it consume the beautiful library until nothing is left, and then it rolls on, attacking everything in its path—one home and another, and another and another. I stand here, frozen and horrified, watching it work its way through the town, and it's then I know that he hasn't been lying.

There's nobody here.

Everybody has gone.

Either the Creature Council has pulled everybody out in secret and over five thousand people have been rehomed, or these monster invaders have murdered everyone. Bile rushes up my throat. It burns when I swallow it back down. I haven't got the luxury of throwing up. I can't move, and I'll suffocate.

I watch as the spell rolls on like a magical storm.

Everything they had, everything they were, is gone.

Every piece of evidence that they lived, loved, and existed in this town has been stolen, and I feel broken.

CHAPTER
TWENTY-ONE

ONCE DAMIEN HAS FINISHED PROVING his point, he looks a little green around the edges. Oh, he pretends to be fine as he barks orders at his men to take me inside. But I can see his soul, and the Dragon's Eye magic has taken Swiss cheese bites out of it.

Is the Grand Claw a short-term position?

Hopefully Damien won't be up for torturing me for at least a few more hours until he's had a nap.

"Take her to the cube," Damien tells the guards.

I'm not going to attempt to run away, so the guards yanking me towards the *cube*, a cell or room, wherever it is, isn't necessary. Even though I've been released from the spell, I can't seem to get my legs to move. I feel as if I've been hit in the head with something hard.

I don't know if it's from the Dragon's Eye magic or shock.

Probably shock.

I feel numb. It's not every day that you realise your entire hometown is dead.

My cobweb-filled mind clings desperately to the environment around me instead of trying to make sense of what I've learned. If I can concentrate on moving my feet, I can ignore everything else.

I was wrong. Not all the buildings in town were gone. The town council's office is still standing. The invaders still need a headquarters, and the ley line gateway is in the basement.

It's a grand Victorian building that I've never been inside. The facade is adorned with large arched windows and intricate carvings of mythical creatures and ancient symbols. The heavy oak doors swing open, and the scent of aged wood and polished brass greets me as I'm bundled inside with my entourage of guards.

It's as if nothing has happened outside these walls and evil hasn't touched this building. I can see where our taxes have gone. People in town have struggled for years, and the council has this. Is that gold wallpaper?

The lobby resembles the destroyed library, with high ceilings supported by ornate columns. Unlike the library, chandeliers hang from above. Their crystals catch the light and scatter it in a thousand directions, creating a mesmerising pattern of colours on the marble floor.

To the left, a grand staircase spirals upwards, its

bannister an elaborate twist of wrought iron and dark mahogany. We ascend the steps and march down a corridor lined with heavy doors. Finally, from the sign on the door, we reach the main council chamber.

The double doors groan open, revealing a vast room dominated by a long, polished table. High-backed chairs, each with intricate carvings, surround it, and the walls are adorned with tapestries depicting long-forgotten histories.

Sunlight streams through the tall windows, casting long shadows and bathing a ten-foot cube of Perspex in a golden glow. The cube is set within a circle. I trace it with my eyes. They used chalk to make the circle. Then they used some herbs, a mixture of blood, and the runes. It must be dragon magic, as the runes surrounding it are very unusual. I recognise a few of them instinctively, and they call to me.

It would be beautiful if it weren't so ominous.

As soon as we get close, I'm boldly picked up—in case I attempt to damage the circle—and launched over the lines and into the Perspex cube.

Landing heavily on my knees, my loose hair flips forward, covering my face, and I cringe when the door slams closed. I feel odd. I can no longer touch my magic. Half of me doesn't care. The magic I have has caused nothing but problems.

Without magic, I'm just a girl.

I rock back on my heels and swipe my hair from my face. There's no furniture, no comfort—just a box, a magic circle, in a beautiful room. I sit on my bottom and hug my knees. I'm left to think of all the mistakes I've made.

What the gargoyle said keeps rolling around in my head, that I'm responsible for the deaths. Whether I pulled the trigger myself or the invaders did. It's my fault. If I hadn't sold the charms, nobody would have got hurt. Nobody would be dead. Has my selfishness caused this? Or would it have happened anyway? The dragon bloods have always been a target, and it was only a matter of time.

I don't know.

I can't help thinking about all my friends, the people from the supermarket, and the old lady who hit me in the face with a fish one Sunday morning because she bought it at a reduction and didn't eat it straight away. So when she came to eat it, it smelt. I know it smelt 'cause I had a good whiff when she battered my face. She's dead.

The teachers from school.

My nan's colleagues at the library who helped me learn about the world and introduced me to fiction. They're all fucking dead. I don't know how to cope with it, being alive when so many good people will not take their next breaths.

Yeah, the guilt inside me is just... Even if I had done nothing, the guilt of my family's being alive when everyone else has died, the relief I feel. I hate myself, and I don't know how to cope with it.

Shit, I'm a complete mess.

I flop back, look at the light pouring in from the window, and wonder if this cube has enough air. Again I don't care. Slowly suffocating is probably what I deserve. I didn't save anyone. I didn't do anything but make them aware of their situation before the invaders killed them.

I groan. This is getting me nowhere. I wipe the tears and snot from my face with my sleeve. I need to woman up and plan my next move 'cause soon Damien Hass will come through that door and he will start asking questions, questions that I need to answer—even if it's not the truth.

What do they say? Everybody, whoever they are, breaks under torture.

I can do one of three things: roll around on the floor and cry, allow Damien Hass to torture the location of the charms out of me and my family, or step up and fix this mess. I need to have a plan and give him some information that makes sense.

Sometimes you've got to use what you've got.

Sometimes you've got to be brave even if you don't know whether you're the villain in the story or the hero. I guess time will tell.

The magic Damien uses isn't his. It's a dragon charm, dragon-made, and the same magic I've been playing with most of my life.

Dragon magic is why the Creature Council secretly locked up everybody with even a trace of dragon blood. If Damien with one charm can create spells that can control minds, spells that can eat buildings, an entire town, I can only imagine what would happen if he used me, used my magic. I'd destroy the world.

He can't know about me and can never find out about my magic. I need to send him on a wild goose chase, and to do that, I need Gary Chappell.

CHAPTER
TWENTY-TWO

The heavy oak door creaks open. I don't even bother to open my eyes. The sunlight is on my face, and it feels nice. I usually try to avoid the sun because of my colouring. I get pink, especially across my cheekbones, with freckles appearing on my nose, and with too much sun, I get sore skin.

It doesn't seem important anymore.

The clunk of boots comes closer. Then I hear the worst voice imaginable. I don't know whether to be angry or jubilant that he's still alive. I knew deep down the guy was like a human cockroach who'd survive anything, including the apocalypse where everybody else died. This proves the theory.

Anton Bloody Hill. He stands there, hands on his

hips, and stares at me as if I'm a goldfish in a goldfish bowl, then he chuckles, and a big grin graces his face.

"Look at this," he says. "Got what you deserved then, didn't you?"

Fuck off, fuck off, fuck off.

I keep my mouth closed. I haven't spoken since Damien grabbed me by the wrist and off the street. I will not break my silence now. Anton Hill is messing with my thinking time, even if a teeny-tiny part of me is glad he's alive.

He grabs a chair from the beautiful, ornate table and drags it across the room. It scrapes against the floor. I wince, worried that it'll damage something. The seat creaks as he sits, and then he leans forward, his hands dangling between his legs.

He watches me. I sit up and watch him right back.

He looks good for a dead man.

He's dressed nicely and is clean. He's wearing a different outfit than he was for the news this morning.

"You're not going to talk? You're not going to confess? The guys out there believe you've got magic, that you found some charms, and that's why they came to our town. The reason they've killed everybody is that you found something that you shouldn't have."

He leans back in the chair, and his heel hits his knee as he manspreads. "Did your nan find something at the library? Is that it? She found something she shouldn't have, and you stole and used it. They say that you know

Gary Chappell. You're in contact with him, and he's been selling these spells."

Look at that. I don't have to speak. He's doing all the work for me.

"What I want to know is where this fellow is. We want to know if he's a witch. Or if he's human and just your artefact dealer. I know you've seen me on the news and what I said about this guy being a hero, but he's no hero. You need to admit what you've done, and you need to sort this shit out. You've done enough damage."

I yawn and rub my eyes.

"Chloe is still alive."

When he mentions Chloe, my heart beats with joy—and then fear for her safety. I swallow, and again I don't speak.

"Yeah, your little friend, the little blondie. She's alive, but she won't be for long. I've been told that they're going to pull her teeth out one by one. Every time you don't answer a question. Every time you don't help, they're going to pull her teeth out. And when they run out of teeth, they'll start on her nails."

I didn't think Anton Hill could get any lower in my estimation, and he goes there. I can't believe he's threatening her. I was all prepared for them to torture me. I had everything planned to give them information about the non-existent Gary, and now Anton is talking about hurting my friend.

We're not close, Chloe and me, but she's always been kind. She's the reason I was on the friend chat group.

Chloe used to lecture everyone about bullying and say that leaving a person out of social things isn't kind.

"Chloe's got great teeth. Are you going to allow her to suffer for you? Give them what they want, Kricket. Give them what they want. Because otherwise, you'll be better off dead."

I press my lips together.

He's quiet; he waits and watches me, and I ignore him as best I can. And then he smiles. "You don't care about anyone apart from yourself, do you? Are you hungry? I could get you some food. I bet you're starving for a nice burger and some fries. Please tell me what you want and we'll get you some food. All you need to do in return is tell us about the charms. If you give me that information, it'll save you a lot of grief."

I turn away.

I expect him to get angry. I expect him to bite, bang on the cube, and lose his temper, but he huffs. Then softly, he says, "I can get you out of here. I can get us both out of here, but you must do what I say. Let me help you, Kricket. Just give me something; trust me, I'm the only help you've got."

I ignore him and continue looking at a painting of a guy riding a weird-looking horse.

The chair scrapes back, and Anton Hill's boots stomp away. The door to the cube clicks open. I gasp and turn my head. Fear flutters in my belly. What's he going to do? Come in here and beat me?

But Anton Hill doesn't come inside. Instead, he

walks away, leaving the door wide-open and shuffling the heel of his foot against the circle's lines, snuffing the magic out. "Get out and send in the big boys, would you?" he says almost inaudibly.

With the circle down, my somewhat dreaded magic floods back into me, and I stare in shock at the open door and the scuffed floor. The main oak door closes softly behind him.

Do I trust him? No.

Should I trust him? No.

But I do trust that he cares about himself more than anyone. He cares about his neck rather than anyone else. That's why he was doing the news reports. That's why he came in here in the first place. So if he's willing to try to help me so that I in turn will help him, that makes sense.

Do I trust him? Nope. But I haven't got a choice. I can stay here, get tortured, or watch them torture Chloe. Or, for Chloe's sake, I can get my arse out of this cube. Out of this room, out of this building, through the ward, and get some help.

If they'll believe me when I get there, that's another thing, but at least I can try. I've got to have hope, and Anton Hill has given it to me.

Which is a surprise.

It's going to be a nightmare, getting out of the building, and if I get outside, it's miles of emptiness. There are no buildings to hide behind, and the ward is miles away. From what I can remember, there are still trees at the top of town. The spell didn't eat them, so I have some cover if I run that way.

Unfortunately, I need to create something new and keep my magical signature low so that if I'm super careful, no one, not Damien Hass or his Dragon's Eye, will notice. I need a charm. The materials I had on me were removed when the guards patted me down; they'd been unable to find any of my hidden charms.

In case I'm being watched, rather than going blank, I keep my eyes open and a contemplating, confused look on my face. I request help and get a ping off a little piece of metal. A broken piece of pen someone discarded under the massive table sings a small, reserved tune that will work wonderfully. I gently feed it magic, a nip of power, nothing like I'd usually do, just enough to create a basic Don't See Me Now spell.

Getting out of here will be like the game red light, green light, where you must run like crazy and then stop and freeze. You're out of the game if you move when the person counting looks at you. Move and then freeze when needed.

If this is another trap, I can presume I'm being watched. Stepping over the circle, I make a show of heading to the desk in the corner and have a dig about. As luck would have it, there are some spells in a drawer. They're the typical crappy council ones. I cup my hand as if I take a couple, and when I walk around the table, frowning at my trainer, I drop to tie my lace, grab the pen charm and head to the big oak doors.

I open the door just a crack and peek through. The corridor is quiet. I listen. Nothing. I refine and enhance the ear charm in my pocket to pick up the barest footsteps and the slightest inhale of a breath.

Listening again, I know I'm alone now. I creep out.

Perhaps I should have left it at least ten minutes after Anton left the room so not to implicate him, but I don't know if he'll change his mind. I'm not going to mess about.

I run down the stairs and into the lobby, and again, it's all quiet. Too quiet. But I don't think about it too much. I've only seen the eight guards and take this as an opportunity. I need to feel fortunate that I've avoided them. Perhaps they've all gone to eat?

The main door clicks open, and I creep onto what was once the street. It's now just dirt. Everywhere is just soil. I see the trees in the distance. They must be a mile or so ahead. I look around. I listen, and again, no one is about, so I run.

I keep running, keep listening, keep moving.

I stop when I get into the trees. I lean against a trunk, my chest burning, and feel a little dizzy. I need some water. I need some food. I hadn't eaten since early this morning, and that sandwich was the first food I'd eaten in days.

The Claw Brotherhood diet is one star. I do not recommend.

There's a noise, shouting, and my heart sinks. I've been made already. I look back at the lonely building, the ward, and the trees. They'll expect me to go for the ward. What happens if I give it a few hours? Use the Don't See Me Now charm. Stay up in the tree.

Okay, let's get up this tree then. Shit. I haven't climbed a tree since I was ten, and even then, I wasn't very good at it. My coordination's not the best. There's a lower branch, and I pull myself up, kicking my legs until I get a purchase, and then I'm up, I'm up, I'm up. I only go about eight feet in the air, and that's seven feet too much. I hate heights, and I'm unwilling to test any of the higher branches.

I don't want to get into the same situation as the jungle gym incident. It's one of my first memories. I was around five, got stuck on some equipment, and couldn't get off it. I remember being stuck, my hands digging into the coarse rope of a suspended net, too frightened to go forward, too scared to go back. My dad had to climb up and rescue me.

The tree is solid, and the trunk forms a V in the centre where the two main branches meet. I move up a little more and cautiously slide my leg over so I'm straddling the thicker of the two and hugging the other.

The Don't See Me Now spell activates, and I disappear.

CHAPTER TWENTY-THREE

THE SOUND of braying wolves makes me jerk, and the rough bark burns my wrists as I wobble precariously and scramble to keep a death grip on the tree. Wolf shifters. Ah, I should have thought of them being on Team Fake Dragon. It makes sense, as the guards are so big. The stink of that charm's magical signature has thrown me off; it hides a multitude of things.

I've made a colossal mistake if they have wolves; I've underestimated the power of their senses. Shifter noses are incredible, and now I'm in a pickle as I haven't tried to disguise my scent. It doesn't matter that I'm hidden. The trail will take them right up to this tree.

I have the cleaning charm in my pocket, and it won't take much—a tiny push of the magic, even at this distance—to eliminate my scent. If I'm careful to use the lightest touch of magic. I can even waft everything around at the front of the building, making it all the more confusing.

I can't.

Then I can use the disguise spell to hide my scent so no one can smell me.

I bloody can't. I'm already pushing it, and if I'm caught, they'll be suspicious. Perhaps I should go all out, use my magic, and give myself a proper chance to escape, but again, I can't give myself away. The secret of my magic is too important to risk saving myself.

I press the side of my face against the trunk and watch for the opportune time to run for the ward. It might be best to wait until it gets dark.

There's a snap of a dry branch and a rustle of foliage. Something grabs hold of my foot, and I'm yanked down. I yelp. I fall oddly, almost upside down, scraping the side of the trunk with my stomach and hitting each branch on the way down.

There's a crack, something snaps in my arm, and there's a moment before the pain registers.

Ow. Ow. Ow.

Damn it, I've broken my arm. Damien gives me a look of disgust as I lie crumpled on the forest floor. No one even bothered to catch me.

"Well," he says, "that was exciting. You only lasted about twenty minutes. You didn't even move towards the ward. You sat there, clinging to the tree like a primate. As if I couldn't see through that rubbish spell."

I blink up at him and his guards.

Ah, I was right to be cautious; they had eyes on me the entire time. I wish I could take a full breath. My poor ribs are hurting so much. I feel like someone's punched a hole in my diaphragm. I just lay there, gasping.

"Somebody grab her and take her back to her cube. Honestly, this was supposed to be a fun training exercise; instead, it was a waste of time. You're a waste of time, such a disappointment. The magic that you found is awful. Primitive. I had thought there was something special about you. I was wrong. The witch, Gary Chappell, why would he want you? You're pathetic. We'll talk about your friend's location soon. Take her away. I can't look at her anymore. She's annoying." He gives me another look of disgust, and on the way past, he boots me in the ribs.

I'm helped inside, or should I say I'm dragged inside. I haven't got time to access a charm to heal myself before I'm shoved back over the repaired and improved circle and into the Perspex box.

I hold my arm to my chest; it's throbbing. My fingers are swollen and look like sausages with a purple tinge. At least the bone hasn't come through the skin, and it's not wonky-looking, so I don't think it needs resetting. It's just excruciating, and my breathing hasn't improved, so I've probably bruised my ribs.

There's another big problem, I have a massive gash

on my side. One of the branches, or several, pierced the flesh just above my hip. I don't think anything vital was stabbed. I'm bleeding, and it hurts.

Everything hurts.

"Can I get some first aid please?" I break my silence. I need to ask because the broken arm needs sorting, and the cut could become nasty if not treated soon. The guards all march out the door; they don't look back. Can they hear me? With my good hand, I tap on the Perspex. "Hello? I really need some help." The door closes behind them, and I'm left staring. I look back at my arm. "Oh well, that went well."

The door flings open, and Anton Hill walks through. He's got a swagger in his step and a massive grin on his face as if he's having a wonderful time.

He's having a wonderful time because he set me up.

That little whispered speech and opening the door, scuffing the circle. I'm an idiot. He set me up. Damien wanted to see if I had any magic, and because I didn't perform any massive magic tricks during my escape, I became useless. It's probably only a matter of time before they kill me. But it's better than the alternative.

I don't want to die. I don't want to be a martyr, but my magic is better dying with me.

At least now I know they can't detect my power when I'm circumspect. If given the chance, I need to refine my magic more and be sneaky, and at least I'm fully recovered from my three-day nap. I frown. Or I was before being pulled out of a tree.

Anton Hill pulls a sad face when he sees me looking at him. His bottom lip comes out in an exaggerated pout. "Oh, did you hurt yourself? Do you need a plaster? I heard that you were a monkey in a tree"—he makes a monkey sound and scratches underneath his armpits—"and you only got so far before you shit yourself and hid. That's hilarious. What? What's wrong?" His boots stomp across the floor, and he gets closer to the circle. His toes brush the edge of the chalk.

"Did you think I was helping you escape? Did you think the Claw Brotherhood wouldn't have a man on the inside? I'm the man on the inside." He thumbs his chest. "The boss said we had to knock that pride and confidence right out of you. What better way than giving you hope and then taking it away?" He smiles brightly, flashing his square chewing-gum teeth.

What better way, indeed.

I shuffle around and turn my back. I just can't. I'm in too much pain to hear him confess he was the town's inside man. I can't. I just can't. Everybody was trapped here, and he'd put himself here on purpose. To spy.

More and more, I think that this wasn't about me. It wasn't about my magic. I wasn't the catalyst, not really. They were waiting for the right time and used the charms as an excuse to act, and now Anton is all smug and happy that he's back with his Claw Brotherhood buddies.

Back still to him, I hobble to the corner, slowly slide down the wall, and sit. The cube's edges do an excellent job of holding me up. I won't be able to lie down. I need to keep this arm elevated.

"Aren't you going to ask questions? Are you not going to talk about what I learned? What I did? Who I am?" He looms over me, watching, and his voice slowly rises. "Don't ignore me, Kricket. I want to know. I want to know what you think. I won. I'm the winner."

"Yeah, yeah, yeah, you won. You're the winner," I hiss. I'd sarcastically clap, but I can't be arsed to do it one-handed.

Surprised I'd answered him, he takes a breath, and then he's silent, waiting.

"You're such a big man, killing frightened, innocent people, our friends and neighbours. You really deserve that pat on the back. Good job..." My voice cracks. I have to swallow a few times to get around the massive lump in my throat. "I hope in the dead of night, when you're trying to sleep, you remember the faces of the people who've been kind to you. Kind even while you were selfish and cruel. You didn't just come to the town, sit in the background and spy. While you were here, you made everybody's life hell, and then you watched them die."

"You don't get to say that. You have to be nice to me because you won't get any food if you're not. I'm sure you're thirsty. I'm sure you need help with that arm. You need to be nice to me. I... I'm... You..." he splutters. "I'll make you be nice," he snarls, stomping out of the room.

The oak door slams closed.

CHAPTER
TWENTY-FOUR

I'M LEFT to stew with the injuries. Damien and Anton have yet to return; the tree incident has made me unappealing, and I must be better as bait. I bet they're hoping to lure Gary Chappell to them. *Good luck with that.* I shouldn't be so amused.

My arm looks a mess, but the swelling started coming down by day two. I had hoped that when I got to use the bathroom, I'd be away from the circle long enough to heal myself. But when I returned to the cube, they had improved and extended the magic and opened a second door to reveal a tiny toilet and sink.

With the gash on my side, I've done my best to flush the wound with water even though it hurts like crazy. I'm not medically trained. I'm sure little bits of wood are still lodged in there, and my body thinks so too as it's producing gallons and gallons of gross pus. I've been using a toilet roll to stem the mess. Not hygienic, but it's all I've got.

Things are happening behind the scenes. There's been some shouting, and all the guards dropping off water and peanut butter sandwiches have lost their swagger. They seem anxious.

I worry they'll forget I'm here.

I need to find a way out of this cube.

ANOTHER DAY, my blood pressure has tanked, I can't seem to get off the floor, and my vision flickers like an old television set. I've got no thoughts of escape, only of taking my next breath. I haven't eaten for a while, and there's a pile-up of plates with various stages of moulding bread.

I want to roll into a ball and sleep, and that's what I'm doing. I curl in the corner, pushing my bad side into the hard floor as I can't lie the other way because of my arm. The weight and pressure of my body help to stem the smell of the wound. The smell makes me feel sick—everything makes me feel sick.

At least it doesn't hurt anymore.

There's a massive blast and the building shudders. *Uh-oh*. That didn't sound good. It takes a huge amount of effort to roll onto my back, and I watch as the ornate lights on the ceiling dance, and the table with its thick, huge legs shifts to the side, knocking over some chairs. All I can do is lie here.

The swinging of the lights makes me dizzy, so I close my eyes.

When I next become aware, I can hear fighting. There's a tremendous bang, a crash, and a gurgling scream. The big oak doors slam open, and there's the thud of an impact, them hitting the wall, and various heavy footsteps stomping into the room.

"What the hell. WE'VE FOUND HER!"

Big feet move into the cube, and plates break as they're kicked out of the way. "You're okay. I've got you." Gentle fingers brush against my cheek, moving my sweaty hair from my face.

I groan. I can't believe somebody is touching me. I stink.

"Hey, nothing girl. You're in a bit of a mess."

Where did I hear that nickname before? The voice is familiar, like a rumble of rocks. This isn't real. I must be dreaming. It sounds like the mean gargoyle trying to be nice. That soft, worried voice doesn't suit him.

Another small groan comes out, and I lift the good arm to batter his hand away. He takes it and gently holds my wrist. I scowl.

"Has anybody got a med kit?"

"Can't you feel it? This entire area is a dead zone. That circle has been inlaid with blood and silver. No magic can be used, and none of our healing spells will work. We need to move her."

My eyes don't work, but I try to talk. My throat burns, but I get the words out. "The other prisoners? Chloe?" I ask.

"There are no other prisoners. We've been through the entire building, and nobody else is here but you and the guards."

"He said Chloe was here." It's not much of a surprise that Anton Bloody Hill lied.

"What did they do to you?"

"I fell out of a tree."

He lets out a strained laugh. "Maybe keep the tree climbing to other people. Can someone prep the gateway? It's not safe here. We need an exit fast. Jeff, hand me that kit. I need some of that dressing."

"Careful, she's got a broken arm."

"I can see that. Brace the limb."

I'm rolled carefully onto my side, and someone's cool hands brace my arm so it doesn't hit the floor. Something soft is pressed against my side, and then I'm lifted and my arm is placed gently across my chest.

"It's okay, Kricket. Keep breathing for me for a little

longer until we get you all fixed up. Jeff, this will need a doctor. Have one on standby."

"Sss o-okay, no long... urts." My words come out garbled.

"Jeff, make sure the way is clear. Let's move out."

He jars me. From his mumbled apologies, he tries hard not to, but you can do nothing when you're as big as him and must charge down a narrow, ornate staircase carrying some random woman.

There's clanking of weapons, banging, and muffled, pain-filled yells, and when they shout all clear, it's our turn to move down another set of stairs into the basement. I can feel the portal and its ley line magic, and the power buzzes against my skin.

Then there is nothing.

CHAPTER
TWENTY-FIVE

I BLINK MY EYES OPEN. Disoriented, I push myself up on my elbows and take in my surroundings. The room is unfamiliar but somehow comforting in its simplicity. The walls are painted a soothing shade of blue. There's a single window opposite the bed, its blue curtains gently swaying with the breeze from outside.

I'm waking up in a strange bed again.

This is getting out of hand and becoming a habit.

I can't believe I'm alive and I feel okay—more than okay. I cautiously check myself out. I'm back in my black jumper and jogging bottoms; the sock has been at it again. I'm also squeaky clean and smell of vanilla soap, so the mop charm has also done an excellent job. My smile fades as, without my permission, my mind flashes back to the hoodie, adhering itself to the gross wound on my side. I lift the top and find smooth, pale skin. It doesn't twinge. There's not even a scar.

The doctor has also fixed my arm, unless... There's a sound, a creak of a floorboard. I drop the jumper and turn to look. How did I miss the door standing ajar and a hulking grey man sitting on the floor, leaning against the hallway wall?

He's staring at me.

Oh.

I notice the ward crackling around the room's walls, keeping him out. He can't sneak in, unlike Emma. Feeling awkward, I adjust the covers and clear my throat. "Hi."

"Hello, nothing girl. I'm glad you're awake." The gargoyle rubs his face. He looks tired.

"This doesn't look like a cell."

He drops his hand, and his lips twitch as he shakes his head. "No, it isn't."

"How long have I been out?" I ask.

"Four days."

"Four. Wow." Four days this time. It's getting longer, although this time, it wasn't the overuse of magic that attempted to finish me off. No, this time it was a tree.

Fuck my life.

"Once we got you out from behind the magic circle, your magic began to heal you. When we got to the hospital, it was already doing weird things, so the doctors thought it best to bring you somewhere safe."

"Safe? Where are we?"

"My house."

"You brought me to your home?" I squeak. My eyes flick around the pretty bedroom and then back to him. "Why would you do that?"

"I didn't have a choice. There was no way to keep you safe in a public building."

"Ah, I'm that bad, am I? Why would you want to keep me safe?"

"Your magic is freaky."

I snort. I've heard that before.

"Your healing charm fixed you, and the cleaning charm cleaned you. The doctor peeked at you through the ward, which appeared out of thin air and had a hell of a kick. He noted that your arm fixed itself within minutes, and your colour improved after a few hours. He explained if you weren't hydrated, you would probably be dead." He rubs his eyebrow and stares at the ceiling. "You're the real deal, aren't you?"

The real deal?

"What?" I don't know what he's trying to say, but I'll try to ignore what he's said about my magic. "Erm." I make my eyes wide and innocent and say, "I don't know what you're talking about. Remember, I'm just a thief."

Remember, he's an arsehole, Kricket.

"Yeah, sure, you don't know what I mean." He

shakes his head and slumps back against the wall. "I'll never live the thief thing down, will I?" he groans.

"Thank you, getting me out of there..." I nibble on my bottom lip. "I'm sorry, but I don't know your name."

"Soren."

Soren. My heart flutters, and I steadfastly ignore it. Well, it's better than calling him the gargoyle or dickhead in my head. I smirk. "Soren, I don't know whether you came to arrest me or kill me, but you saved my life. Thank you."

"I'm only repaying the favour. I was practically dead after the explosion, and you dug me out of the ash and brought me back with your freaky magic."

Ah, he worked that out then. Embarrassed, I fiddle with the duvet cover. I don't expect an apology, but an acknowledgement is kind of nice. "I didn't bring you back, as you weren't dead."

"No? You sure about that?"

I shrug. I've no idea. "I'm not a necromancer." At least I've never tried to bring back the dead. The dead are in fate's hands, and I won't mess with that. You do not poke at the reaper.

"So, Kricket, will you tell me about your magic? Did you find the dragon charms? Or did you create them?"

There's an awkward pause while the gargoyle waits for me to confess, and I fidget. My stomach takes the opportunity to gurgle. He shakes his head and gets to his feet. Looks like my empty stomach saves the day— tummy monster for the win.

"I'm sorry. I'm being a terrible host. Let's leave the interrogation for later, after you've eaten. Is there anything you want?"

I shrug again. I feel very flustered. I've only ever seen those pale green eyes angry, and now he's looking at me with a softness I don't understand. Be nice to the charm maker. Perhaps she'll tell you all her secrets. *Yeah, that's about right.*

"Perhaps we'll try some soup. You haven't eaten for days, and I'm worried your stomach will revolt." He nods towards a door in the hallway. "The bathroom's just down the hall. I'll meet you in the kitchen. Whenever you're ready."

"Okay, thank you."

With a nod, he leaves.

For such a big guy, he moves silently. I don't hear him go down the stairs, but I feel his absence all the same. He's a predator, leaving a prickly sensation in his wake.

I get up. The grey carpet is soft under my feet, and the ward dissipates into the umbrella charm when I reach the bedroom door. I pat my pocket. I'm grateful for my charms. Twice now, they've saved my life; without them, I'd be dead.

Am I concerned that they do what they want while I'm unconscious? Meh, not really. While I lay dying in that cell, I decided to embrace my magic and trust myself. Before I met Damien Hass, I was frightened to death about my magic being evil, but I've seen and felt the

Dragon's Eye and compared to the evil charm, I know my magic is nothing like that.

Now I need to find out what's happening and what the gargoyle knows. I go to the bathroom, tidy myself up, and then shuffle down the stairs. I follow my nose into the kitchen.

CHAPTER
TWENTY-SIX

I stand in the doorway. The kitchen has clean lines and a modern design. The cabinets are crisp, white Shaker-style, and the countertops are cool, speckled grey granite, smooth and polished, reflecting the soft overhead lighting.

On one side, there's a white refrigerator, its surface adorned with a few scattered magnets and a couple of photos. The sleek, built-in oven and matching electric hob sit prominently on the opposite wall.

It's all so normal.

Set in the centre of the room, the kitchen island, topped with a wooden butcher block, serves as a breakfast bar with two high stools. I settle onto one of the stools, lean my chin on my fist, and watch as Soren, the gargoyle, chops vegetables.

He's making me soup instead of getting it from a can. He cuts the vegetables like a chef would, holding the knife correctly and using his first knuckle as a guide. He's also making enough food for an army.

"That was fast," he says, not looking up from his task.

"I'm pretty clean." Thanks to my mop charm, but I don't say that. "I'd like some answers please." My voice is still a little husky.

"Of course you would."

He continues chopping, and I continue watching.

He's a massive man with wings, broad shoulders, narrow hips, and that face of his—beautiful. His wings are a deep slate grey, with veins of silver that glint when they catch the light. My fingers twitch with the urge to touch them. *Gosh, I wonder what they'd feel like.* Every movement Soren makes is deliberate, almost graceful, belying raw power coiled within such a muscular frame.

No other gargoyle looked like that in town. Not that I got anywhere near them, but I know now they can sniff me out. I'm glad I didn't, or I would have gotten into trouble well before this.

Soren slides each pile of chopped vegetables into a pot and continues his prep. From the earthy smell, potatoes are already bubbling away on the hob. In a separate pan, he does something to the onions.

This feels weird. It's like domestic bliss, but instead

of a partner, it's a guy who was trying to kill me a few days ago. Was it days? No, it was probably at least a week, maybe more. I'm all muddled up. It could be years at this point.

"Would I be able to talk to my family and friends? They are going to be worried about me."

"Of course. I'll get you a phone after you've answered my questions."

Ah, there we go. He must have his questions answered. I dramatically blow out a breath and slap a hand against my forehead. "Oh, thank fate. You were being too kind, and you had me worried that you'd been body snatched." I drop my hand over my face to hide the smile. "I thought you were going to feed me first."

"You can talk while you're eating." Again without looking up, he shoves a plate my way. *Bossy.* There's a slice of warm, crusty bread. "Hopefully that won't give you too much trouble," he says.

"Thank you." I pick it up and nibble on the end. A cup of fresh orange juice and a glass of water land beside my elbow. I take a sip of water. "What do you want me to tell you? What do you and the gargoyles know?" Asking outright is perhaps dangerous, but he's dropped enough hints that he knows. Besides, I can't be bothered with this cloak-and-dagger stuff. I'll mess up and end up looking stupid.

"I know that there's no Gary Chappell, that you've been using him as a pseudonym, and that you've been making charms since you were fourteen."

Uh-oh.

So he knows almost everything. I take another sip of water in a poor attempt to delay the inevitable. "I made my first charm at ten," I correct him. "Are you going to write that down?"

I catch something in Soren's gaze, and I realise he's highly amused—though it doesn't show on his face except for a quirk of his eyebrow. But I'm positive I am right.

"I know you use dragon magic, and you didn't know you were using it until the town was attacked. The surprise on your face and the fear in your scent confirmed that. Otherwise, you wouldn't be selling charms to everybody."

"I didn't sell charms to everybody," I grumble.

"No? Just everyone that can pay."

"I bet you don't work for free." I let the words sit.

He can't use his skills as a gargoyle to make money and then be all high and mighty when I use my magic.

"I used what I had to keep my family safe. What would you do to keep your family safe?"

"Anything. But I wouldn't break the law."

"No?" I scoff and wiggle on the stool. Now he's pissing me off. "Whose laws?" I take a big bite of the bread and angrily chew. "I'm sorry I'm not au fait with your world. Do you refer to the laws of this country or the laws of that town we were left in to rot? They killed Mrs Harris for buying an unsanctioned healing potion. Did you know that?"

"No." He leans against the counter, crosses his arms and legs and gives me his full attention.

"She was seventy-three. Her husband had a nasty infected cut on his leg; when she was murdered, he also died. Are those the laws you mean?" I drop the bread on the plate and push it away. I'm no longer hungry. "Or shall we talk about the slave labour? I was forced to work for £2.08 an hour, and on average, I worked ninety-six hours a week. After they removed taxes and my accommodation, I barely had enough money to buy a pack of gum."

I take a sip of water and stare out of the window. "Is that fair? I was never given a choice of what job I did or where I lived. No one had a choice. I couldn't speak out, couldn't have an opinion in case somebody murdered me. I found a way of selling my magic to the outside world, who didn't know we existed, and it was all legit. I have an accreditation and a licence to sell them, and I paid their taxes too."

The gargoyle watches me, wiping his hands on a towel.

"I saw the news and the cover-up. The Creature Council let them take over that town, and all the evidence of the crime has disappeared." My voice cracks with emotion. I want to scream about their deaths, but if I get too emotional, the words will lose their impact. "Like puff, it never happened." I flick my fingers.

"If you pursue that line of thought any further, they will eliminate you as a threat."

No shit. I know that.

"Experienced people are dealing with this. The guilty will not go unpunished."

"I don't believe you."

"That's your choice. There will be no big revenge plans in your future, Kricket. You need to keep your head down and be grateful that you're not dead."

Grateful. The gargoyle is incredibly careful with his words. What he doesn't say, but what is hinted at, is that there won't be any big revenge plans because he won't let me. "I'm not going to be left to live my life, am I?"

Soren's face remains blank.

What the gargoyle has to say and his opinion of me shouldn't matter, and now I feel bad for losing my cool. It was the wrong time to blurt all this out. He doesn't know me, and I should have been smarter, timed it better, and planned what I would say.

He could kill me as easily as look at me.

I need to throw him a bone. "I wouldn't have sold the charms if I'd known all hell would break loose. I had no idea it was dragon magic. Seeing the future isn't one of my skills."

"I believe that as you aren't suicidal. I would have thought Ava Larson would have more common sense. She comes from a family of witches."

"So do I."

He grunts and messes with the onions.

"So what is this?" I wave my hand around the kitchen at the homemade bread and bubbling soup. "Do you still want me to go to prison, to suffer 'cause you think I killed all your friends?" I gulp the orange juice and this time keep my head down so I don't have to look him in the eyes.

"No, I was upset. Grief is a horrible emotion, and I spoke out of turn. I apologise. I thought... I presumed you were just some kid who got hold of some dragon artefacts and sold them. I didn't realise they were your spells until we got hold of a couple of them."

"You got a couple of my charms?"

"Yes, and we tested them. They're nothing like the usual dragon magic. Dragon magic is indescribably dangerous. What dragon magic doesn't do is make you see in the dark or let you read hidden texts, all the innocent things that your charms do.

"We realised it wasn't an ancient dragon who had made them. It was some dragon blood that had tapped into their magic. It's impossible. It doesn't make sense that you can work the magic as you do, but here you are. Do you understand what I mean? It's, it's..." He throws his hands in the air and strangely echoes Emma's sentiments. "It's weird."

"What do you mean it's weird?" Is weird any better than freaky? I'll be starting to get a complex soon. I snatch the bread off the plate and silently chew.

"If you've got power and can make anything, why would you make a charm in the shape of a carrot? Why wouldn't you make something like a death charm?"

A death charm? The bread sticks in my throat. "Or

like a charm that can rip apart an entire town? That claw guy made a charm that destroyed the entire town. You were there, so you must have seen the after-effects. The houses, the buildings, they're all gone. Magic ate away at them. Magic flew up out of his fucking mouth like a plague of black flies, and then it destroyed everything. It ate through everything. And you think it's a shame that I don't make death charms? Death charms? I do not make that kind of magic." *I won't.*

His nostrils flare, no doubt picking up on the fear and anger that's making sweat trickle down my spine.

"No, of course you don't want to make that kind of magic," he cajoles me. "No one in their right mind would want to make that kind of magic. But a carrot, really?"

I narrow my eyes and glare. "What's wrong with the carrot? I thought it was cute and practical."

Okay, next, I'll make a gargoyle that will make the person's skin impenetrable. I almost say it out loud, but my self-preservation kicks in, and I keep my mouth closed.

I've said way too much to this stranger, and you don't have to be a genius to realise he wouldn't like anyone having a skill that makes the gargoyles special.

Soren stirs the pot before placing the spoon down and grabbing two bowls. "But the problem is that magic and potential are within you, and bad people will want that magic. Bad people will want you to do bad things for them and will hurt you. Hurt your family if you refuse."

He ladles the soup into a bowl, placing it before me with a spoon. The steam rises in gentle curls. "Eat up."

Yeah, Yum, yum. So hungry after he's scared the shit out of me.

A change of subject is best. "So this is your house. You live here. Does that mean you didn't live at the peacekeeper building?"

Soren narrows his eyes, and I get the impression that he doesn't like answering questions. Well too bad. He can't have it both ways. He can't be bossy and want to know everything about me, but he turns his nose up when I ask the questions. That's a double standard if ever I saw one.

He doesn't like it. So I plough on. "I'd never seen you before. I saw you that night at the supermarket when everything went tits up. So do you live here and then commute into town?" I actually don't know how far his house is away. I'm guessing it's not around the corner.

"No." His tone of voice says no more questions.

I smile. "Are you an old gargoyle?"

"I'm not particularly old, no." He growls and prods the bowl of soup closer to me. It's full to the brim and splashes a little on the counter.

I pick up the spoon, give him a small smile, and then fish out a chunk of potato. "This looks amazing, thank you." I shovel it into my mouth.

"You've been fortunate that the guys holding you weren't very bright and didn't realise who you were.

You're incredibly lucky. They left you to die in a cage, but it could have so easily gone very wrong."

Uh-huh, lucky. "Why didn't I think of that? I was so fortunate, almost dying. That's good to know. I better count those blessings."

"The realms are blessed that they didn't get hold of your magic. Now you can try to bury your head in the sand and ignore all this. But there's no ignoring it, Kricket. You've got to realise that you've got dragon magic, and it can get you and other people killed."

I'd be in a pickle if I didn't have him gargoylesplain all this to me. How could I cope? "So how am I going to keep myself safe?" I'm sure he has all the answers.

Perhaps he should have let the tree kill me.

"You have a team coming to look after you."

Great. "A team? A team of gargoyles?"

"No. The general has stepped in, and he's sending an elite team for bodyguard duty."

I slump heavily, and the sudden movement shunts the stool and makes it screech across the floor. I grip the edge of the counter, and my fingers blanch with the pressure. "The general. The silver dragon. He knows about me?" I squeak. "He knows about the dragon blood town? I bet that didn't go over well."

"Yes, he knows about you, and he's sending a team of hellhounds to keep you safe while he deals with the Creature Council. I assure you heads will roll. The gargoyles will hunt down the rest of your Claw Brotherhood."

I feel a little dizzy. The silver dragon is sending hellhounds.

Hellhounds.

CHAPTER
TWENTY-SEVEN

Hellhounds aren't from hell or anything. They're shifters, but not just any kind of shifter. They're six to eight hundred years old to be at that power level. Think shifter Terminator. Oh, and we can't forget the magic—fire magic—hence the hell part of their nickname.

Shifters are immortal, as when they shift, their cells regenerate. However, like most creatures, they can be killed, and due to their hot tempers, reaching an age where a shifter can potentially develop fire magic is unlikely, which is why they're so rare.

To exist, hellhounds must be strong and emotionally intelligent, making them scary.

"They're not *my* Claw Brotherhood," I mumble. "There are more of them?"

"There's always more of them, but you don't have to worry about that."

Don't worry my pretty little head, right? I don't know who he thinks he's talking to. I dealt with the Claw Brotherhood myself, knocked them all out, and could have killed them all on my lonesome while he napped in the multi-storey car park.

I have to count to ten in my head so I don't get mad or run my mouth. I can't do that with this guy, as we are still tiptoeing around each other. Besides, I need his help. I side-eye him. *Look at the size of him.* He'd probably kill me if I said the wrong thing.

A part of me wishes I could turn into a dragon and eat people. The other half doesn't want to eat other creatures. I wouldn't even have to eat them; I could chomp on them and spit them out. I wouldn't have to swallow anything.

I'd use my giant dragon gnashers and pulp them a little bit. Or, if I'm as big as the silver dragon, I could squish them with my feet.

Yeah, that would be pretty cool. But of course, "I've got the dragon magic without THE dragon magic."

"I wish you were a dragon," Soren says.

Oh heck, I must have said some of that out loud. I'm still not right, and my filters are broken.

"If you could shift into dragon form, that'd solve many of our problems. No one would mess with you then."

I huff out a small laugh. "No, no one would." Especially Anton Hill. "Hey, did you get Damien Hass?" I ask, taking a bigger mouthful of the soup.

"Damien Hass?"

Great. I should have told him about Damien as soon as I woke up. This is the information that the good guys need. If they're the good guys. I swallow. "Yeah, he calls himself the Grand Claw." I roll my eyes at the stupid title. "He's the leader. He was the guy that abducted me off the street; he has floppy blond hair, a big nose, and is over six feet tall."

He uses a nasty charm called the Dragon's Eye while pretending it's his magic. A charm so evil that it eats away chunks of his soul. I obviously don't say the last bit.

"No, we didn't get him. This so-called leader wasn't there when we came for you, but don't worry. We'll get him; it's only a matter of time. You will be fine. You'll be safe with your twenty-four-hour security."

That sounds fun... twenty-four-hour security. A bossy gargoyle and probably equally bossy hellhounds, all telling me what to do while trying to protect me.

While attempting to nudge me in the right direction of creating spells. Charms that I probably don't want to make. I know, I know. I'm going to get Stockholm syndrome, and I'm going to start liking these people, and then it's a slippery slope.

I drop my head and stare into the soup, searching for answers to my future in the bowl. "I need to ring my mum and dad and tell them what's happened. Well, not tell them what's happened. I can't blurt it all out on the phone, but I'd like to tell them I'm okay and apologise for being out of contact for so long."

Soren adjusts his bowl and taps his spoon. "I spoke to them a couple of days ago. I let them know you've been unwell. You can see them this afternoon if you're ready."

"Really?" I sag in my seat. "You'll let me see them in person? What about the people watching them and the cameras?"

"There aren't any cameras now."

How does he know that? Unless... "The gargoyles have removed them?"

Sheepishly, he nods. "But maybe you should speak to Emma first." He pulls out a phone, presses a few buttons and places it gently on the counter. "She has been calling every few hours, and her mate is getting mad. He's incredibly protective of her and their unborn child."

"Do you know her number?"

He taps the counter. "It's already ready for you to call."

"Thank you."

The phone rings twice, and a soft, gentle voice answers. "Is she okay?"

"Hi, Emma, it's me. I'm okay." I twist the spoon in the soup, feeling a little awkward. I haven't known her long, but she's rapidly becoming a friend.

She sighs in relief. "Oh, thank fate. I was so worried about you. They said you almost died and that your heart stopped."

I stare at the gargoyle, who can no doubt hear both

sides of the conversation. "My heart stopped. Really?" I raise an eyebrow. "He neglected to tell me that."

"Two minutes, fifteen seconds. Your healing charm shocked your heart, along with the doctor who was trying to help get you back."

"Wow, I'm sorry. Was he okay?"

Soren takes the bowl and spoon from me and wipes down the island. "The doctor is a shifter, and he's fine. He said it tickled."

"Tickled. Shit." I pull a face and then continue the conversation with Emma. "I'm sorry about that. I got distracted. I'm fine. I feel great. I'm just a little bit tired, which is ridiculous because I've been asleep for four days. Um, just, uh, don't tell my mum."

"I will not tell your mum," Emma squeaks out. "I've not got a death wish. Your mum's scary."

I giggle. "Yeah, she is a little bit. You should see her with my brothers and my dad. She keeps us all on our toes."

CHAPTER
TWENTY-EIGHT

We approach the gated estate, which is just a stone's throw from the sprawling public park that stretches beyond the boundary. The detached house's facade is exactly like in the pictures, a tasteful mix of smooth white render and red bricks.

I feel anxious as we open the garden gate, walk up the twisted, hedge-lined path, and knock on the black front door. It opens immediately, and Dad is there. "You don't have to knock." He grabs my arms, pulls me in for a hug, kisses my forehead, and then holds me at arm's length with a frown. "You've lost weight. A lot of weight." I pull a face, and he laughs and pulls me back into his arms for the best dad cuddle.

I hug him right back because I need it and do my best

to fight back the tears. I know I'll have to tell him what happened to our town and his friends, but for the moment, I enjoy being in his arms.

"My turn," Mum says from behind us.

Dad reluctantly lets go, and suddenly I'm in her arms. She smells of flowers and home. Her strawberry blonde hair brushes against my face as she kisses me on the cheek and gives me a quick squeeze.

"Oh, sweetheart, your dad and nan have been so worried." She grabs my forearms and gives me a shake. "Never do that again. I have new wrinkles and grey hair from the stress."

"Aw, Mum. You look beautiful as always."

She pulls away and looks at me. "You've lost weight. You're practically skin and bone. You need to look after yourself better." She looks up at Soren and gives him a dirty look. "You're her bodyguard? You have to make sure she eats properly. She's always so busy, and she keeps busy and forgets to eat."

"I'm okay, and Mum, it's not Soren's fault; leave him alone. It's not his responsibility to feed me."

Mum lets out a humph and stares back into the house. "I don't know what your brothers are doing. They've been suspiciously quiet all afternoon. Your nan is at the library and won't be back for another hour and a half. She will be sad that she missed you."

Oh, aren't we staying long then? I frown and duck my head so no one can see my hurt expression.

"Come in, come in. I don't even know why I'm

saying that. It's your house. You can come into your own home." She waves her hand and we follow. At the door, I take off my trainers, and Soren removes his boots without saying a word. I smile at him gratefully.

The house opens into a spacious hallway with dark wood floors in a herringbone pattern. To the right, a sweeping staircase curves gracefully to the upper floors.

"It's not my house, Mum." I ensure the shoes are neatly tucked away. "It's our family home, and I'll sign the deed over to you and Dad as soon as I have time to see the solicitor."

"Oh no, you will not." She stops and turns, and slashes of red brighten her cheekbones. I internally cringe at her angry expression. "Me and your dad are going to sort ourselves out. Robert has an interview next week?" She turns to him.

"Yes, on Tuesday."

"And I've got some plans in the pipeline. We'll be able to afford our own home and will not have to rely on our talented daughter." Why does the word talented seem to come out as a slur? "We will be moving out as soon as possible."

I frown. "Congratulations on the interview, Dad." I pat him on the arm with a forced smile. "I know you'll smash it and get the job." I turn to Mum, take a deep breath for courage and try again. "There's no point in the house being empty, and it's too big for me."

"Well, then sell it. Honestly, girl, sometimes you

think too big." She stomps off again, and over her shoulder, she says, "Would you like a cup of tea?"

"Yes please." Tea will fix everything.

"Aleric, Ledger," Mum bellows. "Kricket is here. Come down, boys, and greet your sister." She waits for a beat, and when there isn't the sound of obedient running feet, Mum huffs and marches up the stairs. "Robert, get ready to turn the Wi-Fi off."

Dad chuckles, puts his arm around me, and steers us towards the kitchen. "Let's put the kettle on, shall we?"

The open-plan living area is arranged around a low coffee table and a contemporary fireplace. A plush, oversized, L-shaped sofa dominates the space. The dark grey kitchen has state-of-the-art appliances integrated into sleek, handleless cupboards. Adjacent to the kitchen, the dining area features a long wooden table and sliding doors leading to a spacious patio and garden. It's nice.

Soren follows us quietly.

"I'm sorry I haven't said hello to you yet, Soren. Thank you for keeping us informed about Kricket's situation." Dad leans around me, and both men shake hands. "I'm Kricket's dad. Would you like a cup of tea?"

"Yes, that would be lovely, thank you."

Oh heck, my manners aren't the best. I'm sure I'll get it in the ear later from Mum. "I should have introduced everyone, but I don't know where my head is at. I'm sorry."

"You're still not recovered," the gargoyle says kindly.

Above us, there's a door bang, and then Mum runs

down the stairs. Out of breath, she flies into the kitchen. "They've gone," she says. "They've—they've gone."

"Gone where?" Dad asks, putting down the kettle.

"I don't know," she wails. "They're not supposed to leave the house. We have strict instructions and bodyguards to protect us when we leave the house. Emma arranged everything," she tells Soren. "But they've gone. They've snuck out. Robert, they've snuck out, and there's another thing"—her eyes fill with tears and dread—"I checked, and I think they've been in the safe."

The charms.

Oh no.

I give Soren enormous eyes while I wrestle with my emotions. I need to keep calm. "I'll go and have a look. See what's missing, if anything." I bolt out of the room and take the stairs two at a time. I know where I'm going. Even if I hadn't seen the layout and photos, the main bedroom is easy to find because the magic in the safe calls to me.

I fling open the wardrobe and drop to my knees. The safe's ward opens with a touch, and then I pull out the bag of charms.

A box containing twelve charms is missing. My brothers took them 'cause the box is fancy, and inside, the charms are inlaid with foam. I put everything else back in the safe and hurry downstairs. I know what I can do. I can track the charms and, if they're still near the box, find Aleric and Ledger. It'll be fine. Everything will be fine.

They're more than likely messing around with the charms outside.

"Yes, some charms are missing. They've taken a box full of them."

"Oh no," Mum says, slumping against my dad's chest. "Where have they gone, and why would they do that?"

"I don't know, love. Perhaps they've got some new friends and wanted to show off."

"They haven't met anyone yet, no new friends. They haven't got a phone. I don't know what they were thinking." Mum pushes Dad away, bunches her fists, and then her anger is aimed at me. "Kricket, this is your fault. All this is your fault. Your blood money and this stupid house. Your baby brothers wouldn't be in trouble if it weren't for you and those stupid, dangerous charms."

Blood money, wow. I stumble back in shock, wrap my arms around myself and look at my mum as if I've never seen her before. "Mum, I..." What can I say? I can't—I can't give excuses, and I can't claim innocence. Mum's right. This is my fault. I should have tweaked the ward so not even my family could touch the charms, or better yet, I shouldn't have sent them with them in the first place.

"Mary, that's not fair," Dad says, his voice pleading. "You can't blame her for this. Your Mum doesn't mean it," he tells me.

"Don't you dare talk for me." Her nostrils flare, and she glares at Dad. "I do mean it. I'm sick of walking on eggshells for our daughter."

Eggshells?

I'm sorry the annihilation of our entire town inconvenienced you. I rub my chest as I remind myself that she doesn't know. She wouldn't say all this if she knew. My parents are aware that I've not been very well, and it has something to do with the invaders, but they don't know all the details, which was why I came here in the first place.

Mum moves towards me with her hand raised.

"No." With a soft growl, a blank face, and his wings rustling, Soren moves to stand between us.

He's doing the bodyguard thing. I don't know why he's bothering. Mum has a temper, but she wouldn't hurt me. Right? Prickles of pain dance across my forearms, and the skin on the underside becomes itchy. I scratch, and bumps can be felt underneath my fingertips. Am I having an allergic reaction? I pull my sleeve up.

My arm looks perfectly normal.

"Do they have a computer, a datapad?" Soren's voice has slipped into professional mode, and it cuts through the bullshit.

"Yes, they both have datapads and a gaming console," Dad answers.

The gargoyle nods, pulls out his phone, and calls someone. He quickly explains what has happened, and when he hangs up, he says, "Ava will ring back after she's checked their accounts."

Ava, that's good. She's the best at computer stuff.

"I can track the charms—" My voice cracks and my

hands shake. I hide them by tucking them into my armpits. This with my mum has thrown me. I need to get over myself and track my brothers.

Soren turns to me and his expression is kind when I meet his eyes. His big hand tugs one of mine out with a gentle squeeze. "You can track your charms?"

"Yes."

"Interesting." So *interesting*. Great, we'll discuss this at length when we are alone. "If you can find the location of the charms, I'll help you get your brothers home."

"Thank you."

"If you don't find my boys, I'd better not see you again," Mum snarls.

"Mary, that's not helping."

I think she's talking to Soren, but no, she's looking at me.

It's going to be incredibly hard to concentrate with the vitriol that my mum is shooting at me and the blame in her eyes. Love hurts like this sometimes. The crack inside me that's been growing, splinters a little bit more. I'm dealing with the consequences of my actions.

Every day, I feel more like the villain.

Fear for my brothers, along with guilt and my mother's nasty words, make me shut my emotions down. It's not about me. None of this is about me. I let all thoughts of what is happening drift away. It's beyond my control, and I can only afford to concentrate on tracking those charms. I block everything out.

I hear Soren's phone ring. I ignore the conversation

and force myself into the blackness of searching. The dots in the vast ocean of black come much easier now that my mind has calmed, and I quickly pinpoint where the charms are scattered like little fireflies in the sky. I immediately find a cluster far off my mental map—the twelve charms. I realise then we have a problem: the box of charms is not in this world.

No. It's in Faerie.

CHAPTER
TWENTY-NINE

Whoever has taken them has gone through a gateway. My brothers aren't just in the park playing football or messing with the charms; they're in an entirely different realm—another realm I know nothing about. The horror almost overwhelms me.

I can't believe it. They've never been out of our town, and the fae somehow kidnapped them? It doesn't make sense. My head feels like it's going to pop off.

I stare at the gargoyle as he finishes his phone call and addresses my parents. "Ava said there are conversations on their game console."

"Threats?" I ask. My voice is an emotional rasp.

"No." The gargoyle drops his voice to a gentler tone. "It looks as if Aleric and Ledger have been bragging online about the charms. Gary Chappell has almost a cult following, and someone, one of their game buddies, told them they were lying about owning charms and asked them to meet up in the park to prove it."

"How could they be so stupid?" Mum moans.

"The creatures they were meeting weren't the teenagers they pretended to be," Soren continues.

"The Claw Brotherhood?" *Have they taken my brothers?*

"No, Ava doesn't think so. She said in her initial investigations and tracing of the messages, they appear to be from elves. The meeting was over two hours ago. She's gone through all the records and security feeds, and there are no cameras where they met. Aleric and Ledger haven't been seen again by any cameras. At this time, we're presuming that the elves have taken your sons."

My mum moans and covers her mouth, and Dad's eyes fill with tears as they cling to each other.

I nod towards them. "Can Ava send them all the information—"

"If that's what you want?"

I nod again.

"I'll forward everything to your dad."

"Thank you."

Soren gives me a chin lift in acknowledgement and sends Ava a message. At the same time, my parents begin to argue, blaming each other for not watching the boys. It's pointless pointing the finger as my brothers are old enough to watch themselves.

"It's her fault," Mum harshly whispers.

I smile bitterly, nod, and turn on my heel. "Soren, are we okay to go? I have a location."

"Sure." He frowns at me as we head for the front door.

"If the offer to help was genuine, I hope you've got a ley line code to get us into Faerie, as we need to go to the Autumn Court."

"Hang on a second." The gargoyle pauses, tying the laces of his boot. "You can track them to other realms?"

"Yeah, the other-realm tracking is news to me too." I shrug and go to grab my trainers. "Oh, just a second. Would you wait for me…" I bolt up the stairs, enter my parents' room, open the safe, and remove the bag of charms. Their presence here has done enough damage. I close the safe and head back down. My feet feel like I've got lead shoes, my legs are like jelly, and I can hardly walk. Everything is catching up to me. Gosh, I feel a hundred, not nineteen.

"She didn't mean what she said," my dad says when I get downstairs.

Yes, she did. Mum was angry before we even knew the boys were missing. She never wanted to leave our town, and I've ruined everything. I dragged her family away from a perfect life. I can hear her sobbing in the front room.

"I love you, Dad." I kiss his cheek and shove my feet in my trainers. "I'll get Aleric and Ledger back. Soren will send you all the information. We still have to go over what happened with the town. It's bad, Dad, but we'll talk about it when the twins are home safe." I pat his arm and then pat the rucksack, which I throw over my shoulder. "And I've removed the rest of the charms from the safe. You can tell her none of my dirty magic is left in the house. Apart from the ward. If she doesn't want that, I can send a proper witch out to put up a permanent one."

As that's the magic she prefers or she can do it her bloody self.

"Don't be like that, Kricket. You wouldn't understand as you're not a mother. She's stressed. She's frightened. It's been a long few weeks, and she wants to go home."

Home. I laugh manically inside my head but hope the madness I'm feeling doesn't show on my face. "Dad, we didn't get to talk, so you both don't know. There is no—"

"Get out. This is all your fault," a voice snarls. With red, swollen eyes, Mum stumbles out of the living room and towards us.

Ah, well, that was good timing. She saved me from saying things I might have regretted. I open the front door, and Soren and I step outside. I dare not look at the gargoyle. I'm so embarrassed. Behind us, Mum continues to rage.

I'm no longer listening and I clamp my mouth closed. Arguing and shouting back is not the solution. All it's going to do is make the situation worse. Of course, I want to scream at her about what has happened, about how everyone's dead. Everything is gone, and if she goes back there, there is nothing but soil and dust.

I can't tell them any of that while I'm this angry and hurt. If we had a civil conversation, that would be completely different. I could deal with it with sympathy and compassion, but now I'm too scared about my brothers. I can't deal with her pain, her worry, and her anger along with my fear.

I was protecting my family. I did protect them. Because if they hadn't left, they'd be dead like everybody else.

"Kricket," Dad says, his expression wary.

"It's fine. We will get them back."

Soren and I walk down the path, and I gently close the gate behind us. I take a deep breath. "Okay, we've got no video footage, so we don't know what the elves have done. What we do know is that the charms are in Faerie."

Soren waves his phone. "I've got a gateway code. I'm still waiting on permission. The paperwork should arrive in the next half hour or so. Ava also sent me the details of where they were supposed to meet. Let's go and take a look at where they were taken. It might help. Oh, and the hellhounds are coming."

I shiver and push my fear of them away. I'll take all the help we can get. Granted, it's like using a nuclear bomb to stop a catfight, but I'll take the backup. "Okay, let's go and have a look."

"Okay then, nothing girl." On the way past the car,

Soren takes the backpack off my shoulder and puts it in the boot. "They will be safe in here, won't they?"

"Yeah. They'll be fine." As a precaution, I tell the charms to hide and protect themselves. I still have a pocket full of charms, so it isn't like we're unprotected. I glance to the side and my eyes go up and up. I take in the massive gargoyle who matches his long stride with mine.

He's about two of me—huh, maybe two and a half—and built like a tank.

Yeah. I don't think we're going to have much of a problem.

"Are you all right?"

"Yeah, I'm fine." *No, I'm not.* I have a knot in my throat that I'm trying to swallow down, and my chest hurts. I'm frightened to death that something awful has happened to my brothers, and my entire life is falling apart, and I'm wondering why I keep fighting so hard when I fuck everything up. I hate this, and I hate feeling sorry for myself.

"Your mum's a bitch."

I rip out a laugh, then a hiccupy sob, and then I'm bawling my eyes out.

"Ah, shit." A big arm lands across my shoulders. He drags me into his side, and I bury my head into his shirt. "It's okay," he whispers. I feel his wings' warmth and weight as they come around and shelter us, cocooning us from the outside world. "It's okay."

He rubs my head and gently massages my neck. All

the while, he whispers and murmurs inconsequential things while holding me tight.

CHAPTER THIRTY

WE GO over the post-and-rail fence into the park rather than wasting precious time by walking around to the gate. I can't be bothered scrambling over the top of it. I've already established that I lack coordination or any luck with wood. Fortunately, the gap is wide enough that I climb between the rails.

Of course the gargoyle just vaults, and I can't help smiling at him when he does it. "Show off."

He grins back at me, and then my smile fades. I shouldn't be laughing when my brothers are missing. Soren catches the switch in my mood as we silently walk across the grass and onto a stone path.

The park has two outer paths: one has a sign for horses and bikes, so it's a bridleway and cycle path, and the inner track is for walking, so we choose the inner path.

I've never seen a horse in real life before. I don't think horse riders would want to stumble onto a gargoyle, and I've no idea how a horse would react. I have a massive urge to ask him, but I clamp down on the words. He's been kind, and I don't want to offend him.

When this is over, I'd like to get a pet—not a horse, of course, but a cat or a dog.

After ten minutes, we come to a copse of trees on the edge of a small duck pond. "Here." Soren looks up from the directions on his phone.

I don't know why my brothers thought it was a good idea to meet these gaming buddies here. I'm sure the park has safer places, but Ava said they were elves, so they wouldn't want to be seen.

My naive, sneaky little brothers would also like to avoid the eyes of our mum, which has put them in danger.

There's some flattened grass and uneven and muddy ground closer to the pond, but nothing—no blood, no evidence—nothing to indicate they've been here. I wish I could scent like a wolf. "Can you smell anything?" At least one of us has a super sniffer.

"No."

I stand there while the cold breeze plays with the loose strands of my hair and freezes my face. My nose and eyes are sore from crying. *Think, Kricket.* The charms are no longer here. They've left through the gate. I can trace them, but then something doesn't seem quite right. I narrow my eyes. Why would the elves take my brothers when they got what they were coming for?

Many of the fae deal with human trafficking. But would they risk taking two young boys to the portal? Ava would have checked that. Plus, they could have used a disguise spell.

"Oh," I say, looking around again. I realise what I'd overlooked. I can see other people's magical signatures and not just mine. I have no idea if other creatures can do that, but I've always presumed they can. If I can see the charms on my mental map... "Can you see magical signatures?"

"No, that's not a thing."

I rub between my eyes and groan. *Really? No one else sees magical signatures? Only me?* This is getting ridiculous. Me and my freaky magic. I could have saved myself a lot of hassle and time if I had known.

When I was in the cube, I told myself that I was going to embrace this magic shit. *You better get to it then.* Okay, well, I start by finishing that last thought. I can see other magical signatures, so maybe I can do the mental map thing to track my brothers.

My stomach flips. It won't work, and the idea is ridiculous, but I try anyway, concentrating on picturing my brothers and their budding witch magic. I close my eyes and bring up that map—the one I usually reserve for charms—and use it to search for magic similar to mine. Their magical signatures are so familiar it's easy. I find my mum still in the house and my nan travelling from work, and then I spot two pale green threads twisting together, moving apart, and intertwining again. I smile. Two lines twisted and mixed, that has got to be my twin brothers.

I follow the thread of magic, and my knees become weak with relief. They aren't in Faerie with the charms. My brothers are still bloody here in this park. *I think.* I lick my lips and my hand shakes as I point. "I can see their magical signatures, and they went that way."

"You can? You can see magical signatures? Since when?"

I nod, drop my hand, and shrug. "Since forever. I can see them, and now I can track them. Come on." I wonder if this is a useful skill or another reason people will want me dead.

"And I thought your brothers didn't have any magic." His voice gets a suspicious edge, and a flash of anger rolls across his face. His immediate anger makes me uncomfortable and mad. I do my best to ignore it, but I can't help feeling hurt. I don't know why. I shouldn't. After the run-in with my mum, I'm a little sensitive.

It doesn't matter to me that he doesn't trust me.

It shouldn't matter. But it does. I don't even know this man, and we aren't friends. "Their magic is dormant and *normal*." I head in the right direction, stomping through the trees, skirting the pond and onto the walking track. "I didn't lie to you; they are technically both witches, so they will be capable of stirring spells or making wards if they want to train in that direction."

They're still young enough for training. I wonder if, now that the town council no longer controls us, my parents will put them in the Witch Academy.

"Don't worry, their magic isn't like mine. But they have a light, magical signature that I can track." Even pure humans and animals have magic.

Following the trail that only I can see, we keep walking. Our once comfortable silence now feels uncomfortable. I'm not trying to give him the silent treatment. I just don't know what to say.

This has been a crappy day, and part of me wishes I could just go back to sleep.

After about fifteen minutes, the gargoyle grumbles. "I apologise. I didn't mean to upset you."

"You didn't upset me," I tell him, trying to keep my voice blasé. He did upset me. But I'm not going to say anything. I'm lucky he's letting me do this, and I'm grateful he's helping.

Then, "I did upset you," he says as if he were plucking the thought from my mind.

"It's okay."

"We need to stop for a break. You're still weak from being poorly."

"I'm fine, I'm fine. I need to get to my brothers." I trip over a stone and almost fall on my face.

Soren's hand snaps out, grips the back of my top, and pulls me into his massive chest. "Nothing girl, you're exhausted," he whispers. His massive grey forearm, which wraps around my waist, stands out starkly against my black top. I shiver and lean into him a little, even though I shouldn't. He smells so good.

"Please, ten more minutes. They're just up here."

He growls and lets me go.

We continue to walk. But now he's closer. I'm almost brushing against him.

I don't know the park, and apart from checking crime statistics before I purchased the house, I didn't look it up. But now we are out here walking it and I feel a little bit silly. We've already been out here for a while. We should have gone back to my parents' house, got the car, and driven around, as I have a feeling that Aleric and Ledger will be closer to the main road than they will be to our parents and the house.

We turn around the corner, pass another pond, and then come to a minor road. To the left is a hotel, and to the right is the main road around the park. And then I see them, two redheaded boys messing around.

They're throwing stones in another pond, joking and laughing with each other like nothing has happened. Like they didn't convince me, a gargoyle, and our parents that they'd been kidnapped. If I had the energy, I'd run over there and give them a dig. But I can't do that because I'm knackered.

"O!! You two! You are in so much trouble!" I yell while we amble across the road. They both jump and spin around at the sound of my voice.

"Kricket!" Ledger shouts with a wave.

"Don't you Kricket me," I say as my arm moves of its own accord and I give him a wave back.

"We've missed you. Are you all right?"

"Never mind am I all right. What are you doing outside? You're supposed to have bodyguards, and why did you numpties meet elves and give them my charms?"

Aleric slaps his forehead and groans, "She knows."

Ledger throws his hands in the air. "Of course she knows. It wasn't our fault," he whines. "We thought that they were our pals. We were telling them about the charms. We didn't mention you or anything, but we said that they were really good. They called us liars, and we said we weren't, and we had an argument, and then we met here to prove them wrong, and they robbed us." Ledger shrugs.

"They robbed you?"

Aleric groans. "You were useless. Yeah, they robbed us, but sis, they were elves, and one of those guys, the blond one, was scary."

"I chucked the charms in a bush and then ran. We ran to the road, and they couldn't get us without people seeing, so at least we did that. I'm sorry. Are you mad? Were they worth a lot of money?" Ledger innocently blinks at me.

I've seen that expression on my face in the mirror a time or two. I hold my hand up. "You chucked the charms in a bush, and you ran?"

"Yes, of course we did!"

I grab them both around the neck and squish them to me. I kiss one sweaty redhead and then the other. "I'm so proud of you. Please do not meet strangers off the internet next to duck ponds in the middle of nowhere. Don't meet random weirdos anywhere, as that's a great way to get killed. They could have been vampires and eaten you both." I hiss and flash my blunt teeth to make a point. "But you thought on your feet, and I'm so proud of you. I don't care about the charms. I'll either get them back or I won't. But I'll never get you two back, now will I?"

I give them both a squeeze and they groan and push me away. I laugh when they pull the same face. "Get off!" Aleric shudders, rubbing his head as if he can rub the residual kiss off. "Can't believe you kissed my head." Aleric looks Soren up and down. "Bloody hell, you're a big one, aren't you?"

"Oi, Aleric, don't swear."

"You always swear. Hell's not swearing, not really. Fate, man, you're huge." Both boys stare at Soren.

I tut. It's not like they've not seen a gargoyle before. "Don't be rude to Soren. He volunteered to help me look for you. "

"Thanks, Soren," Ledger says.

"Yeah, thanks, pal," Aleric grumbles.

The gargoyle gives my brothers a manly chin lift while he watches me with a soft smile.

"Come on then, you two shits, we'd better get you home."

"Aw, do we have to? She's going to be so mad,"

Ledger whispers, and his eyes flick about as if Mum is going to leap out of a hedge any minute.

"Yes, she's going to be mad. But now, she's going crazy because she's worried about the pair of you. Come on. Let's get you home. I'm sure you're hungry, and Nan should be home by now to protect you."

"Are you going to stay for dinner?"

"Not tonight. I have things to do. Perhaps another time."

"We've got a lift over there, so you don't have to walk back." Soren points to the road and a waiting vehicle across the grass playing field.

"Oh, thank fate, I'm knackered," I say.

We head over to the car. The ground feels mushy underneath my trainers.

At the car, we are greeted by a colossal shifter. I can tell he's a wolf straight off. The magic oozes off him, and I get fur and flashes of purple. Purple? Huh, that's strange. I expect the man's eyes to be cruel and arrogant, but I'm shocked to see against his dark skin, his striking pale grey eyes are soft, warm, and kind.

He holds out a giant hand and shakes mine. "You must be Kricket. I'm pleased to meet you. My name's Owen." The hellhound smiles at my brothers and even shakes their hands too.

Introductions over with, we all scramble into the car.

Owen's magic is different, odd, and *more,* and I poke around a little bit. I can taste ashes and fire on my tongue and, for some reason, marshmallows and chocolate. I've never tasted magic before, but his is incredibly unique.

Well, now that's interesting. As my dragon magic has bloomed these past few weeks and I've become more aware of it, I've never met a hellhound, but I can see clearly from his magical signature that the fire magic he has is a dragon-touched gift.

CHAPTER THIRTY-ONE

Huh. I'd wondered why the silver dragon oversees the hellhounds. As he's semi-retired and inactive, I'd thought it was a desk job to appease him. Him being a war hero and all. No, I wish it was that easy. The hellhounds are his. *He made them.* They're walking, talking, shifter charms.

I shiver. Of course, he probably didn't touch them all to make the magic happen like I do. He might have changed one or two a few thousand or so years ago, and they evolved. Once dragon magic is out in the world, sometimes it takes its own initiative. I've seen that happen myself.

I'm not a dragon, but with my charms, if I'm being honest, I struggle to let the magic out of my sight, and I never wanted to sell them in the first place. But at the time, it felt imperative.

Everybody knows dragons have treasure. I wonder how many people know the hellhounds are the silver dragon's horde, just as the charms are mine. That thought is enough to scare the absolute crap out of me.

The idea that the silver dragon is so powerful to *charm people* and no one knows about it makes me want to run for the hills or the nearest dark hole. I'll never breathe a word of this to anyone, and I'll take that knowledge to my grave.

The gargoyle in the front of the car must sense my anxiety because he turns his head to give me a reassuring smile. I smile back and wave away his concern.

Could I make a shifter into a hellhound? I wiggle in the seat. I don't know. No, I couldn't immerse my magic into a person. Not that I'd want to. I stare at the back of Owen's head in awe. The magic could have gone horribly wrong. Hellhounds are what happens when you mess with power. It's only because the silver dragon is incredibly strong and wise that hellhounds are the good guys. He set parameters, which might be why they seem to live so long when their lesser-powered brethren end up dead. They might have *super control* buried in their DNA.

I almost poke at Owen's magic but force myself to stop. It wouldn't be good for my health. The general will find out. I know if anyone messes with my charms, I feel it. Owen doesn't notice my attention. He drives carefully, and we're back at my parents' within minutes.

My brothers fling themselves from the car and run up the path with belated thanks at the two guards. The gate swings, and my hand stings when I catch it before it smacks me in the leg. I don't want to see my mum again—not for a while anyway. But for my own sanity, I need to make sure they get home and don't get themselves in any more trouble from the kerb to the front door.

I follow behind them, a few steps away, when they shove open the front door and yell that they're home. My parents are there, and the boys are getting hugged and kissed and then shouted at, and I stand there and watch.

My dad looks at me over their heads and smiles. "Thank you."

I nod, give him a small goodbye wave, and turn to go.

"Kricket!" my mum shouts. I spin on my toes. "Thank you," she says, and the door slams closed.

The silver door knocker wobbles and then settles. "No apologies for me then." For a few seconds, I stare at the door and rapidly blink. "Yeah, thanks, Mum." I'm surprised my heart doesn't crumble as I shuffle back down the path and close the gate softly behind me.

The gargoyle is leaning against the car—his car. Owen is standing nearby.

"Are you all right?" Soren asks.

"Yeah, yeah, I'm fine, thanks." My lips wobble as I try to smile.

Will I ever be all right?

No tears this time. I'm floating on exhaustion and relief that we aren't fighting elves in Faerie.

I reach the passenger side, get in, click on the seat belt, and lean against the door in an exhausted heap. The two men chat briefly. The gargoyle pats the hellhound on the arm in a very male, buddy fashion, and then he gets in and starts the car.

"Owen will follow us back. We've decided to move houses in the morning, and we'll move every few days."

"Okay." That's fine. My books and movies education aren't going to cut it. I'm happy for them to handle logistics as I didn't last even a few hours when Emma left me to it. I'm delighted to hand it over to somebody who knows what they're doing. "Thank you for your help today."

We slowly drive out of the estate. "You're welcome. It's no problem. Now tell me again about you seeing magical signatures."

My leg jiggles. I don't know how to explain it without putting another big giant cross in the middle of my forehead for someone to murder me. *X marks spot. Here, kill the freak.*

I lick my lips and blurt it out. "I can see magical signatures. I've been able to see them forever. I know when a person creates a spell—not the person who uncorked it, but the person who made it. I can see the creator or the creator's fingerprint, their signature. Sometimes I can see a creator's signature on the ground or in the air, like when a shifter changes shape. I can see the magical signatures in most people." I presume most, as

I've not met a massive number of creatures because I've been sequestered in a prison town.

I won't go as far as to tell him that I can see other people's magic acting on others and combinations of magic. The signature of the witch who stirred the spell of a healing potion or if someone has cheated on a test with a memory spell. And I can see what the dragon did to the hellhounds.

I shut that thought right off. I'm not even going to go there.

I must bury that knowledge deep and ensure that, for my self-preservation, I need to be blind to any uber-powerful magic in the future.

My spike of fear has the gargoyle's nostrils flaring. "You're frightened."

"Yes, of course I'm frightened. I'm sorry, but I don't trust you. Everybody is concerned about my magic, and now I'm giving you more ammunition, more things to be concerned about. You're going to run to your bosses, and they're going to want to either lock me up and throw away the key, or they're going to use me until there is nothing left."

Or worse, they're going to want to pull me apart to see how I work, and then they'll want me dead.

He asked the question. I might as well finish now and give him the answer. Otherwise, the gargoyle will keep picking, and I don't want to be the Kricket-shaped scab he flicks off.

Not being forthright will make this entire situation

worse. "I can see my charms. I can close my eyes and do a mental map to see all the charms I've created and find out where they are, if they're happy, if they've been used correctly, and if anything is wrong. I can even add my power to them so that if a ward is struggling and someone's going to die, I can boost it. Or if there's a carrot charm, say, that has an issue"—I glare at him; he's mentioned my carrot charms a few times, and I'm feeling overprotective of them—"I can pull that magic, I can take my power away, and the charm will become inert."

"You can do all that? Destroy them with a thought."

"Yes." I think so. "So I thought if I could trace my charms and see magical signatures, it wouldn't be much of a jump to see if I could trace my brothers, and it worked. Instead of just being information like a fingerprint, the magical signatures that I normally see ended up being like a trail. Like a magical string that stretched off into the distance. A string that we followed."

"You're a magical tracker."

Huh. Is that what that is? Well, this is the first time I've heard of anybody being able to track magic. It seems right.

It's my turn to change the subject. "What's going to happen to my family? They're supposed to have guards. They let my brothers slip out the back door. What if the elves return, or the Claw Brotherhood decides they're an easy target to make me do what they want?"

"The general has spoken to a few people, and one of our colleagues has contacts with a special place where your family can go while things are resolved. Have you ever heard of the Sanctuary?"

"No." I've never heard of the Sanctuary. "What's that?"

Soren flashes his lights and lets another car go ahead of us. "It's an otherworld hotel within a pocket realm, and the host who runs it has another world and will allow your family and others to stay. It's the most secure place imaginable. The host controls everything, and your family will be safe. Your brothers will be able to study, and there are other kids. They have facilities that you can only dream of."

"That's great. Hopefully, my mum and dad will agree to go. It sounds like the perfect solution. Thank you. I wouldn't like staying in a pocket realm if you told me last week. I hope it'll be a nicer environment and won't be the same as being stuck behind the glass prison ward." I guess it will be a different feeling as the stay will be temporary and I'll feel less trapped.

Soren's hands tighten on the steering wheel and the leather groans out of protest. "Ah, well, unfortunately, it's going to be just your family. You need to learn more about your magic, and you won't be able to do your spells there as the magic in the realm and your dragon magic wouldn't mix. It's been decided it will be best for you to stay here with guards."

Stay under their control.

"Okay, that's fine." *Well done, Kricket. How stupid of you to think that they'll let you go.* I'm mortified. As if they will let me have a holiday in a pocket realm where everything's safe and fun.

I lift my eyes to gaze at the roof so my frustration doesn't leak down my face. I need to do an anti-crying charm. Something that will stop me from bawling my eyes out. I'm sick of emotion making me look weak.

All this is overwhelming, and I don't know what to do. I can't run away, and I don't have the skills to look after myself... I stop when it hits me. *Ah, yes, now that is a good idea.* I have people helping me, and a whole host of other guards will be coming in to keep me safe.

So what's saying that I don't learn?

Who's to say I don't learn these skills from those at the top of their profession? My stomach twists. Who wouldn't want to learn how to fight with a hellhound? They'll get bored, and it won't take too much for me to convince them to teach me how to keep myself safe.

I'm already the question queen. I've been suppressing that part of myself for years, but if I just let myself go, ask the questions, get the answers, and learn, perhaps this is only temporary.

According to my grandad Gary, the witches' biggest fault was their reliance on magic. They couldn't fight, and if given the chance, other creatures would rip a witch's head clean off before they could unstop a vial or finish a chant.

If I'm going to survive crazy dragon-loving zealots, the Creature Council, and a silver dragon's suffocating safety, I need to learn to fight.

I also remember asking my nan about how people could control elephants. They're such massive, beautiful creatures. They can weigh up to six thousand kilogrammes. How could people control them? Was it animal magic? Nan smiled sadly at me and told me we see fluffy baby animals as adorable and that elephants see people the same way.

I'd asked her, "Is that why the elephants obey? Because they think that we're all cute?"

And she said, "No. I don't know if it's everywhere, but from what I've read, they will tie the elephant to something incredibly strong. Like a metal pole in the ground, and when the elephant tries to pull away, the human stands there, and in the elephant's mind, they believe the human is so strong that they can't win."

It's learned helplessness.

Part of me recognises that's what they will do to me. They're going to develop and nurture this learned helplessness in me so I don't fight back, and I'll never realise how strong I am and what I'm capable of. My magic is vast, and I can probably do anything. Who is to say that I don't do everything? That I don't make my own pocket realm and live there like a queen?

I close my eyes and take a deep breath.

If I look at things with fear, I'll always feel fear, and the same if I feel like a victim. But if I look at things logically and am smart, I can protect myself and destroy anything that's out to get me.

What did Soren say? *"I wish you were a dragon. If you*

could shift into dragon form, that'd solve many of our problems. No one would mess with you then."

I need to be a dragon—a dragon blood. I might not turn into a scaly beast, but who's to say that I can't be scary and powerful and keep people away?

With power comes safety.

Both forearms itch this time, and I ignore them. I'll use everyone for now, like they're trying to use me.

Soren drives us back to his house, and the passing traffic and the flickering view from the window makes the tiredness I've been holding back come at me full throttle. My body's still recovering. Even though magic can cure everything, it can't replace nutrients, and from healing and dealing with my injury, I'm a little bit low on everything. Perhaps I need to get some vitamins?

I close my eyes for a second. I don't mean to fall asleep, but I do.

When the gargoyle gently nudges me awake, I almost poke myself in the eye as I quickly wipe off any drool. Hopefully Soren didn't see that.

Groggily, he helps me out of the car and guides me into the house. Then I'm lying in bed. He removes my trainers, covers me with a duvet, and I'm out like a light.

CHAPTER THIRTY-TWO

A RUMBLY VOICE calls my name, and when I open my eyes and turn my head, I see Soren outside the bedroom door. He stands there glaring at me and then glaring at the ward. "I wish you'd get your charms under control. As your bodyguard, I should be able to enter your room."

"Well, if no one else can, I'm safe, right?" Oh, the snark. My pep talk before and a proper nap—unconscious, poorly sleeping for four days doesn't count as rest—has done me a world of good. I stretch and yawn. "What time is it?"

"It's just after eight o'clock. I wanted to let you sleep, but you need to come and meet your other guards as we'll be moving locations early tomorrow."

"Okay, sure. Have I got time to use the bathroom?"

The stressed gargoyle nods.

"Okay. I'll be down in a minute."

"I mean it, Kricket. This ward—you've got to stop your magic from interfering with my job."

I groan. "I know, I know. Before you repeat it, it's weird. My magic is weird"—I wiggle my fingers in the air—"and I can't help it when I'm unconscious. I'm exhausted, Soren, and my magic is worried about me. At least the ward only stays within the confines of the room. It just protects me. It can be a hell of a lot worse. Crikey, it could have warded the entire street."

So the gargoyle needs to give the charm more credit. Plus he can get lost if he thinks he can burst in here whenever he likes. I know it's his home, but I should have some privacy.

"You'll have to live with it for a little while until I'm back to full strength."

The gargoyle makes a humph sound under his breath and quietly disappears down the hall. I listen intently and shake my head. I've got to learn to do that. No noise, not a floorboard creak or anything. It's a skill. And he calls my magic freaky when he moves like a ghost.

Gosh, he's mad this evening, or back to his usual grumpy self. I'm betting he doesn't like strangers in the house. My being here and all these dangerous people downstairs must make the gargoyle uncomfortable.

I don't know much about gargoyles, and I've tried to pick his brain, but he's not one for talking. Do they have territories? I'm not sure, but having all these people in your home and messing around with your stuff must be unpleasant. I'll try my best not to do anything to wind him up until we leave.

I jump in the shower and get changed using the sock charm. I need to get some clothes soon. There's a scary thought in the back of my mind that if my magic fails or something happens, I'll be naked in public. Not that the charm doesn't produce fabric—it's fabric, and it doesn't disappear when I take it off. But you never know.

I think about the chalk circle and the cube and remember that the entire area was a magic wasteland. I wasn't naked then, so perhaps I'm worrying for nothing.

Heck, I'm going to save a fortune! I can conjure one up if I want to prance in a ball gown. It's so cool. I grin as I head down the stairs.

My hair is wet, so I quickly separate the strands and pull them into a messy plait. This time I follow the voices to the living room. I stand at the door, finishing the plait. I have no hair tie, so I leave it. Hopefully the length will keep it tied up, and if it doesn't, it'll slowly unravel, and I can do it all over again.

Then I remember the sock charm. I ask for a hair bobble, and it lands in my hand.

Yep, that's so cool.

Like the rest of the house, the living room is nice. The walls are soft grey, which makes them warmer than white, and the navy sofa looks comfortable.

A group of creatures takes up most of the room,

chatting away. Owen's there, and another gargoyle I recognise from the multi-storey car park—the one that flashed his teeth at me, and I knocked him out with a well-timed sleep spell and slapped a null band on his wrist. I internally smirk. I enjoyed that way too much.

There's also a woman—a wolf shifter. Female shifters are a rarity, and when I say rare, I mean incredibly, treated like princesses and locked up in castles and encouraged to be baby-making machines. I can only imagine how stifling it would be.

No, I don't need to imagine anything. I know how stifling that would be. I cross my arms and lean against the doorframe.

To see a female shifter here in Soren's home is unexpected. But what is interesting is that she's so petite.

Shifters are born—sometimes they can be bitten, but it's not the same, and the bitten men never shift or last long. Women always die from a bite. That's what makes shifters so dangerous.

Shifters are always enormous creatures. They're usually well over six feet. Even the women. They're warrior huge. And yet here is a beautiful female shifter with a mass of pale *pink* hair that must be past her waist when it's out of the simple plait she's wearing, and she's around five feet tall. She turns and looks at me, and her eyes are an odd shade of yellow, with one having a splash of green at the bottom.

It's as if a wolf is staring back at me.

I realise then that her hair and small stature are a

disguise. She could easily appear young, pretty, and perhaps a bit dense if she flutters those long pink lashes. *Look at me with my pink hair. Aren't I sweet?*

She is tiny and delicate.

And the most dangerous person in the room.

I can feel her magic and stop touching anything or analysing it further. She's got... yeah, I'm not going to go there. I've promised myself that I won't poke around with scary magic. Knowing too much can be problematic, and she must be the most terrifying person I've ever met.

Oh, she looks friendly enough, and I don't feel she's going to leap across the room and break my neck, but fear prickles up and down my spine and my heart rate increases. I have to concentrate on keeping calm.

Before I drop my eyes to the floor, I see the corner of her mouth tip up, and her eyes sparkle when she notices me standing here.

"Hey, dragon girl."

I wince. Her rough, broken voice doesn't match her face, but it matches her power. Here I was, worried she'd have a little girl's voice, but she doesn't. She sounds like someone ripped her throat out and it's healed wrong.

What did she say? Oh, she called me a dragon. "Oh, no, no, no. I'm not a dragon." I twist my hands. "I just have some of their blood, some latent DNA."

"Sure, sure." She waves her hand and grins at me.

"Why did he send you?" Soren grumbles, coming

into the room from behind me and handing me a mug of tea.

"Thank you."

"We don't need shit blown up." He rests a heavy hand on my shoulder and steers me into the room.

"Oh hush, rock boy. He sent the best." She holds her hands out to present herself and grins.

Soren shakes his head, and the car park gargoyle grins. "He sent us a pain in the arse." The *he* they're talking about must be the general, aka the silver dragon. They grin at each other.

"Kricket, this is Forrest. Forrest, meet Kricket. Owen and Jeff, who you've met before."

Jeff is the car park gargoyle. "Pleased to meet you," I mumble. I hope he won't hold a grudge.

"This is the main team that is going to keep you alive. We have others, but you won't spend time with them. It'll be just us."

"No one will hurt you," growls Owen, the giant, grey-eyed hellhound who had been quiet until now.

"And while we are waiting for things to kick off," Forrest says with a grin.

"We are going to teach you to fight," Owen finishes.

Forrest claps her hands.

Ah, look at that. I didn't even have to say anything. This is brilliant. I knew I liked Owen, and Forrest isn't scary. She's awesome!

Soren shakes his head. "No. Absolutely not. She's not learning to fight with you two."

I grip my tea and return Forrest's smile. "Please, Soren, I'd like to learn."

The gargoyle takes in my fluttering eyelashes, beaming expression, and groans in defeat.

"But just to warn you guys, I'm not that coordinated."

"That's okay. We can work at your pace," Owen says.

"You've got your work cut out. A tree almost killed her," Soren grumbles.

I scowl at the gargoyle, and Forrest wrinkles her nose. "Killed by a tree? Like a tree monster? Is that a fae creature? Like a bad dryad? Where can I see this monster tree?" She bounces on her toes like an excited puppy.

"No, not a monster. A normal, bog-standard tree. She fell out of it and decided to hit every single branch on the way down. A broken arm and an infection bad enough to cause sepsis."

"I didn't fall out of the tree. I was dragged out of the tree by some bad guys."

"Her heart stopped."

"Oh," Forrest says, tilting her head to the side. She gives me a thumbs-up. "Oh well, we can work on that."

"We will take things slow. Oh, and Tues..." Owen pauses with a shake of his head, "...the host of your parents' realm has asked you to call your mum. I have set up a datapad for you to use." He nods at the new datapad on the table.

They've already left for the pocket realm. I rub my face and groan. "I don't want to speak to them." The conversation we still have to have will not be fun. "My mum's not happy about what happened with my brothers, and then on top of that, telling them that everyone they know has been murdered is not in my skill set. Aren't there people better trained for that?"

"What?" Owen looks completely confused.

Ah, perhaps he doesn't know. "Everyone's dead. Everyone was killed in our warded town. The Claw Brotherhood killed them, and the Creature Council covered it up."

Everybody looks at me as if I'm talking in tongues.

"They all died, right?"

"No. The host made a new pocket realm to contain the people who lived in your town. She made an exact magical copy and moved everyone via portals when they woke up. She can make them out of thin air. We evacuated everyone who wanted to come, and they are safe. Apart from the deaths in the initial attacks, they are all safe, Kricket. Your family joined that realm. They're staying in a replica of your house, and for now, people are discussing their options. They will be given time and a budget and treated like refugees. They can go anywhere or stay in the pocket realm indefinitely."

I wobble and find myself sitting on the sofa, unaware of how I got there. The mug of tea is no longer in my hand. I see Soren place it on a side table.

"Shit, Soren, did she think they were all dead? Why didn't you tell her?" growls Forrest.

"I didn't realise. I thought Emma had told her. I

didn't realise she didn't know. I would never let her think that."

Whoa, I've let my imagination run wild this time. I never said to anyone that I'd believed the entire town, the whole town, was dead. I must have implied it, right? I go over all the conversations in my head and realise I went on about a cover-up, but that could have been construed in many ways. I never even asked; I'd just presumed everyone was dead.

Soren must have thought I was talking about my time in the Perspex cage when I went on about telling my parents.

I've been very internal—all that internal guilt has been impossible to voice. The woe is me; my actions have killed everybody. The deaths of so many people have been a weight on my soul, and now I feel stupid I didn't ask questions. I didn't ask the crucial questions, and I wrongly assumed everyone knew. You know what they say about assuming: you make an ass out of yourself.

I groan.

But most of all, I feel so relieved.

They're not all dead.

"I'm sorry," Soren tells me. He's sorry that he didn't mention that everyone had moved to another realm, a realm I'm not invited to. I should have said something. I was just so... I stare at the lights on the ceiling.

I was just so ashamed.

"It's not your fault." I drop my eyes and blink at Owen. "They're all in a pocket realm?" Alive. Safe. My parents, brothers, and nan joined them. "The host saved them?"

She made an entire realm for them. Wow, that's real power, and I've been worried about my little charms. I'm surprised I can fit through doors with my big ego-inflated head.

"What are you leaking for?" Forrest tries to hand me a clean, fancy, monogrammed handkerchief.

"No, thank you." I wave it away and wipe my face on my sleeve. "I'm not leaking," I say in a rough voice.

Gosh, I feel so relieved.

CHAPTER
THIRTY-THREE

THE WHIMPER DIES on my lips as I bolt up in bed, the covers fall around my waist, and my body shakes. I feel sweaty, as if I've been running on the treadmill all night. The gargoyle stands in the doorway. He's been calling my name. The ward is barring his entry.

He lets out a low growl, and his wings twitch. He's wearing pyjamas; the stripy bottoms cling to his thighs, and the T-shirt clings to his abs. For some reason, wearing nightwear makes him look bigger, bigger than he does during the day.

Soren presses his hand to the barrier. His skin sizzles and he pulls it back with a wince. "Let me in," he grumps, his voice rough from sleep.

The ward dissipates, and he silently pads across the room and sits on the edge of the bed. "Are you okay?"

I rub my face. "Bad dreams. I'm so sorry I woke you. I dreamt that everyone from my hometown was dead, and it was all my fault. This time I watched them die."

Instead of buildings, the Dragon's Eye ripped people apart while I stood there frozen and let it happen.

"They're not dead."

"No. They aren't dead. I know everyone's safe. It's just hard to tell my brain that." My voice cracks at the end, and I rub my face again and swallow a few times. I don't want to cry. "I'm sick of crying. Why can't I just be normal?"

"Emotions aren't bad," he tells me. "It's normal to be frightened. I'm surprised you're not having more flashbacks with everything that you've been through. Come on." He gets up and offers me his hand.

"What?" I ask, my nose wrinkling as I move to the side of the bed to get out.

"We're going to have a cup of tea, and I'll make you some cookies."

"Cookies?"

"Yeah, cookies. I have a recipe for sticky toffee pudding cookies. They're gooey in the middle, oozy, and amazing. Do you want me to make them for you?"

"Yeah, that would be nice." I can eat cookies.

"Come on then, nothing girl. Let's go downstairs, make cookies, have tea, and chat."

"What do you want to talk about? My dreams and fears?"

"If you want."

"You'll listen?"

"We're friends. Of course I'll listen. I might be a foolish man. I deal with such evil that I'm glad you can't comprehend. I'm forever fighting, and sometimes I forget how to deal with genuine people. I'm sorry our start began so bumpy, but I hope that we can be friends."

I grab his hand and I follow him down the hall.

"I'd like to be friends."

This new safe house kitchen doesn't have an island, but it does have a wooden table. I sit down and watch him move around, opening drawers and closing them with a grunt when things that should be there aren't. But it's well stocked, and it doesn't take him long to get everything he needs.

Then he starts making cookies, and I watch while drinking my tea. He really is beautiful.

"Tell me about your dream," Soren asks as he adds the measured dry ingredients into a mixing bowl.

To explain my dream, I have to explain what first happened with the Dragon's Eye. Then I tell him about my nightmare. As I talk, he listens intently while he makes the cookies.

I was back in the town square, and I'd just woken everybody up from the spell. I turned to run to the library. I could hear the helicopter coming. Damien appeared, his mouth opened, and magic roared out like a black plague. The buildings were eaten and destroyed in real life, but the people were eaten in the dream. They screamed and cried, and then they were all gone.

"It was horrendous."

"I'm sorry."

"Thank you for listening."

There's a crash outside. Soren walks to the kitchen window, moves the blind, and peers outside. He grunts.

"What's wrong?" The house is warded. It's not one of mine. It's an excellent witch ward that'll keep the baddies out.

"Oh, some unwelcome visitors." The gargoyle winces and then chuckles. "We'll leave for another safe house in the morning. We'll try another town."

Oh no, they found us. I go to stand and he waves me to sit down. "I'm making cookies," he says. "Drink your tea." He goes back to the oven, nods happily, and pulls out the baking tray. The kitchen smells divine as he sets it aside to cool.

The back door opens and Forrest prowls inside with a soft, relaxed smile. At first glance, Forrest has freckles across her cheeks. Freckles? She doesn't have freckles.

No, is that blood splatter? I realise that, yes, there are spots of blood all over her face. She's wearing black, so you can't tell if it's on her clothing.

"Ooh, cookies!" she says. Her smile gets bigger. "Ooh, can I have one or twenty please?"

"You can have two," Soren says as he puts another tray in the oven.

"I've been on guard duty all evening and fighting for a solid five minutes. I deserve more than two cookies." She stretches and rotates her wrists. "It was brilliant. I don't get to do this much. I love chasing shifters around and frightening the fae to death. But sometimes I need a good no-holds-barred, hand-to-hand fight. Granted, they weren't the best, and I had to fight six at once to get a proper workout, but it was great."

Forrest nods and wipes her face. She frowns at her palm, shrugs, and wipes her hand on a dry spot on her leg. "Yeah, it was great." Forrest grabs my cup and takes a swig. "Oh, it needs more sugar," she says, pointing at the cup as she sits and smiles at Soren. "Are those cookies ready yet?"

CHAPTER THIRTY-FOUR

It's been three weeks, and we've been in this town for the past week, jumping from safe house to safe house. A couple of days here, a couple of days there. I like it here in this town. It's magical. The powerful signatures of the creatures around us make the hairs on my neck stand proud. Scary, but in a good way. If something kicked off here, there'd be a lot of creatures, powerful creatures, dealing with it.

That's probably why we're here.

I'm at the wax-on, wax-off stage of training. If I hadn't seen Karate Kid, I'd be very disappointed. All Owen keeps going on about is muscle memory and the correct form. And there's a proper form for *everything*.

Forrest has made me go on an exercise bike and run.

Next time I have to run for my life, I'll do it a bit faster and be able to breathe at the end.

When I told them in all seriousness that I could use magic to improve my speed and strength, they both laughed.

Forrest explained that fighting would be the ultimate last resort and that cardio was king. I needed to learn to run away, move out of the way, block, and run. She has this mantra: "What do you do?" and I answer, "Block and run." When I asked her if she blocked and ran, she gave me a crazy smile.

It's her job to run towards the fights.

The bodyguard information consists of the following: We deal with the problem, you find a safe space and ward, and we'll get to you. The central theme is: Do not help us. If you get in the way, you'll get us killed. Run and hide.

When an expert—a hellhound—tells you to run and hide, you better do it.

I'm learning to be a good body to guard, and I'm getting physically stronger. I'm not a warrior—that is apparent—but if I keep training, I'm not a soft target either, even if I'm bolting for the hills.

Forrest bounces on her toes and gives me a big grin. "Come on, dragon girl, come on." She does the fight-me hand wave—the one that's in all the martial arts movies. "Come on."

I groan and slump to the floor. I'm a sweaty mess, and this is just... "Ugh, I think I can feel every single muscle in my body, and they're all complaining." For the past couple of weeks, I've done everything without a peep of complaint, and the number of times I've used my healing charm—I've even tweaked it so it gets into the muscles first.

"Come on. You need to run another three miles before lunch."

I snap out of my moaning puddle of sweat and give her a look, my mouth dropping open. "Three miles?"

"Yeah." She claps her hands. "Chop, chop."

"Please, Forrest, I can't. Mercy. Mercy." I flop back with a dramatic groan, and she snorts. "Today, I'm just done. I feel like a sweaty slab of jelly."

I hear her soft footfalls leave, and when she comes back, there's a clank of something hitting the floor next to me. "Here."

I open my eyes to see her prodding at a small case. "What's this?" I groan. "I hope to fate it's not a weapon." I'm not ready for weapons. I can't control parts of my body while training, and I won't fare well holding something pointy and sharp.

"Ah, no. I'm not allowing you near weapons. You'd only stab yourself."

True. "Hardy har har. Thanks for that."

She drops her voice to a whisper. "Um, I borrowed it, and I must give it back probably in about the next half hour." Forrest looks at her arm and taps it, which is odd because she has never worn a watch, and there's nothing on her wrist. "But until then, you can have a poke at it." She gives me a grin and backs towards the kitchen. "Okay, well, I'm just going to leave this here while I make myself a nice cup of tea, and when I get back, I'll take it away." Forrest prowls out of the room, humming a song under her breath.

She does that a lot, and she likes theme tunes.

She's a little odd, but I like quirky people. I like her. She makes me laugh, and she's lovely when she's not twisting my arm behind my back or trying to pull my fingers out of their joints. And that wasn't even when we were training. It was not my fault I ate the last chocolate bar.

I side-eye the case.

Up until now, I've not had any magic training; it's all been physical, aimed at getting me fit, and when I'm not passing out from one of Owen's torture sessions, I've been working on things. I have been surprised that nobody has taken the charms away from me. However, the risk has made me think about how to carry them with me safely.

I've always created them, so if anybody has any jewellery, they'd automatically attach themselves to it. They'd make a lovely charm bracelet, necklace, or even a key ring if the person using them wants that.

I never really thought about how I'd carry them.

In my head, like a proper hoard, they'd be in a safe and secure storage room, and I could sit there and look at them. It's not like I'm carrying a couple. I have a lot, and there is no safe space to store them with all this moving about.

I've been thinking about pocket dimensions and my need to examine the magic more closely. I spoke to Forrest, who told me that she's good friends with a witch and that the witch has a sister who can do realm magic. It's very rare, and all hush-hush, and I can't tell anybody. Doesn't that sound familiar? But Forrest did say she'd get something for me to have a look at.

This must be it.

I stare down at the case, sit up, flick the catches, and lift the lid. Inside, there's an innocuous bag—thin and silky black—nothing unusual about it. But when I try to look at it with the power inside me, magic-wise, I see something powerful.

Huh.

I stand up, grab a towel, and wipe my hands. I don't want to leave little sweat patches on the fabric. I shuffle to the main light switch, turn on the light, and then sit cross-legged on the floor with the case under the bulb to see the bag better. No, it's not a bag; it's a mini pocket dimension. Of course I can see with my magical senses, but I need to look with my eyes too.

I grin, my heart pounds, and my stomach flips with excitement. Is this what people feel when they hold my magic? The bag only does something visual once you open it, and within its black depths is a storeroom the size of a wardrobe.

Wow. That is amazing. It's so unbelievable, and it looks like an optical illusion.

I shrug away my caution and shove my hand inside the bag. I can feel the space, and even when I swing my hand from left to right, I can't touch the sides.

It's incredible. It's mind-bending magic.

I pull my arm out and angle the bag so the light shines inside. I'm sure you could stick anything in there. However, I'm curious if the width of the bag limits you.

My eyes flick about, and I find a pole on the wall. I don't know what it's called, a staff? It's a jousting, fighting thing. I jump up, grab it, and then sit back down. If I feed it via the end, it will go right in, but what happens if I try to put it in sideways? The pole is about seven feet long.

Will it work? Will you only be able to shove narrow things in here? I push the pole against the lip of the bag, and it grabs it, and even sideways, it disappears. You could store an entire settee in here. Gosh, I'm glad it didn't suck me inside when I stuffed my hand in.

I'm still firmly holding on to the stick. It will have security and safety parameters, and I don't know if you need to connect to the magic or attach it to you somehow for it to work. I don't want to risk losing Owen's stuff.

I pull the pole back out.

That's cool. Even if I could make a bag, even a bag as cool as this one would be useless for my charms. They'd be easily captured, and even if they couldn't get into the pocket dimension, they'd still be able to transport my charms and keep them away from me.

It's not suitable for my hoard.

I place the pole on the floor next to me and hold the bag up to analyse with my other senses. The bag isn't as alive as my charms, but I feel it doesn't approve of being studied. "Hush, I'm only looking," I mumble. Bloody hell. The magic is incredible, and I'm beyond impressed.

It's an intricate weave of magic. Time and space knitted together in godlike complexity and power. I reverently put it back in its box and closed the lid. I can see how the magic works and know there is no way, absolutely no way, I could build anything like that.

It's too complicated, too intricate.

Whoever weaved that magic is incredibly powerful.

I huff out a breath. "So that's what that feels like." I've always been magically gifted and thought my magic limitations were only my lack of imagination. But this magic here makes me feel human. This is how ordinary people feel—overwhelmed and awed.

It's an interesting feeling.

So my magic does have limitations. It's a relief I can't create everything like the beautifully made pocket dimension. I laugh, grab the towel, and wipe at my sweaty head. If a bag that's a glorified wardrobe is beyond my reach, I won't be making a pocket world, that's for sure.

My skill is charms.

My skill is charms.

I strum my fingers on the case as I think. I know I

can't make anything invisible because that's impossible, but I can make... make a pocket of air. I could make it like a balloon which could float next to me. A charm that can hold all my other charms out of sight. Then if I needed a charm, I could pluck it out of the air pocket or, I bet, use it without touching it.

Would that be possible?

Oh my gosh, I'm going to make a mini cloud. I grin.

I have a new cloud charm when Forrest returns and collects the case. It's not a charm. What I mean is that it isn't a material thing. No, I've somehow charmed the air to create a netted bubble. A bubble that answers only to me, and all the charms are up there in the cloud. They can't be seen with the naked eye, and the magic is so light and delicate that no one should pick it up.

"Sorted?"

"Yes, thank you."

"Come on then," Forrest says, holding out a hand. "Do you know what we're going to go and do?"

"What?"

"I need to drop this case off, and then we can go for a hot chocolate and chocolate cake." Her eyes twinkle. I've only ever seen that look on her face when she talks about her mate.

"Both? A chocolate overload. Won't cake and hot chocolate make you feel sick?"

"I worry about you. How could chocolate on chocolate make you sick? With thoughts like that, you will get your girl card revoked. Hand it back if you don't think a chocolate explosion is the best thing ever. Come on." She grabs my hand and pulls me up. She doesn't even strain, and I pop up like I'm in a jack-in-the-box. Gosh, she's strong. She hums as she drags me out of our makeshift training room.

"I need to get changed. I stink."

"No, you don't."

"Yeah, I do. One second." I bolt up the stairs, shower quickly, wash my hair, and use a charm I've made to dry it in record time. I get dressed and then run back downstairs ten minutes later.

Forrest stands at the bottom of the stairs, her foot tapping. She's all clean.

"How did you get clean so fast, and isn't that the same outfit?"

She grins at me. "I shifted. I can shift into a wolf and pop right back. It cleans my clothes and everything. I've got a clothing retention spell that my friend Jodie made for me. It's brilliant."

I shake my head as we walk outside. When a shifter turns into their animal form, they rarely keep their clothes. However, many spells on the market allow them to shift with their clothes, and when they return to human form, the clothes are still on their bodies, so there are no naked incidents.

"Some days, I don't even brush my teeth."

What? "Ew, Forrest, that is gross."

"Yeah. My mate thinks so too. He chases me around the house with the toothbrush, insisting I brush my gnashes. I'm like, no, babe, I've shifted, and he doesn't believe that's enough and makes me brush them. So then I leave the toothbrush in random places. It drives him nuts. Toothbrush wars, it's hilarious."

Owen appears out of nowhere, shakes his head, and opens the rear car door. "Come on then, you two. Where are we going?"

"We're going into town," Forrest says. "I need to drop this case off with Jodie, and then we'll get hot chocolate and cake from the café."

I think Forrest is obsessed with chocolate. I'm just happy to be getting out of the house.

CHAPTER
THIRTY-FIVE

After Forrest dropped off the pocket dimension, we weave through the crowd of shopping creatures, and the air is thick with varied magical signatures and mingling scents. The bell above the door chimes, and we walk into the loveliest café I can imagine.

I look up at the ceiling, and there are branches with big pink blossoms and twinkling lights. I realise the blossoms are real, as I can see the magic. It's the dryad tree, and I've never seen anything like it. The smell of flowers, coffee, and cake makes the atmosphere homely.

I like it. This is great.

There is a massive cake display in the window and a counter with all the different sweet treats. Forrest bounces up. "Hey, Jen." The blonde girl behind the counter smiles.

"Hey Forrest, how are you doing? Your usual?"

"Yes please. Can I have two and a boring black coffee? And oh, can I have some squirty cream on mine? Kricket, do you like cream?"

"Yeah, cream's nice."

"Cream on everything, including the hot chocolates. Oh, and can we have marshmallows and a flake?"

"Yeah, yeah, I'll do everything, Miss Chocoholic. I'll get them sorted and bring them to your table."

"Thank you so much." Forrest hands over some cash and tells Jen to keep the change.

Then Forrest guides us to the back of the café. An empty table is tucked into the corner beside some bookshelves and the floor-to-ceiling windows.

Forrest sits down with a happy sigh, her back against the shelves. She's positioned herself to look outside and see everything around her. Owen takes a seat on the opposite side of the table.

"Do you not want anything else, Owen?" I ask him, nodding towards the counter.

He shakes his head. "Thanks for asking, Kricket. The boring black coffee is fine."

Forrest gives him an oops face. "Oh sorry. I didn't order you a cake."

"Notice that, did you? It's fine." Owen growls. "You were in a chocolate frenzy. I forgive you."

Forrest and Owen begin to bicker like children; they're hilarious, and every second that ticks by, Forrest anxiously bounces more in her seat, her eyes watching Jen's every move.

I absent-mindedly rub the table with my fingertips, mapping all the dents and scratches. There's an old indent. I trace it and realise it's the letter L. I turn my head to the side because it's at an angle—the person who carved it was sitting where Owen is now. L-I-Z. I trace each letter with my finger and eyes.

Liz. I wonder who she is and if Liz put her name there, or if some spurned lover decided to score her name into the table in a fit of rage. I also wonder if it was a claw or a knife that made the mark.

I don't know why people do that, damage things. Mum had said when she was a kid, she used to use a compass to write her name on everything. I can't imagine Mum being young and reckless.

"I'm just going to go to the toilet." Forrest waves me away. I get up, weave around the tables, and step into a narrow corridor. I pass a strange black post box randomly stuck to the wall and walk into the lady's room. I don't need to go to the loo, and I'm glad they'd let me go as I need to check something out.

I miss being independent. I've returned to childhood, where someone always told me what to do. It's hard. I lean against the sink and stare at myself in the mirror.

I look tired.

I check the stalls using the reflection and find they're all empty, just like I thought. I secretly put up a ward and wash my hands. "You can come out."

She appears out of nowhere.

There was no scent, no magical signature. This creature was genuinely invisible until she's standing in front of me, and I'd have never believed it was possible if I hadn't seen it myself.

Her skin is pale green, and her hair has black roots blending into a dark green. She has wide, large green eyes and cheekbones for days, and her mouth is full and wide. She's gorgeous.

And dangling from her wrist on a chunky, cheap-looking bracelet are my charms. She's the charm thief and the reason I came into the bathroom. I felt them. What are the chances of her being here today?

"How did you know I was here? No one has ever detected me before." Her voice is soft, and her accent is Northern English. She doesn't sound like she comes from the Faerie realm, and she's also not an elf.

I'd almost say with her colouring a troll, but trolls are massive and don't have her level of magic. Her magic signature fits firmly into the do-not-look-at category.

"The charms," I say, folding my arms and leaning against the sink with my hip. I can act all casual, but I have charms that can knock her on her arse if she tries anything. "You stole my charms."

"Oh wow." She touches the bracelet and the charms jingle. Her expression is genuinely horrified. "These are yours?"

"Yes, I made them, and they were stolen from my little brothers three weeks ago."

"Oh. Are your brothers okay?"

I nod.

"Good. That's good. Before you try to kill me..." She holds her hands up. "I didn't touch your brothers. I, um, I stole a bag from a nasty group of elven slavers. Creature trafficking. They caught me in Faerie while I was working and tried to make me into a slave. I got away. When I ran, I took a bag."

She blinks, and her long lashes sweep down—they're so long they almost touch her cheeks. "I didn't mean to take the bag," she says softly. "I took it because I was frightened. They'd stolen all my stuff, and I was frightened and so mad. I grabbed the nearest bag and ran with it. I didn't realise until I got home that it had something important inside—your charms." She gives me an anxious smile. "I'm—I'm sorry. I didn't purposely steal them, but I have used them, and you won't believe how much they've helped me. It's a story, that journey. They have saved my life." She lets out a little gasp. "If you made them, does that mean you're Gary Chappell?"

I let out a huff of surprise.

"The charms told us their maker's name," she continues. "Well, not me, but a friend who is a witch. She said they were very chatty."

Huh. That's a new thing, and I glare at the charms. *Telling witches our pseudonym, eh?* At least they stuck to the story and gave Gary's name instead of mine. *Don't be giving away all our secrets*, I tell them. "Yes, I made them."

"Well, it's a pleasure to meet you. My name is Pepper. Oh—" Her eyes widen. "I gave one away, the one shaped like a cat."

The cat is a grumpy magic reflection charm. It's one of my favourites. It reflects magic back, so say someone chucks a nasty spell, the cat sends it back to the caster. Great for the charm user, but not so much for the person who attacked.

"He wanted to go with the unicorn, and I had a feeling that it was for the best, but I'm sure Tru will give it back if I ask her. She wasn't very impressed. Here." She starts to slide the bracelet off, and I hold my hand out to stop her.

"They've saved your life?"

"Yes."

The charms are happy with her—not that she needs them with all that magic bubbling inside her. "And you stole them from the elves?"

"Yes."

That makes my week. If the elves still had them, there's no end of harm they'd be able to do. If I hadn't found them so soon, I would have had to pull the magic eventually, but now I don't have to. "Keep them."

"Really, are you sure?"

"Yes, do you know where the elves are now?" I still have an urge to hunt them down. *They stole my treasure.* I'm sure Forrest will help.

Pepper smiles sweetly and rubs her forearm. "They put a slavery rune on my arm. I couldn't in all conscience let them hurt anyone else."

CHAPTER THIRTY-SIX

My worry about the stolen charms and the elves targeting my family settles inside me. As I weave back through the tables, I struggle to remember her name. It's on the tip of my tongue, but I just can't... Who was I thinking of again? I shake my head, and the thought disappears like smoke as I'm greeted with a sight that makes my lips twitch—a cup of hot chocolate and an oozy chocolate cake.

The chocolate cake is almost as big as the plate—a massive slice covered in squirty cream.

Forrest has already eaten half of hers; her arms are covering the entire plate as if someone will dare to steal it away as she snatches little bites with a cake fork. I do not doubt that if Owen leaned forward in his seat a bit, she'd start growling.

"Wow, that's impressive," I say as I pull the chair out. "What a treat."

Forrest hums.

I sit down, get the long-handled spoon, and start digging into the hot chocolate—it's got a flake and pink and white marshmallows. There's probably more stuff on top than hot chocolate in the mug. It's a real meal.

The utter disappointment on Forrest's face when she finishes her cake makes me want to lean across and pat her head, but I'd probably lose my hand. Her eyes glow a little as they lift from the squeaky-clean plate. Did she lick that without me noticing?

"Aren't you eating that?" she says, pointing her spoon at my cake.

I feel like I'm feeding a giant predator as I nudge the plate towards her, and she snatches it, hunches over it, and goes to work. "Thank you," she says after the second bite.

"No bother." I grin at Owen.

"I don't know why she didn't buy two slices or the entire cake."

Forrest gives him her middle finger mid-chew, and he chuckles.

It doesn't take much to imagine Forrest dropping the fork and mashing her face into the cake. It must be her toothbrush-wielding mate who insists that she's dainty with utensils.

I continue eating my hot chocolate and the never-ending whipped cream, and when I get to the liquid chocolate part, it's thick and delicious. I'm not halfway through it before I begin to feel sick. I wouldn't have been able to manage the chocolate cake as well.

The door opens, and they must jerk it a bit as the bell rings slightly off. I wouldn't think anything of it, but Forrest and Owen stiffen. More worryingly, Forrest forgets about her remaining quarter of a cake and moves to stand in front of me in a guarding position.

I twist in my seat and see seven policemen spreading themselves around the café, and another two are outside the window. *Well, that's odd.* Human police don't interfere with creature stuff. Their job is to handle the humans. They use magic to protect themselves, but that's as far as they go. They don't get involved with creatures.

They aren't looking at anybody else. No fugitive human is hidden under a table. Instead, I have their full attention. They are looking at me.

"This isn't good," Owen says under his breath. "I'll keep them busy. You get her out the back."

Forrest takes hold of my hand, and as if it's rehearsed, the police officers whip out their guns. She freezes.

We don't have guns in the UK except for the specialist police and the human armed forces. You're more likely to get your head chopped off with a sword or boiled alive with a nasty spell than shot. Firearms are useless against most creatures, and you'd more than likely make the creature you're shooting at angry than kill them.

But the guns aren't pointing at Forrest.

No, they're pointing them at me.

I wiggle in the chair and keep my hands where they can be seen. I have charms I can use to protect us. I could knock them out or throw up a ward, but I don't want to make this harder than it needs to be. I don't want to make this problem worse.

A policeman with brown hair and blue eyes walks up to the table. His tanned skin looks sweaty and pale. He nods to Forrest and Owen, then turns his attention to me. "Kricket Jones," he says, "you're under arrest."

I blink a couple of times. "Pardon? Me?"

"Don't say a word," Forrest says out of the corner of her mouth.

The sweaty policeman ignores her and continues with his spiel. "For events that happened at the enclave four weeks ago, you're wanted for questioning about the gargoyle deaths and the murder and abduction of the remaining protected dragon bloods."

Are they blaming me? "Me?" I point at my chest and then, taking Forrest's advice to heart, snap my mouth closed. There's no point in talking or expressing innocence because innocence doesn't mean shit when you've got police pointing guns at you.

"Hang on a minute. You can't arrest her; she's under the hellhound's protection by order of the general," Owen says with a snarl.

"We can. She's human, and this is our jurisdiction."

"She's not human. She's more creature than me. She's…" Forrest pauses and looks at me. "Oh."

Dragon bloods are classed as human, and we can't advertise my magic to the human police.

"We know she's of dragon blood and half witch, but the witches won't claim her. So according to the law, she's human, and she's coming with us." The chatty police officer puts his hands up in the air when Forrest narrows her eyes. His hands shake. "Look, Warrior Hesketh, we don't need any problems. We don't want to mess around with you, the dragon, the hellhounds, or the fae. All we want to do is take this girl in for questioning. She's been accused of murder and abduction. Even if you believe the charges are false, they must be investigated. You know this more than anybody. It's the law. We'll be at Central Police Station." He places a business card down on the table. "Send her solicitor here, and you'll probably have her out in a couple of hours."

Owen growls.

"I'm just doing my job, sir. I don't want any trouble. I certainly don't want trouble with hellhounds. Please."

Forrest has lost that cutesy, crazy air, and I can see her assessing the situation. She's ready to take on the world for me. I can see her cataloguing where everyone is: the older man in the corner who's reading his book, the two ladies to the left who were chatting and joking, and one of them has a pram with a baby in it. The mother is out of her seat and is shielding her child.

We all know what will happen. People are going to get hurt. The police are going to die, and I can't have that. I can't have other people dying for me. I'm still dealing with the guilt from the attacks.

The police officer said I'd be out in a couple of hours. It will be easy to prove that none of the dragon bloods have been abducted, and the gargoyles more than likely have evidence proving my innocence. Otherwise, they would have prevented Soren and Jeff from acting as my bodyguards, and they would have locked me up in a cosy prison cell.

Are a few hours of my time worth somebody's life?

Of course not. Definitely not.

I rest my hand on hers. "I'm going to be okay," I tell her. "I promise. It'll be all right. Just let me go, and I'll see you both later." I smile. "Everything's going to be fine, and anyway, you've taught me how to run. Block and run," I say her mantra in a singsong voice.

"Block and run." Forrest snorts, and her body relaxes —which is a good sign, right?—and she says, "Yeah, I've taught you how to roll around on the floor."

"Yeah, but at least now I can roll around on the floor, and you can bend my finger backwards, and I'm not going to cry. I'll be fine."

The police are getting impatient. One guy with thin arms must be holding a heavy pistol as his hands shake. The hot chocolate sloshes in my stomach. "I'll see you soon. It'll be fine." I get to my feet.

Owen gets on his phone. I'm sure he's ringing Soren.

"Hands behind your back please, Miss Jones."

Before I can move, his colleague grabs hold of me, spins me around and smashes me against the table. All the air comes out of my diaphragm with an *oof,* and everything on the table goes flying.

"Hey, careful. She's not resisting." Owen growls.

"Leave her alone. I know a gargoyle with a crush that will rip your head off if he finds out you've mistreated her, and as we said before, she's under the general's protection. You're making a mistake, officer. You will handle her with utmost care, or Soren and I will hunt you down." Forrest snarls.

What? Wait, does Soren like me?

"You do not have to say anything. But it may harm your defence if you do not mention when questioned something which you later rely on in court," the handsy police officer whispers in my ear while he twists my wrist and squeezes my arm.

I've seen a lot of internet programs and cop shows where people fight the police. Worse, they fight the Hunters Guild and hellhounds. There is no way you should fight people like that. You're never going to win.

I don't struggle and allow him to manipulate my hands behind my back, putting them in a backward prayer position so they don't strain my wrists. The cuffs have some null runes, and I can feel the drain on my magic as soon as they're snapped into place.

Why do the human police have rune cuffs? They're nowhere near as bad as the null bands Soren slapped on me, but they're strong enough that an ordinary creature would be unable to use magic or shift.

Handsy pats me down, checking my pockets thoroughly. "She has nothing on her, no magic, sir."

No charms. Thank fate I stored them today. I test the cloud, and I can feel all my hidden charms. Phew, I can still use them.

I'm pulled up off the table, and as I'm dragged out of the café, Forrest pulls her phone out. As the door closes, I hear her saying, "Emma, we have a problem. We need Mr Brown."

Then I'm forced into the rear of the police car. The chatty police officer buckles my seat belt. It's awkward sitting with my hands behind my back, and the handcuffs hurt no matter what wrist and arm position I try.

We drive past the police station. Okay, that's fine... I know I'm in trouble and begin to silently freak out when we get to the motorway.

Soren will be so mad, and today is his first day off in weeks.

With the cloud reassuringly floating above my head, I can sort myself out at any time. I hope I'm being paranoid and they're taking me to another place—perhaps another town? I don't know how human policing works.

After about twenty-five minutes, the car turns onto a service road and parks next to another vehicle. I sit in the back silently as the engine ticks. "I'm sorry about this, but it's my family, Mike," the chatty police officer says to his colleague. He pats his shoulder, and both get out.

That sounds reassuring. I need to watch what's happening. I awkwardly lean forward, wedging my shoulder against the door and my cheek against the glass while trying not to think of the germs. I can't see much as the headrest is in the way.

The police officers talk to two other people; the angle is wrong, and I can't make out anything else. I think they're both male.

I attempt to use my magical senses to determine what type of creature they are, but that comes to a grinding halt. I can't pick anything up. I scowl at my hands; the blinking rune handcuffs are interfering.

They must reach an agreement as the police officers return to the car. The back door is opened, and the chatty police officer unbuckles the seat belt and uses my elbow to pull me out of the vehicle. We march towards the other car, he opens the back door, and I'm shoved inside.

"Lean forward," he says to me. I do, and he undoes the handcuffs and removes them. I bring my hands to the front and rub them. I glare at him as he slams the door and walks away. Now I haven't got the cuffs on, so I can at least test the magical signatures, but before I do, the door is opened, and a new guy slaps a null band on my wrist.

I groan.

"Great, nice one, Kricket." The null band doesn't knock me out, but it makes my head throb, and for some reason, I can't touch my charmed cloud. *Someone knows about my magic.*

There's shouting, a flash of light, and then I see the chatty officer fall. He falls back like a chopped tree, hitting the ground with an almighty thud. I wince and cover my mouth with my hand at the sound his head makes as it strikes the concrete—even through the door, it makes the sound of a melon hitting the floor.

Oh fate. That's horrible.

The front passenger door opens, and a man gets in. He leans around the front seat and waves. "Put your seat belt on, eh love?" He smiles his nasty smile.

I'm too shocked to react.

It's Anton Bloody Hill.

Oh no. What is he doing here? I obediently put the seat belt on, and he gives me a nod of approval. "It's nice to see you again, Gary."

CHAPTER
THIRTY-SEVEN

GARY. Oh no. I've royally messed up. I sit frozen. If Anton Hill knows Gary is my pseudonym, then the Claw Brotherhood know who I am. Damien. *Shit.* My head is all mushed up, and I don't know what to do for the best.

I can't let them use me.

"The boss charmed the null band, so there's no getting it off. The police should have already confiscated everything, but we didn't want to take a risk," says Anton as he puts his seat belt on, and the other guy starts the car.

The tyres grind against the road's uneven surface as the vehicle turns around. "We took his family," he says casually as if he's talking about the weather, and like a bad tour guide, he points at the dead, once-chatty policeman as the car rolls past him and his colleague. Both men are dead and left on the road like rubbish.

They didn't deserve to die. They also shouldn't have been meeting baddies on the side of the road for a dodgy prisoner exchange, but they didn't deserve to die. Maybe if I'd done something earlier, they'd be alive?

"We took his family and suggested to get them back, he'd have to come and collect you." He looks back at me and grins. "He needed all those cops to come for you because of your guards. We've been unable to get anywhere near you and lost a few guys. That pink-haired chick is absolutely mental. She's only a diddy thing, but jeez, she's scary."

I hum, agreeing with him but not saying anything aloud. Forrest is my friend, but I still have a healthy fear of her.

"So yeah, you've been ruining all sorts of things, and the boss is angry with you."

"The policeman's family. Are they safe?"

Anton huffs. "Nah, they're not safe. What kind of people do you think we are? I told him he'd see them again. I didn't say that they'd be alive. Don't worry, Kricket, they're all together now. A happy family. In heaven." Both men chuckle, and the silent guy gives him a fist bump. "The boss wants your magic. Who knew that you're powerful, that you can make charms? I certainly didn't. I would have been a lot nicer to you, really nice, if you know what I mean." He winks. "Might have been your boyfriend, and then I could have just manipulated you, and everything would have been fine. But no, you had to be difficult. You had to be cocky and play hard to get."

Hard to get. That wasn't hard to get. For him, I was impossible to get. *Ew.*

"But you, Kricket Jones, are a magical marvel. I can't quite believe it. Now he will use you to go after the silver dragon."

My heart misses a beat, and I must have misheard. "Sorry, what? Damien is going after the general?"

"Yep."

"But... But why would he do that? It's a suicide mission."

He lets out a self-deprecating laugh. "Have you heard her, Dave, as if it's that easy to dissuade the boss. Why? Hell, if I know. Look, Kricket, I'm a minion, and we don't get to ask the questions. If it were up to me, I'd rather be buying pizza and Coke at that shitty supermarket you worked at. I wish all this had never happened." He shakes his head. "This is shit."

"Well, if it's shit, why don't you both walk away? Let me go?"

Anton Hill bangs the back of his head against the seat and groans. "I can't let you go. If I haven't got the protection of the Brotherhood, I'm a dead man. The Executioner, that unicorn bitch, is hunting us all down. She's getting all the stragglers first. Plus if the boss's magic doesn't finish me off..." He pats the driver's leg. "...Dave here will kill me. Wouldn't you, pal?"

"Too right I would," says Dave.

"Oh, and that's not counting your guys: the tiny pink terror, the hellhound, and the loved-up gargoyle. Everyone's gonna kill me. I might as well carry on the way that I'm going. Either way, I'm fucked. Trust the process, eh, Dave?"

"Yeah, pal."

"I can talk to them on your behalf if you'd help me. I can… I can try to protect you."

Anton scoffs. "You can't even protect yourself." He leans around the seat and stares at me. "Look, Kricket, I know I've been a dick to you, and you're a nice girl. Smart too. Do what they say, and you'll be fine. You never know. You might make it out of this alive."

I've heard all this before. "Last time we talked, you tried convincing me that you had Chloe. I don't believe anything you say. You do what you must, but please don't pretend you're a nice guy."

He slumps back into his seat. "Yeah, well, it was worth a try."

"I thought you had her there for a minute, pal. I thought you had her." The driver chuckles and shakes his head.

"She has such a bleeding heart." Louder, he says, "Don't think I didn't notice you slipping money and food into your family's coffers while you were starving. Bet you never got any thanks for it, did you? That's why no one ever plays the good guy, 'cause good guys are the people that die first."

I bite my lip and stare out of the window.

"I've never been a nice guy. I enjoy the heat and bet hell's toasty and warm." He leans forward and turns the radio on, and that's the end of our conversation.

I slump back in the seat. Both my forearms and right knee are itching. I hope I'm not coming down with anything. I bet it's the bloody null band. I feel odd. I tug up my sleeve and glance down at my arm, and—oh, that's interesting.

I cover up before Anton Hill can see my lovely new green scales.

What the fuck is that? I surreptitiously rub my forearms on my itchy knee and then take another peak. Yep, the scales are still there.

Don't freak out. Do not freak out. Don't freak out.

What the heck is happening to me? What is the null band doing? Is this Damien's magic? Is he turning me into a monster?

To prevent myself from climbing out of my skin, I close my eyes and try to see if my tracking magic will work. It does. Thank fate. The null band is only blocking my access to charm magic. I immediately find Soren and instantly recognise the three other unique magic signatures with him: Owen, Forrest and Jeff.

I take a deep, relieved breath, then another. I hope they don't get in trouble with the police when they find out I'm missing.

I'm going to be okay. Soren insisted that I drink an

untraceable tracking potion. They'll be able to find me. I need to hold on and give them time.

I pluck at the null band and hiss as the bloody thing shocks me. They will have to remove this at some point, and I've got a ton of charms they are unaware of. I'm not defenceless. Even if I've only had three weeks of self-defence lessons, I need to be ready, and when I get the chance, I need to hit hard and then stick to Forrest's mantra: block and run.

I've no real choice but to wait this out and wait for rescue or rescue myself. I can be my own white knight.

We don't go to my old town. They must have abandoned it after the gargoyles attacked them and rescued me. We park, and I'm dragged out of the car; as soon as my feet hit the pavement, I feel the ley line magic.

Uh-oh, there's a portal.

No one will find me if I'm taken to a different realm!

CHAPTER THIRTY-EIGHT

INSTEAD OF GOING STRAIGHT to the gateway, as I fear, I'm tugged left and through the back door of an old office building that has long been abandoned. The mould in the entryway is ridiculous, and the walls are almost black.

Anton pokes me in the back and forces me up some stairs.

The narrow staircase creaks under our combined weight. The wooden treads are worn, and with the trip hazard of a ratty maroon carpet holding on for grim death, I have to be careful where I put my feet.

When we get to the top, there's a square landing. Anton opens the only door and walks in first. Dave, the driver, prods me to follow.

The abandoned office occupies the entire floor. Weak, natural light filters through the dirty windows, casting eerie shadows on the walls, marred by peeling paint and more mould patches. Cobwebs drape from the ceiling and the dark fluorescent lights. An ancient filing cabinet stands open in one corner, its drawers askew. Behind a wooden desk that has seen better days is Damien Hass.

Nice place you've got here, Damien.

We stare at each other.

The silence is thick, broken only by the distant hum of traffic from the street below and the occasional creak of the building settling.

Damien isn't looking well. His eyes and skin have got a yellowish tint as if he has liver failure, and when he opens his mouth to talk, I notice he's missing a few prominent teeth.

"Ah, here she is," he says, leaning back in his chair and crossing his ankles.

I do my best not to wince. I don't know if I succeed as Damien's eyes narrow and his jaw ticks. Worse than the tone of his skin and his teeth is the damage to his soul. His soul is a complete and utter mess. It's black and bubbled with huge gaping holes. It's as if the evil Dragon's Eye magic is eating him.

He's dying.

Goosebumps of horror pepper my arms, and I want to back away from him with a scream but force my feet to stay still. *It's not like I can go anywhere.* Anton moves behind me to stand next to the filing cabinet. Dave's bulk blocks the door, and another guard in the room blocks the windows.

Damien's only got three guys. Is that the extent of the Claw Brotherhood? I hope so. I close my eyes and with my magic I count, there are fourteen.

"Did you have any problems?" Damien directs his question over my shoulder at Anton.

"No, sir."

"Good lad." Damien smiles and leans across the desk. Again I have his full attention. "If I didn't need you, Kricket Jones, I'd beat the ever-loving shit out of you. You need to learn some respect, girl." Some spit dribbles out the corner of his mouth as if he's not yet used to missing teeth. He pulls the Dragon's Eye from his pocket, and for the first time, he openly shows it to me.

The monstrous thing sits almost innocently in the centre of this palm.

"You made a fool out of me pretending you had no magic. I had you, and you tricked me. I've been running around after you for weeks. I've lost men, good men." His hand tremors slightly as he holds the Dragon's Eye out. "I'm sure Anton has told you of our plan. We are going to use you until you burn out."

Burn out like you?

I keep my mouth shut while inside, I shudder. I mentally put my brave knickers on and dare to give him a look I borrowed from Forrest. It's a look that can't be copied, but I do my best. It's her combination of you're-shit-out-of-luck and are-you-kidding expressions.

Classic badarse.

Damien huffs and leans back in his chair. "The Brotherhood was made for dragons. It's our duty to serve them."

"To serve them?" I splutter. The words rush out of my mouth without thinking. "So why are you trying to capture him—" I yelp as Anton reaches over and smacks me on the back of the head.

"Don't be rude, Kricket," he reprimands me, grabbing my shoulders and pushing me down into a chair. "Now, sir?"

"No time like the present, lad." Damien nods his approval, folds his fingers over the Dragon's Eye in his hand, and under his breath begins to chant.

Oh no. Fuck that. I'm not sitting here while he works his magic. I've seen what that thing can do, and I do not want that power aimed at me. I scramble to my feet.

Anton grabs ahold of my neck and violently slams me back into the chair. Seconds later, the Dragon's Eye shoots black sparks, and at Damien's command, the sparks thicken to smoky black ropes. Through the air, they crawl towards me, pulsing with diseased magic.

I can't think, and I struggle to breathe with Anton Hill's hand gripping tightly around my throat. I whimper as the smoke touches me. It solidifies, and bands of magic coil around my body like a snake attacking prey.

It pins me to the chair.

Damien walks around the desk.

He seems to take forever, and all the while, he chuckles like a Disney villain. "I'll kill everyone you care about and anyone who cares about you." His voice is conversational. I don't know what expression he's reading on my face, but Damien takes great delight. "They will die, and you'll know it's your fault."

I hate him.

I squeak as he hooks his index finger into my top and, with a perverted smirk, pulls the fabric away from my chest. His other hand comes up, and he drops the Dragon's Eye. It lands on the bare skin of my chest and adheres to my collarbone.

My heart pounds as if he chucked a scorpion into my bra. If given the choice, I'd prefer the scorpion. I don't want that thing near me. I hiss. *Ow*, it's painful. Tiny little barbs are digging into my skin, burying into my collarbone. I do my best to stay calm. I won't give him the satisfaction of screaming.

"Ah," he says. "I almost forgot." He smiles as he snatches hold of my forearm. Due to the magical rope sticking me to the chair, he can't lift my arm high, but he yanks it up as far as it can go and leans towards me. Damien smells of rotting meat. His fingers rub against the soft skin on the inside of my wrist where the null band sits. The null band heats and dissipates, returning to the Dragon's Eye as he drops my wrist.

Oh, thank fate.

I haven't got time to waste. Immediately, I pull all my

magic away from the Dragon's Eye and chest and further into my body. Then I nudge the cloud, asking the ward charms to help. Several answer my call, and instead of warding me or the room, I delicately gather the power and slide it inside me, directly underneath the Dragon's Eye, to ensure that it can't dig any deeper.

In response to my defensive magic, the barbs in the Dragon's Eye bite down harder. I grit my teeth as pain rolls down my chest and into my shoulders. I can feel its frustration as it meets and batters against the wards.

Damien doesn't notice. Of course he doesn't. The men are talking and laughing, but I can't understand them while I'm battling with this disgusting thing.

It's stronger than three of my wards working together to protect my soul.

But it's not stronger than me.

It's not stronger than my magic.

You've had your chance. Now let's see what I can do with you.

It's my turn to dig my metaphysical fingers into its filthy power, just like I did weeks ago when, on the fly, I turned random jewellery into charms to heal the town. Right after that, I deactivated the power, rendering the charms inert and returning them to their original state.

I do the same thing.

My magic grabs hold of the Dragon's Eye, and I unmake it.

CHAPTER
THIRTY-NINE

THE DRAGON'S Eye fights me. Oh boy, does it fight me —the Dragon's Eye rips, bites, and claws. The pain is so bad I'm surprised I'm not bleeding. I worry it's shredding my soul, but I keep going. I don't have a choice. I must fight.

I once again gather my wards and flood them with power, making them thicker and like a dome. They surround it entirely while I pick it apart. Its magic is like a tangled knot—a knot I must unravel.

It has had so much autonomy for such a long time that it doesn't want to relinquish its power. It has been allowed to do what it pleases for centuries. It isn't like my charms, which are happy and eager to please. I need to learn a lesson from this charm and make sure to give my magic thorough guidelines.

I need to add something to the charms scattered throughout the world that they can protect but not inflict harm. It might be tricky, and maybe I'll need help from someone who knows what they're doing. Someone like the silver dragon.

He must have knowledge and skill. Shit, he charmed the shifters. I think he'll be able to help me.

The Dragon's Eye continues to fight me. I tried this for the first and only time with my magic, and the energy wanted to come back to me. It's not like I destroyed them when I pulled the power out. That power, that essence, has created other charms over the past few weeks. My charms never die.

But this thing, this evil, nasty charm, corrupts everything it touches while taking life force. It needs to be destroyed.

I can see in the centre of it, and perhaps once upon a time, it was beautiful. But now there's no trace of what it should have been. It's like a corrupt, festering wound full of nasty bacteria. I work my way through the ooze and the rot. To the centre, find its heart, and then I pull and twist.

The magic holding the Dragon's Eye together snaps.

My ears ring with the sound of its rage, and then power rushes to me. I mentally take a step back. *Oh fate.* What am I going to do with this power? I've only done this once, and I'd sucked the magic back into me, but I don't want this rotten magic. I don't want it at all, rotting away at my insides.

On the cusp of panic, I swallow down my fear. I don't want to do this anymore, but this is my responsibility. Even if I only want to curl up in a corner and cry. Who else is going to do this? Who else can? I wish the silver dragon would come and sort this shit out. I'm sure it's his bloody duty.

Instead, here, now, there's just me.

I groan, and then I do something brilliant. Or I do something terrible.

I remember what I've learned about magical signatures and tracing people. As I unmake the Dragon's Eye, I keep a solid metaphysical grip on the wiggling, rancid power, and with my next breath, I push it into the creatures with the Dragon's Eye's magical signature.

All the magical signatures connected to the Dragon's Eye get a dose of power.

Every last remaining member of the Claw Brotherhood. All fourteen are here guarding this building. I know it will be too much for their bodies to take, but I do it anyway.

It doesn't take long. Damien wobbles on his feet, and his gap-toothed grin freezes on his face. He coughs, gargles a little bit, and then there's a *puff*, and he's gone.

A black substance falls to the floor in a small pile, as if he's been instantly cremated. I stare at the pile. The magic holding me in the chair disappears, and I lean forward and nudge the pile with my foot.

Oh okay.

Where Anton Hill was standing, there is another pile of dust. And another near the door and another by the window. I rub my prickly arms and then cover my mouth as I gag. I have a sudden and unexpected bout of dry heaves.

Fate, I killed them.

I stare at the four little piles, which seem inconsequential, such tiny things from four scary guys.

There's a bang as a door downstairs gets kicked in.

Then almost silent footsteps.

The door opens, and the breeze wafts the piles, so they're not piles anymore but kind of spread out a little bit.

The gargoyle is here.

Unbeknownst to me, one of my wards has taken it upon itself to spring up to protect the room, and Soren walks right through it. "Huh," he says in surprise as he continues to move towards me. *The umbrella charm lets him in.* An acknowledgement that he's trusted.

That I trust him.

I don't know how many times he's been blasted by my wards while I've been unconscious, but the stubborn gargoyle didn't think twice about walking through it to get to me, to help me.

He drops to his knees, gently takes my face, and his big thumbs brush my cheekbones. "Kricket, are you all right?" he asks. "Did they hurt you?"

I stare into his beautiful pale green eyes and can't form words.

The dying screams from the Dragon's Eye still echo in my ears. The dead charm stuck to my chest crumbles. Leaving black shards and ash in my bra and across my chest. It's uncomfortable, but I ignore it for now. My cleaning charm rescues me. The smell of lemon and vanilla fills my nose as the mop charm whisks it away.

"Kricket? Nothing girl, are you okay?"

"They're gone," I say softly. "I, I, um, I, I killed them."

"Good." He kisses me on the cheek. His lips are surprisingly warm and soft, and I lean into his touch. "We were so worried about you. I was worried about you. Forrest, Owen, and Jeff are outside hunting the other Claw Brotherhood members, but they seem to have gone. Come on, let's get you back to the house."

"Anton Hill killed two police officers and... I, I, I killed them."

"I know about the police officers, and if any people deserved killing, it was them."

"All fifteen of them."

Soren's eyes widen, but he doesn't ask any further questions. He gently holds my hands and helps me up. My legs feel wooden, and when I try to take a step forward, I can't.

"They're, um, they're on the floor. They're the dust. That's them." I point. "They're on the floor."

Soren eyes the floor, at the dust in front of my toes, and then back at me with compassion. His big hands creep around my waist, and he lifts me. He holds me above the floor, sweeps me into his arms, and carries me princess-style across the room so I don't have to stand on them.

I know it's stupid, but by doing that, I fall just a little bit more in love with him.

CHAPTER
FORTY

Soren carries me down the stairs and out of the building. He puts me down and waits until I've regained my balance before he lets go. The door hangs off its hinges. He picks it up and awkwardly closes it. It won't close. It bounces open when he tries and leans a little to the left. He shrugs.

Owen gives me a once-over, and Jeff nods. "Glad to see you're okay. Come on. The car's parked around the corner."

Forrest—or should I say wolfy Forrest—appears. Her nails click as she pads across the pavement, and her coat gleams in the sunlight. She's white, and the tips of her fur are red or reddish pink. I haven't seen a shifted wolf before. She's quite big, around waist height.

We didn't have shifters in town, so this is kind of cool. My hands twitch, and I want to pat her head and tickle behind her ears. "Oh fate," I tell her, "you are so beautiful."

Her mouth opens, and her tongue lolls out. Forrest gives me a wolfy grin, and her tail wags in a circular motion. With her ears flopping to the side, she just looks adorable. She sneezes three times in a row, sniffs, snorts and uses her paw to itch her nose.

I pout when the visual treat is gone. From one breath to the next, Forrest stands there in her clothed human form as if she weren't some grand, furry beast a second ago.

"I'm glad to see you're all right. I don't know where they've gone. They've disappeared into thin air and left these weird little piles of ash everywhere. Do you think they can teleport?"

I hold my hand up. "Yeah, that was me. I, um, vaporised everyone."

Forrest grins and gives Owen a high five. "Look at that! Look at our training. Vaporised. Get in!" She gives me a double thumbs-up. "When we get to the house, you'll have to give me all the gory details. I want to know everything, dragon girl."

Owen shakes his head, Jeff laughs, and they all continue to joke with each other as we wander back through the narrow alleyway, away from the ley line gateway to the back of the buildings and the cars.

They talk about what they will eat for dinner and

decide to pick up Chinese on the way home. Once they take my order, Soren opens the door, and I crawl into the passenger seat, suddenly exhausted.

I wave to Forrest, who bounces to Owen's car, and Jeff follows them. They're gone, and we drive away from the office building through the small, run-down town and back onto the motorway.

I spoke to my mum yesterday, and she's still unhappy with me. Oh, she's happy because she's back at home with her things, even though they're not really her things. I love my mum dearly. She's used to seeing me as a child. She needs to start seeing me as an adult. She disapproves of my magic, and she doesn't understand me.

She's disappointed. Not with me helping people and not with me saving our town. But she's angry with me for being a martyr. That I should have originally kept my mouth closed. If I hadn't tried to save Soren, if I hadn't used my magic in front of him, then he would have never known it was me, and all this being protected and guarded would never have happened if I'd just done what I was told.

I can beg to differ, but not to her face. Fate has a hand in everything that happens. Sometimes things have to happen.

Like destiny.

I look at the gargoyle who likes me and smile to myself.

Yeah, destiny.

That's when my entire back starts to itch. I surreptitiously wiggle and rub my shoulder against the side of the car seat. It feels uncomfortable and sore. I try to ignore it, but then my arms start to burn. I hiss, and then I groan. *Why do I have to be in so much pain?* My head feels like a migraine is coming as my vision becomes blurry. I frown as I wiggle my left foot. I've now got pins and needles in my toes, and both my arms feel like they're on fire. "Soren," I say. "I don't feel well."

He glances from the road. "What's wrong? You've gone pale."

"Something weird is happening to me."

"Your magic weird or normal weird?"

My nails dig into my thigh. I trusted him enough that my ward knew he was allowed through. I'm positive I'm in love with him. I need to trust him now. I swallow down my nerves and roll up my sleeve.

I show him because he won't believe me unless he sees for himself. I show him the green scales. The scales disappear under my sleeve, covering my entire arm. When I tilt my wrist, they sparkle in the light coming through the windscreen, like the colour-changing paint on fancy cars: green, blue, and a little silver.

One-handedly, Soren gently cradles my arm and rubs his thumb across the scales on my skin. "Scales? Did this happen just now? Did they do this to you?"

"No, it's happened a few times, in patches."

"You should have said something. How long? How long has this been happening?" He pulls the car into the first lane and takes the next slip road.

"I'm sorry. I was scared and confused." I shrug and pull away from his hand. "A couple of days? Maybe a couple of weeks?" I wince. "I'm not sure. Soren, I'm freaking out, and my skin is itching. I can't remember when they first started happening. It seems to be when I'm stressed."

We come off at a roundabout and continue driving silently for a few minutes. The gargoyle's jaw ticks, and his big grey hands clench the steering wheel.

"They're itchy, and I didn't think much of it, but my back is hurting, and I feel like..." I bend over. "I'm going to be sick." My stomach revolts, and Soren stops in time for me to open the door and throw up all over the road. "Oh, I'm sorry. I don't feel good."

I can't make sense of what he says until Soren sweeps me into his arms. "It's not safe here."

"No, please don't." I push against a massive pec. "I might throw up on you."

"I don't care," he says, and then he's running.

Why is he running? When we have a perfectly good car?

Oh fate, I hope my stomach doesn't revolt again. I love this guy, and he can no doubt smell my sicky breath. He bolts through an industrial estate, past a few rotten-looking buildings, and over a service road, and then there's a road made from concrete that looks like something from the 1970s and an old Harris fence. I don't know what he's going to do until his wings snap out, and he lifts into the air, and we are over the fence.

He flies another fourteen feet; then he's back on the ground and running again.

He continues to use his wings for balance as he runs incredibly fast. I didn't realise gargoyles could move like this. We come out from between a copse of trees, and we're in a field. In front of us is a beautiful, old aqueduct that continues off into the distance.

Soren gently places me down on the grass, and I'm gasping. He isn't even breathing hard. "You're okay," he says, brushing the sweaty hair from my face. "I've never seen this before. But I have a feeling that you're shifting. You're turning into a dragon."

Shifting? What?

"What are you talking about? No, that's not possible." I let out a moan as my insides roll and squeeze, and I feel like I'm falling apart. "It hurts," I cry.

He holds my hand. "I've got you. I've got you. Just breathe. Kricket, you need to stop fighting and let go. Please love."

Let go! Is he nuts?

"No. Can I not have a healing potion?" I pull on the cloud, and the charms do nothing. They do nothing! "Why are my charms not working? Why aren't they healing me?" I whine.

"Because there's nothing to heal." He holds me in his arms and whispers, "You're okay, you're okay, I've got you, you're okay. Just breathe. Can you see yourself when you use your magic to look at magical signatures?"

"No, I can't see myself," my words emerge as a growl.

"Try."

I scowl at him. "I don't want to talk about the magical signature. I don't want to talk about magic at all. I want my healing charms to help me."

I want him to save me.

"Nothing girl. Please check," he says with his own growl.

I huff and close my eyes. I find my magical signature to be completely different. It's fluctuating and changing. It doesn't look like my brothers' anymore; it's different, somehow fuller. I've never met the silver dragon, but I've seen the imprint of his magic within the hellhounds and can see similarities.

Soren's right. It's a dragon's signature.

Oh fate. Oh no.

I'm too young to shift into a dragon.

According to the books in Nan's library's reference section, dragons are old when they shift, and they don't change to a dragon form because they are dragons. No, they turn human, but gaining the magical strength can take a thousand years.

Oh no. I'm doing it the wrong way. And I'm not a dragon! I have some magic and a little DNA. It must be the charm. Have I inadvertently sucked down some energy?

The Dragon's Eye has messed me up, and now I'm going to die. *Do people die from shifting wrong?* "Am I going to die?" I must say the last words out loud, because a rumbly rockfall voice tells me I won't die and to let go.

The pain ceases, and I can't feel anything. I can't hear him. I can't see him. I'm floating. I'm swallowed up by the blackness in my head. There is blackness around me, and all I can see is my magical signature pulsing.

I trust him and let go.

I allow it to happen and stop fighting. It becomes easy, like walking across a room. My body flows like water; it feels like a relief. What I am cracks open and falls apart. The little microparticles that make up my spirit and body twist and break.

The particles re-form and I grow bigger.

I grow *much* bigger.

Soren's no longer holding me. I worry that something has happened to him, but I pray he got out of the way 'cause I'm no longer me.

Well, I'm no longer me with my human skin and my red hair.

I'm different.

I'm not human. I'm *dragon me*.

I dig my toes into the grass, and it parts easily against the pressure. I've got toes on my hands. I lift my hand, and within the iridescent green scales are long, catlike, incredibly sharp black nails. Claws. I've got four toes. I wiggle them. Huh, I'm missing a digit. I glance underneath me, and the toes on my back feet are the same—four toes. Wow. I look at my other hand—no, my other foot—and see the same.

Gosh, this is weird.

I'm green, and I'm not that big. I heard the silver

dragon's left nostril was as big as a car. But I'm not big at all, perhaps the size of a car? I wonder if female dragons are smaller than males, but it might be just my age. I know the silver dragon is thousands of years old, so it must be that. Maybe I'll grow bigger as I get older?

I stretch and wobble. It's weird to have four legs, and I look out the side of my eye and see a wing and, on the other side, another wing—dark green wings. Bat-like. No, dragon-like. I toothily grin. I turn my head. Oh, my neck is long, and I can almost, yeah, I can get it back really far and look at my bum.

I have a long tail with a spiky thing at the end.

I cough and blow out a breath. It's air, there's no flame. I don't even know if dragons do flames. I roll my eyes to look up and think I've got horns. I lean to the side, and my back leg comes up, and I carefully pat around my head.

Oh yes, I've got horns. They're only small. That's kind of cool. I stretch and yawn. I'm tired from shifting. But I'm not worried about being in this shape. I know I'll easily be able to turn back.

There's a noise to the left, and a smaller version of Soren stands there, his mouth wide-open, pointing. "You did it. You are a dragon," he says. "You're a beautiful dragon."

Yeah, no shit, Sherlock. I'm a dragon.

And then he starts to laugh.

Dear Reader,

Thank you for taking a chance on my book! Wow, I did it again. I hope you enjoyed it. If you did, and if you have time, I would be *very* grateful if you could write a review.

Every review makes a *huge* difference to an author—especially me as a brand-new shiny one—and your review might help other readers discover my book. I would appreciate it so much, and it might help me keep writing.

Thanks a million!

Oh, and there is a chance that I might even choose your review to feature in my marketing campaign. Could you imagine? So exciting!

    Love,
    Brogan x

P.S. DON'T FORGET! Sign up on my VIP email list! You will get early access to all sorts of goodies, including: signed copies, private giveaways, advance notice of future projects and free stuff! The link is on my website at **www.broganthomas.com** your email will be kept 100% private, and you can unsubscribe at any time, with zero spam.

ACKNOWLEDGEMENTS

A special thank you to Gary Chappell, who first gave me the idea of a reflection charm while I was writing Rebel Vampire. Who knew I'd have so much fun with it? Thank you so much for the idea and for allowing me to use your name! I hope I've done both justice.

To everyone who contributed to *Cursed Dragon*, your support and encouragement have meant the world to me. Thank you.

Love Brogan x

ABOUT
THE AUTHOR

Brogan lives in Ireland with her husband and their eleven furry children: five furry minions of darkness (aka the cats), four hellhounds (the dogs), and two traditional unicorns (fat, hairy Irish cobs).

In 2019 she decided to embrace her craziness by writing about the imaginary people that live in her head. Her first love is her husband, followed by her number-one favourite furry child Bob the cob, then reading. When not reading or writing, she can be found knee-deep in horse poo and fur while blissfully ignoring all adult responsibilities.

facebook.com/BroganThomasBooks
instagram.com/broganthomasbooks
goodreads.com/Brogan_Thomas
bookbub.com/authors/brogan-thomas
youtube.com/@broganthomasbooks

ALSO BY
BROGAN THOMAS

Creatures of the Otherworld series

Cursed Wolf

Cursed Demon

Cursed Vampire

Cursed Witch

Cursed Fae

Cursed Dragon

Rebel of the Otherworld series

Rebel Unicorn

Rebel Vampire

The Bitten Chronicles

Bitten Shifter

Made in the USA
Columbia, SC
15 July 2025